BEHIND
THE SMOKE
CURTAIN

A NOVEL SET IN VIETNAM 1967—1975

DUYEN NGUYEN

BEHIND THE SMOKE CURTAIN

A NOVEL SET IN VIETNAM 1967—1975

DUYEN NGUYEN

PUBLISHED BY

 Escrire

A FICTION IMPRINT FROM ADDUCENT
ADDUCENT, INC.
WWW.ADDUCENT.CO

TITLES DISTRIBUTED IN
North America
United Kingdom
Western Europe
South America
Australia
China

Behind the Smoke Curtain

A Novel Set in Vietnam 1967—1975

By Duyen Nguyen

ISBN: 9781937592523 (PAPERBACK)

Library of Congress Catalog Number: 2016930159

PUBLISHED BY ADDUCENT, INC. UNDER ITS ESCRIRE FICTION IMPRINT

JACKSONVILLE, FLORIDA

WWW.ADDUCENT.CO

WWW.ADDUCENTINC.COM

PUBLISHED IN THE UNITED STATES OF AMERICA

This book is a work of fiction. Names, characters, places and incidents are the products of the author's imagination or are used fictitiously. Any resemblance to actual persons, living or dead is purely coincidental.

Dedication & Acknowledgments

To the fallen and wounded soldiers of all sides, and the innocent civilian victims of the Vietnam war.

With special thanks to Dinh Quang Anh Thai, Roy Russell and Dennis Lowery for your assistance with gathering facts, proofreading and editing this book.

"Duyen Nguyen brings us a Vietnamese American love story that is woven from the threads of history by a man who watched the fabric unravel. Who, in *Behind the Smoke Curtain*, attempts to tie up the wars loose ends of politics, betrayal, and human loss."

– Roy Russell, First Lt., US Army,
Vietnam 1968 to 1969,
editor Typhoon magazine.

"*Behind the Smoke Curtain*" contains all of the hallmarks of a great masterpiece: war, love, deception, truth seeking, action and suspense. Truly a great read for all generations."

– Joey S. Zizileuskas,
Attorney at Law

SPRING 1956

The young woman entered the village. She was in the wrong place at the wrong time as heavily armed insurgents attacked the nearby plantation. Trying to flee she was in the crossfire of automatic weapons and stream of bullets chased and caught her stitching a line of red, ragged, holes up her back. She fell beside a low, earthen, wall near where the village fields began and watched as the plantation burned. Men raced by without helping her. She'd told her daughter, that morning, only hours before.

"I won't be long." She brushed the 8-year-old girl's long black hair.

"Let me go with you!"

She took her shoulder and turned her so she could see her face.

"You must stay here."

"There's fighting... father said so." Though so young and slender the strength in her daughter's arms always surprised her.

"There's always fighting... always some conflict or another." She sighed and smoothed the tears from Mai's face. It showed the legacy of a colonial French grandfather who fell in love with a Vietnamese woman. His fine, Gallic, features had passed to his granddaughter. Mai was a perfect blend of the two countries: Vietnam and France.

"Father says it's like we're in the middle of a tug-of-war." Mai had stopped crying but was still frightened.

The sound of a mortar or grenade explosion shook the memory. The vision and sound of her daughter, from this morning, faded, but the thoughts didn't. A new memory shifted in. She heard his voice. Mai's father, the young man she'd married. Even though she feared losing him to the fight against the French, had survived years of battle after the Second World War as France tried to regain colonies they had lost to the Japanese. He had studied his country's history at the University. "Control of Vietnam is the gateway to Southeast Asia. China, Russia, France... they know this." He often lectured on the subject and Mai was an avid listener. She learned of the French finally capitulating with their defeat at Dien Bien Phu only two years before and knew, from others, he was a hero from that battle though he never spoke about the fighting.

She felt the dirt beneath her clinging to her legs, clenched a fistful and brought it up to see blood-soaked mud. Her thoughts spun on. But those nations' intrigues, France specifically, had brought her French father here to fall in love and have a child. She'd been born as a result. The fighting with the French had brought a young man into her life who became her husband. And Mai was born. So many connections...

her mind drifted. She heard a voice and could see a shape forming.

"Má..." Mai knelt beside her. Tears, again, coursing down her cheeks.

She wiped them away with the back of her hand feeling their wetness. "Đ?ng khóc em bé c?a tôi... Don't cry my baby..."

"Why?" Mai cried.

"Why what my little girl?" She was tired but did not want to leave things unanswered for her daughter.

"Why must there be fighting?"

Mai's shape flickered and darkened. "I don't know Mai... I don't know." Her daughter's face blurred and began to fade. She spoke her last thought into the darkness, "Will it ever stop? Will my daughter discover love and a time of peace and happiness?"

* * *

11 YEARS LATER

The smell of gunpowder was as pungent as it was unexpected in the small classroom. It and the smoke hung like a dark, wet cloak in the air, choking the students and obscuring the fleeing terrorists. The microphone squawked loudly from feedback as the student audience scattered from the room like a flock of ducks taking flight at the sound of a round chambering in a shotgun.

One man lay on the stage in a pool of his own blood. Another, next to him on the floor, was lifeless as a rag doll. A young woman was struggling to stand. The three intruders, into what was to have been a special night of music, took flight. Dressed in fitted black pants and tight black, short-sleeve shirts, a familiar uniform of sorts, they disappeared into another gentle and poetic evening fractured by death. Sections of the ceiling had come down, striking the young woman in the center of the room. A young man, bleeding from gashes in his back, knelt next to her crying.

"Mai... Mai...!" He collapsed over her.

Chapter 1

To Scott Reynolds, she was the most sensual and alluring woman he'd ever seen. She glided like a cheetah—lithe and graceful—always moving across the campus with intent. Mai Trinh, a second-year student in the Literature Department at Saigon University, was on a mission that morning.

Crossing the quad, she saw the young American she had shared several English classes with since the beginning of the semester. He intrigued her, arguing most anything she brought up, she felt, often just to keep her from walking away. Though she loved a good debate, she'd already admitted to herself, she also wanted to extend their talks. Just to look at him and listen to his voice, which was deep and resonant, filled her with something she'd not felt with other boys. She knew he was taking several classes toward his master's degree and had come to Vietnam as a freelance writer.

Scott watched as Mai approached where he was sitting her black sandals flapping against the concrete, hair bouncing from shoulder to shoulder, swaying and keeping time. He had come to be able to tell her frame of mind by the way she walked. She seemed in a good mood.

"Mr. Reynolds," she said quickly in a pseudo-formal voice with an emphasis on the mister, "would you like to go to a concert with me this evening?"

To Scott, it sounded more like an order than a request but he didn't mind. Her manner and way of speaking came honestly. Mai's father had raised her since her mother died when she was eight. A Lieutenant Colonel in the South Vietnamese Army, he was also the acting Deputy Province Chief of Pleiku, a strategically important province in the central plateau of Vietnam. Scott knew of him from his press work with the 633rd Special Operations unit based there.

"Hello, Mai," he said, rising from the bench. His six-foot-three frame and sun-bleached hair made him an unlikely campus figure. He paused before answering her question. He knew she was so self-assured, he would naturally say yes without hesitation, and wanted to make her consider there weren't any strings on him. He stroked his chin and looked up at the bright blue sky, and then back, down, to her. "Who is it? Where and what time?" as if his calendar might be full.

"It's a Trinh Cong Son concert. You know who he is, don't you?"

"Uh, yeah, sure, of course." He didn't know who the singer was, but he would've gone if it had been a Polka with costumes required as long as it was with her. Just to be with her was intoxicating.

"It's not a big and noisy type of concert like you're used to in the U.S. Not like the music you listen to. It'll be intimate, tasteful. It's going to be in the literature building, actually in one of the classrooms."

"Are you saying my music isn't tasteful and uplifting?" he said and grinned at her, "Yes. I'd like that. What time?"

"Seven."

On the surface, she gave only the slightest hint of a smile, "Good. I'll see you at seven." Her face was a softly blended palette. A mix of her aristocratic half-French mother and handsome Vietnamese father that resulted in a light olive complexion with just a hint of natural burnt umber in her cheeks. Long, straight, black, silky hair draped over her shoulders, framed a stunning face with skin as soft as the petal of a magnolia flower. Dark brown eyes, the color of chocolate, balanced with high-arched brows and a face that never felt the dab or rub of makeup. At five-foot-five, taller when wearing shoes, she wasn't the typical Vietnamese woman in stature or temperament. Inside she was beaming but her slight grin at Scott didn't reveal that as she studied him for a moment before turning away.

"See you then," he said, as they parted each going on their way, feeling, today's a great day!

* * *

THAT EVENING
SAIGON UNIVERSITY

Trinh Cong Son was a Vietnamese legend and phenomenon. A poet, singer, songwriter, musician and activist likened to Bob Dylan. Son's tunes were poignant stories about peace, love, and hope. Mai and Scott entered a classroom meant to hold thirty, but tonight's audience of sixty used every desk and all the standing room left after a makeshift stage had been placed at the front of the room.

Scott and Mai stood on the periphery opposite the door. After six songs, there was a break. The soundman off to the side left the microphone and speakers on and joined the students standing up from the folding chairs. As they applauded and began to stretch their legs, two men and a woman walked through the door dressed head-to-toe in black, tight ba-ba outfits. Anyone who noticed them assumed they were part of the show. The students had been singing along, upbeat and energized by the artist when the mood in the room suddenly went sour and quiet as the students realized who the three were.

The newcomers immediately commandeered the stage. The female, though slight and almost frail looking, grabbed the microphone from the stand and bellowed, "Today is December 20th, the anniversary of the National Liberation Front."

With that declaration, the students—sensing the danger—began to edge toward the single door. All of that motion stopped when the trio waved handguns in the air, shooting into the stained ceiling tiles. One of the men, most of his face covered with a black cloth, seemed startled when his eyes caught Mai's. They moved to the arm around her waist. He looked at Scott, raised his pistol and aimed. Mai screamed. Scott froze.

* * *

SAIGON HOSPITAL

The building and the room were old and musty, left over from the French occupation, made from concrete and cinderblocks with only a few windows. Scott drifted deeper into the dream memory. Back to Los Angeles:

"Kid are you crazy?" The man's cigarette danced as he talked. Scott didn't know how it managed to hang on his bottom lip; not fall off or be swallowed. "It's dangerous over there." The man shook his head and leaned forward ash falling on the papers strewn across his desk. "And how are you gonna come up with stories? You don't have any experience..." he glanced down at the one-page résumé Scott had handed him. "And that also means you don't have a pipeline to feed you leads." He was beginning to regret giving the kid five minutes, but he had admired his perseverance.

Scott had expected that question. He had spent the last two hours rehearsing his answer as he waited, for the third straight day, on the off chance he'd get in to see this man and speak to him. "I have a friend, a journalist, who just returned from Vietnam. He covered the 9th Air Commando Squadron at Camp Holloway, the Air Force Base in Pleiku. He told me he could get me in with the 633rd Special Operations Squadron writing pieces for their Public Affairs Officer and he didn't mind freelancers. Most of the writers they've had hustle off to cover combat stories—they want someone who'll stick around for a while."

"Don't those units drop leaflets and such? There's not much news in that, son." He scratched his eyebrow. "That doesn't sell newspapers and magazines."

Scott leaned toward him. "I know, but that gets me in the door—I'll get experience and make contacts— they also do Search and Rescue, sir." Scott sat back. "I'll find stories."

The man finally took the cigarette butt out of his mouth and crushed it into an overflowing ashtray. He smiled. "That's not much different than how I started 25 years ago... covering the stuff no one else wanted to until I hit with a breakout story."

"I know I'll find something newsworthy, sir." Scott sensed he'd gained some ground with him. "I just need a chance..." he swallowed; next was the hard part. "And credentials... so I'm taken seriously."

The man's smile faded but didn't turn to a frown. He had a thoughtful look. "We have correspondents that string for us... they won't like a new guy—a young kid like you—stepping on their toes."

"I wouldn't do that, sir."

"How would you keep from doing it?"

"In Saigon, I'm also going to work on completing my masters in literature at the University there. I'm not going to be hanging out where other journalists are. And I think the young people—the young Vietnamese— are going to give me a different perspective. I'm not going to chase the same stories that other, older, journalists are going to chase."

The man rubbed his chin. "A young person-civilian in Vietnam slant on the war. That might work." He pushed back his chair and stood. Scott rose with him as the man drilled him with a hard look. "I do this and you send your stories straight to me. Don't waste my time with crap. You do and I'll pull your press cred so fast it'll leave a burn on your neck. Got it?"

"Yes, sir!" Scott had met his stare and shook his hand.

He slipped out of the dream and into a deep sleep.

* * *

Mai sat staring at Scott in the hospital bed wrapped in bandages but sleeping more soundly now. The tears rolled down her cheeks. If only she hadn't invited him. In the otherwise quiet room, a ventilator hissed and sucked air above Scott's head, filling the oxygen mask covering his face. An IV hung from a pole on each side of the bed. Mai watched the trail of plastic lines as they disappeared at the end of the needles into Scott's arms. White gauze covered his shoulders and most of his torso and arms. Several large, red stains indicated he was still bleeding, despite the pressure and the coagulants.

I'll stay all night, every night until he wakes, she thought. Mai knew she'd never forget the concert scene as long as she lived. It all happened too quickly. When the woman on stage began to yell her message into the microphone, it had registered that the men and woman were Viet Cong, what most South Vietnamese referred to as the VC. She had watched as the emcee wrestled with one of the men who was about to take the microphone from the screeching woman. The emcee was shoved to the floor and the man in black pointed a .45 automatic pistol at him. As the stunned and motionless students watched, he shot the emcee four times in the stomach. Then she saw the man look at her and aim his gun at Scott. But he had lowered his handgun standing rigid staring at her as the other man pulled the pin on a grenade.

Mai turned toward Scott as she watched the grenade hit a desk, bounce and then land on the concrete floor only three feet away. In the panicked rush of people, she had been separated from Scott. Everything was happening so fast; she couldn't reach him against the press of bodies.

Pushed to the other side of the room, Scott ran toward her as she froze. Mai seemed a mile away as he struggled vainly trying to get through the screaming students. He felt like he was running in thick mud, reaching, reaching—knowing he only had seconds. When he was eight feet away, he jumped and threw himself at her, his arms outstretched as if in a cliff dive, draping over her body as they began the fall to the floor together. The grenade went off in a shattering explosion, hurtling chunks of steel through the air in a dozen directions, much of it tearing into Scott's legs and back.

The sound was deafening in the confines of the small room. Smoke immediately billowed up and filled the classroom as one desk caught fire. Mai's ears were ringing; she could see the expressions of terror on the students' faces, but couldn't hear them screaming. She saw a young girl next to her, lying on her back, her face completely gone.

Large shards of glass from the windows high above began to fall, like sharp foot-long icicles, bursting and splintering around her. She kept her eyes closed and shook her head, trying to orient herself when something hit her on the head and all went black.

She came to feeling a heaviness... something was pinning her down. She realized it was Scott who was lying on top of her, unconscious—maybe dead. Oh God no, she thought, struggling to move his 215-pound dead weight body off her. Quickly pressing the artery in his neck, she sighed at the feel of a faint pulse as she pushed herself out from under him. She heard the sirens of approaching police and ambulances. Relieved help was on the way her mind shifted to something she couldn't figure out. She'd looked into the eyes of one of the attackers. And she knew she'd met him before.

* * *

"Ms. Trinh, I'm sorry to wake you," the doctor said, touching her shoulder lightly. He stood over her in his white coat with the insignias of a major in the South Vietnamese Medical Corps, a stethoscope swinging in Mai's face, his voice concerned. "I gave you a mild tranquilizer three hours ago and you've slept a while. Your friend is heavily sedated and he will not wake until morning. It's very late. Perhaps you want to go home and come back then. There is nothing you can do for him now."

Mai sat up, smelled the alcohol and cleaning materials, saw the drab gray walls, the doctor's smock, and realized she'd been dreaming.

"No, absolutely not; I'm not leaving until I know he's okay," she said adamantly, rubbing her eyes and straightening in the chair. She felt she was responsible. If she had never asked him, he wouldn't be lying here.

"As you wish, Ms. Trinh. As I told you, one of the pieces of shrapnel nearly cut his femoral artery, but we were able to stop the bleeding. He has three other wounds in his back. They should all heal well in time. He's a very lucky man."

Chapter 2

JULY 1967
SAIGON

Scott had arrived at what was little more than a single, gray concrete building with large plastic letters lit but flickering: Tan Son Nhut Airport. To either side of the terminal were aerial ports, aluminum one-story structures primarily used for military storage. It was a small but busy commercial airport shared by civilians and military. Given the constant takeoffs and landings of the helicopters, it was dusty and hot, as it always was during the summer.

Scott stepped out of the Continental Airlines 707 from Manila. He carried an old leather suitcase with a frayed strap and buckle securing it; a keepsake his grandfather had given him. Under the other arm, he had a taped cardboard box that contained his Remington typewriter, some ink ribbons, and a ream of paper. He had no idea what he would need when he left California. He pushed the distinctive Ray-Ban sunglasses with the bright green lenses up onto his forehead. An old brown leather valise was slung over his shoulder, another keepsake, this one from his mother. He'd taken the bag to all of his college classes and many of his trips to Mexico, always ready with paper, pens, and journals.

In a pair of Levi's that looked like a miner had worn them during the gold rush, he was an unlikely visitor. He hadn't dressed up for the long haul from California to the Philippines, and now to here. In fact, he rarely dressed in anything but jeans and a t-shirt.

Stretched over his lean frame was his favorite navy blue t-shirt with a logo silk screened on the back that read, Day-Glo Surfboards, Huntington Beach, California.

Glancing around, trying to get his bearings, Scott saw several Air Force C-123 transports along with at least ten Huey B-1 army helicopters and two army Cobra choppers on the tarmac. Two other Continental jets were sitting idle nearby as well.

After passing through the small building, Scott saw a driver standing on the curb holding a sign with his name on it. He waved as the driver opened the back door of the old French Citroen and smiled. Scott placed the box and his bags on the back seat and jumped in, noticing the clean, unscratched leather. On the other hand, the front seat was old tattered cloth stained from years of wear. The driver naturally tended to his passengers first. On the dash and hanging from the visors were, at least, thirty various trinkets. A collection of crucifixes, charms, photos in plastic holders, a set of dice trapped in an hourglass, and pictures of what seemed to be his family.

The driver began adeptly sliding through the chaotic traffic. Scott looked at the buildings, thinking the city resembled a larger version of a midsize coastal town in Mexico, near where he and his friends sometimes surfed in the winter. The buildings were mostly concrete, vintage French/Spanish architecture.

Nguyen Van Thoai Street, the sign read. The street came almost directly from the airport parking area and then made a straight shot away to the west. Even though it was still light out, late afternoon, lit neon signs dominated the front of many of the one- and two-story buildings. It looked like every other storefront was a bar. GIs hung out in front, drinking beer and talking with Vietnamese women who Scott quickly realized were hookers.

It was a seedy scene with a background babble of conversation, music blaring out the windows, a sea of human traffic, and cigarette smoke. The smells were sour, the women's clothing garish.

At the end of Nguyen Van Thoai Street, the backdrop was different. On the busy intersections, two Saigon traffic cops stood in white short-sleeve shirts and khaki pants. Each trying to direct the near anarchy of traffic like seasoned conductors using the flick of a wrist to keep a trumpet quiet or the wild waving of arms to head off a trombone blast. There were far fewer GIs, mostly Military Police, and the city seemed to settle into itself.

Scott was both watching and engaged in the battle. The entire history of late-twentieth-century automobiles filled the pavement, horns blaring and honking. Abused old mopeds, beat-up trucks, battered buses, and rickety three-wheeled taxis fought for the head of the line, wherever that was.

To Scott, it all seemed like a perfectly choreographed frenetic, New Age dance, where the purpose appeared to be to get as close as possible without hitting another vehicle.

One of the cops stayed in the tiny protective stand, in the middle of the intersection, apparently taking his break. He was protected from the traffic by steel poles mounted on what looked like a large overturned bucket with a round tin roof that provided a small disc of shade.

Glancing side to side as the car continued through the city, Scott noticed the many street, vendors. Some were just children, hawking their vegetables and fruits from crude encampments made mostly of baskets and cardboard laced together.

They also passed a large central outdoor market where other vendors shared a common corner selling rice, fish, fish sauces, and food he'd never seen. One seller stood near an enormous pig's head. On a plate in front of the head were four hooves.

Since Vietnam was an agrarian society, this is what they had to sell along with some items of clothing and miscellaneous trinkets mixed with Pho signs, cafés, and repair shops, Scott thought. It all seemed an incredible, perspiring mess that somehow worked—a city that, at least in this part, had not yet decided if it wanted to be too civilized.

Scott turned his head rapidly as he used his camera to try to capture as much as he could. The many walls made of sandbags. The Presidential Palace. The American embassy, which looked like an effort to mimic the New York Public Library. The Continental Hotel. Tu Do Street and then turning the corner suddenly, the poverty, the underbelly and the not so neat part that reminded him of Tijuana.

He felt lucky to be the beneficiary of a car instead of one of the hundreds of three-wheeled taxis that Tai, the driver, told him were cyclos: essentially glorified rickshaws that vied for asphalt.

The cyclos were all different, almost customized, and seemed handmade from miscellaneous but utilitarian parts. A seat mounted on two large tires accommodated two people. A man sat behind on a third wheel with an attached bicycle seat and handlebars and either peddled or, in some cases, motored his passengers through the city. Scott could imagine the industrious owners scavenging for seats and tires from old cars and then spot-welding part of a bicycle frame together with some steel poles to create a living.

A satisfying presence of military vehicles competed with the taxis and pedestrians for space. Many of them MPs in armored Jeeps, or troops in deuce-and-a-halfs, 2.5-ton army trucks with canvas covers that reminded Scott of the Conestoga wagons of early America.

Tai, knowing Scott was an American and sensing he'd never been to Saigon, perhaps not even Vietnam—saw his passenger's fascination. He took it upon himself to speak, his English honed from thousands of fares.

"I see your interest in Saigon; is this your first visit?"

Scott pulled himself out of his trance and answered, "Yes."

"Are you a journalist?" Tai probed.

"Yes, how did you know?"

"Lucky guess," Tai said with a knowing smile, glancing again at Scott's press pass hanging around his neck.

"What was the area back there on Nguyen Van Thoai?" Scott asked even though he was sure he knew. "Sure was different than here."

"That is where most of the GIs spend their time. Except the MPs, they don't venture out from there very far. That's their comfort zone—women, drugs, and alcohol—not much more they want after they've come to Saigon from some gruesome fighting. And, it's close. They can walk from the base, use the PX there, and not have to go into the city for their cigarettes, beer, and other necessities."

"Most people in Saigon don't have that much interaction with the military for that reason. They stay on Nguyen Van Thoai, and we move around the rest of the city."

Scott looked at Tai in the rearview mirror. He was intent now on the traffic. He appeared to be about fifty with a thin gray mustache, creases around his eyes, probably from so much sun.

"Do you speak Vietnamese?" Tai asked.

"Not yet. I'm going to be taking classes at the University, though."

Tai decided to pass the time by acting the part of the guide as he continued to question Scott.

"Ah, when you begin your studies, remember, Chinese has influenced our language, writers, and artists for more than a thousand years. So it's important to understand Chinese to some extent."

"That's good to know. Thank you."

Tai continued to dodge traffic and cyclos, seemingly without even looking at the road as he glanced back and forth at Scott.

"Vietnamese won out, however, and I'm glad. Being a journalist, you should be, too. Our language is far subtler than Chinese and English," Tai continued as if he were a professor. "It is tonal in nature. A change in tone alone can completely alter the meaning of a word. It is like poetry without the punctuation."

The car finally left the busy intersections and continued on a quiet street. Tai had Scott's attention and since he'd told him the ride would take forty minutes, Scott decided to learn something.

"Your English is excellent. Where did you study?" he asked.

"At the University. Now there are no jobs, so I've become an excellent driver."

Sensing this was a great opportunity to tap into Tai's experience, Scott asked, "What other insights can you give me about your people?"

Stopping at the last light, and glad to be engaged, Tai said over his shoulder, "Small question, and big answer— too big for one ride. Maybe you call me again for more stories. I can tell you some things. You should learn how to say please and thank you first. Then, learn how to ask questions like, where is the bathroom, how much is this thing, how far is it from here? So, learn: Who, How, When, Why, Where, What, and then you can learn the names of things like phone, taxi, food—those kinds of things. You don't need to put together sentences; the people will understand."

Scott thought for a minute how much that was like journalism: "Who, How, When, Why, Where, and What."

"Important," Tai said, holding his index finger up for emphasis. "Names are different here in Vietnam. We use our family name first to reinforce the importance of household over the individual. It comes first, then the person's name second. For example, if Mr. Nguyen calls his son, Tai, then the boy will be known as Nguyen Tai. Simple."

Suddenly, Scott heard a commotion, the chattering and yelling of several male voices off to his right. He rolled down the window and watched an odd sight. In a park about fifty yards away, men were standing in rows resembling a checkerboard. Two men in the center were quarreling vehemently, but not physically. The other men on either side of them were stoic, not moving, not getting involved.

One of the street cops continued to hold his hand up; halting traffic. Something that could often take ten minutes, so Scott continued to watch what he thought might turn into a fight.

"What are they doing over there?" Scott asked

Tai twisted his head to the right and said, "Oh, they are playing human chess. Each man is a piece and when a piece is taken, a fight ensues."

"A real fight?"

"No. It is play. They pretend to protest. It is all part of the fun."

Scott was interested. There was so much to see and experience. He was like a sponge when it came to learning.

"Do you have a card?" he asked Tai.

"Yes, but it only has a phone number. If you need more rides, make sure you call me first. I'm the best and the cheapest. I have lived in Saigon all my life," he answered, reaching into his pocket and handing Scott a crumpled white card. It had his name, Nguyen Tai, and a phone number.

"I'm a guide, don't forget. I can escort you to many things," Tai said as he drove off.

* * *

It couldn't have been a better time for someone striving to be a journalist. Scott was always inquisitive to the point of being obnoxious—a good trait for a reporter though he considered himself more than that. He wanted to discover and expose the smokescreens in every story he wrote and it seemed, if he really looked, there were always plenty of those. He looked at every potential article by first asking what each player's motive was. If he knew what the true motives were, he generally got the real story—mostly those motives were greed, ego, power, or lust, but more often than not, money.

Before he had left for Vietnam, Scott had either written or read about China's first hydrogen bomb test explosion and many other significant events. The Shah of Iran crowning himself and his wife in Tehran. Martin Luther King's march in New York. And U.N. Secretary-General U Thant, revealing that a Vietnam truce, proposed by him that was approved by the U.S. and South Vietnam had been rebuffed by the North Vietnamese.

For a journalist, 1967 was a busy year, a perfect storm of mythical proportions, in particular for the U.S., its allies, and South and North Vietnam. It was the story of his generation, and Scott knew it. However, it sickened him that American lives were tallied on a weekly and sometimes nightly basis and then broadcast on the major networks as nonchalantly as the numbers posted after each inning of a Major League Baseball game.

What was the point? He wondered. The media had never played this role in any of America's wars; not in Korea and certainly not in WWII when there was no television. To television producers, this was entertainment. The war drew huge nightly audiences as American families sat around the dinner table and listened to the drone of the body counts from their sets. And always there was the triumphant note of winning, in the most gruesome way, and it was often wildly inaccurate: the home team only lost 205; visitors, 923!

Was the media trying to influence public opinion against or for the war? In his experience, both, depending upon your politics.

Politics. Scott hated that word. It was a dirty profession in his mind, pursued by those who wanted a "revered" title and a lifetime hall pass from real work.

He had his own ideas and his job was to be objective, or, at least, that's what he'd been taught in journalism. Not an easy thing to do. Especially if you were 24-year-old, naïve, American in South Vietnam learning of the atrocities. Like Viet Cong guerillas tossing grenades into a helicopter on display at Saigon City Hall that killed seven and wounded forty-seven innocent bystanders.

Even some journalists who lived for objectivity were incapable of seeing flaws in their heroes. Scott didn't want to just regurgitate the daily diet of bullshit the military commanders or the State Department dished out; and, as for heroes, they often turned out to be fairy tales. As might be expected of a military eager to keep civilians out of their business, war correspondents were criticized heavily. Especially by General William Westmoreland, who said, "Fifty-one percent of 'them' were under twenty-nine years old and, for the most part, had little or no experience as war correspondents." Others said, "These so-called writers were mere messengers, translators, cameramen, or backup staff, but not true journalists and not really legitimate. Most were there for a short period of time, often less than a week. Just long enough to give their work at home some semblance of cachet, but hardly enough for them to learn much about the war."

Scott knew what he would face trying to get the real story, and he knew he was in it for as long as the paper kept him on assignment. But he would not allow himself to be lumped into Westmoreland's description. Or worse yet, become the type of journalist he'd described.

Chapter 3

Mai had visited Scott in the hospital every day between classes and then again at the end of the day until midnight. Then she went home, studied for her classes, and fell asleep in a chair until the next morning. Each day, she pushed the doctor for more news, better news, but Scott remained the same, slowly healing.

It was late in the afternoon and Scott was asleep as she sat next to him and put her hand on his forearm. The doctor told her his vital signs had stabilized, but he was still on heavy doses of morphine. Outside the window above his head, she could see storm clouds forming and smell the moisture. It was muggy and warm out and the rusted old air conditioning box seemed to cough out more water than cold air.

She couldn't shake the violence of the concert or witnessing the man she thought she knew as one of its perpetrators. She kept trying to place his eyes, the only part of his face that had been visible. Where had she met him before? The sounds of the gunshots and explosion still echoed in her mind. They brought back vivid memories of the death of her mother. Those were likely the last sounds she heard. It was in 1956, just two years after the French defeat at Dien Bien Phu when her mother had taken a short trip to a village. Armed insurgents, the VC, attacked a nearby plantation and she was killed. She had overheard the authorities tell her father she had bled out from her wounds. Dying a slow and agonizing death as the fighters retreated, leaving the wounded to die.

Though she was only eight at the time, even then she understood the politics of her country from her parents. Her father had said it seemed as if Vietnam had been in one kind of struggle or another forever. Nations were always vying for influence in Southeast Asia and that meant controlling Vietnam. Authority, power, greed, call it what you will, it was all the same. Her mother had always told her, "Mai, there will always be hope. That is why our country is still called Vietnam and not France, China, or Russia."

She knew that in 1954, the French were defeated and the Geneva Accords were signed to separate Vietnam at the 17th parallel. After the country had been split, thousands of Viet Minh stayed behind in the south to help with a proposed reunification election that was never held. That meant there was really no political demarcation between South and North. The Viet Minh, later referred to derogatorily as the Viet

Cong, blended in with the Nationalist South. By then, her father, Hung Trinh, had already risen to the rank of captain in the military. After Mai's mother had been killed, he was left only with Mai—his princess—and a cold rage she sensed as she grew old enough to become aware.

Mai struggled to understand it all, the many influences—the French, Americans, Russians, Chinese, and now the North Vietnamese as a separate entity, but not different people. All Vietnamese shared the same DNA, but ideologies were more important. At heart, and especially after her mother's death, Mai was a South Vietnamese military brat with a bent for politics and hatred for Hanoi and the Viet Cong. As she got older, she slowly began to understand America's involvement in her homeland. They seemed to be saviors. Maybe the Americans would be the first ones without an ax to grind. Perhaps they would be the first without greed or self-serving agenda. After all, they came to defend her way of life. Right?

* * *

Scott's arm jerked and his eyes slowly opened. Moving his head side to side, trying to figure out where he was, he fixed on Mai. She jumped up and put both hands on his upper arm, the only spot free of bandages.

"Oh, Scott, thank God," she said. Not answering, Scott looked at Mai's face with heavy lids then down to his bandages. "Scott, do you know who I am?"

He slowly raised his eyes back to Mai and said with a shaky voice, "Yes. Of course. You're room service, right?" He grabbed Mai's hand and drew her closer. "It's good to be alive," his smile steadied.

Mai held his hand tightly. "And I'm not room service." She leaned over to kiss his forehead. "How do you feel?" she asked even though she could tell he was in terrible pain.

"Did you get the license on that deuce and a half?" he joked, "the truck that hit me." He coughed hard clenching his jaw with the spasm. "What did the doctor say? When can I get out of here? Is it Christmas yet?"

Mai moved close to his bed.

"It's passed already. Do you remember what happened?"

"Vaguely. I remember the concert I remember three guys in black."

"Do you remember saving my life?"

Scott's eyes opened fully. He started to push himself up.

"No. Lie down. The doctor hasn't checked you yet. It wasn't three guys, it was two men and a woman— Viet Cong. They shot the emcee and killed a female

32

student. I wouldn't be here if you hadn't covered me with your body—Scott, you saved my life."

"Oh, so that's why I feel like shit?"

The two laughed nervously, but Scott clutched his side, wincing.

"Okay, no more jokes," he said.

"Your femoral artery was cut and there was other damage, but they stitched you up and according to the doctor, you just need time to heal fully. You're lucky this is a military hospital. Otherwise, you never would have survived. These guys have seen everything." Mai wanted more than anything to reach over and embrace him, but she knew she couldn't. "Do you remember the guy aiming a gun at you?" Mai asked, still trying to shake loose an identity in her brain.

"Why at me?"

"I don't know. Possibly because you're an American, perhaps because you're a blonde, maybe because you were the tallest one in the room."

"Or they don't like surfers," Scott smiled.

"The weird thing is I feel I know that guy," she said. "I could see his eyes—and I've seen them before. I just can't place them."

"And if you could, what would you do?"

"I'd hang him by his toes and cut off his... his tongue; something to match his crimes," she said. She stomped her foot in anger. "The VC are so filled with hatred there is no room for light to get in. There is no place in their darkness for any other ideas." Turning back, she added. "And then I'd set his accomplices on fire."

"Wow! I wouldn't want to get on your bad side." Scott said.

She was never subtle when she expressed herself politically. She had already lived through two wars and studied political science and history, first through her mother's stories and then at the University. "You may not know it yet, but the Viet Cong and the North Vietnamese regime want to force us back to the days of serfdom and land reform. They want to keep us ankle deep in paddies, plunking down rice shoots in the muddy water. To keep our mouths shut and our hands out, and if that doesn't work, they want to annihilate us even though we are all Vietnamese."

Scott had noticed she chewed on the fingernail of her right index finger and walked in circles when she was nervous or angry. She stopped and turned toward the door.

"I'm going to go find the doctor," Mai said. "I want to know when you can get out of here."

Scott watched as she walked out of the room. As he lay there helpless, his mind went back to the concert and the three Viet Cong, who had disappeared after they inflicted their proclamation and violence on the students. When he'd left California months before, the war protesters were becoming more vocal and violent. His younger brother, who was very close, had been drafted that June, right out of high school. He was only eighteen, for Christ's sake. He was lucky though and got stationed in Germany; so far so good. He'd been in the army since 1965 and hoped to be discharged unscathed.

Nothing ever changed. Boys who couldn't wait to fight for their country dying here, or going home without a leg or two. And those who fought a different war at home, protesting vehemently against the imperialism, the barbarism, the civil war of it all—more vehement against America than North Vietnam. That might have been the beginning of Scott's distrust; not just of the media that employed him, but of the American government, and even more specifically, the career politicians. Did he fall in the middle, he wondered? I won't enlist, but I'll go and do my part? I'll survive. I'll come home and be proud to say that I served in Vietnam. Then, as he had done so many times since landing at Tan Son Nhut, he caught himself; felt the guilt running down his spine. Who am I kidding? I came here to find and tell the truth. I didn't come here to be able to go home and tell everyone I was a hero or just that I served.

"Knock it off," he said aloud as Mai came back with the doctor in tow.

"Who are you talking to?" Mai asked, looking around the room.

"Just me."

Mai stood on the right side of Scott's bed, smiling with subdued excitement. The doctor walked around to the left side of the bed as a nurse entered the room. He smiled, used his stethoscope on Scott's carotid artery and then his heart, and then turned to the nurse and said, "I think another week or so and this young lady can take him home."

* * *

The nurse slowly pulled out the IV. That and a change of the bandages, and Scott could get dressed. Mai reached down to pick up her tennis bag. It held Scott's jeans, t-shirt, and his deck shoes. It was a uniform that he alternated when he needed to, with the army issue fatigues he'd worn when flying with the 633rd.

"We're going home," Mai said. Though she would head to her father's house and Scott would have to go back to his hotel, the Caravel, where the embassy had commandeered two floors for some of the press.

"No, we're not going home. We're going out to dinner at Pho Hien Vuong," the only restaurant name that Scott could pronounce. "Nothing but the best for you. We need to celebrate," he said as Mai helped him pull his t-shirt over his bandages.

"Boy! You'd think I'd saved your life," Mai laughed. She wore a traditional ao dai, a fitted, long, red satin tunic top that was very popular with South Vietnamese women because the style accentuated the figure with the top draped over the pants. Around her neck, a mandarin collar was closed with knotted buttons—a pop of red accented her mouth. Most of the University students wore white during the day. For nonstudents, the daily wardrobe consisted of black, blue, or white, but for special occasions, more color was called for: red, bright green, or even orange.

Scott turned and held her shoulders as he said, "You have."

On the street they took a cyclo and though the restaurant was one of the best, seeing the front, any foreign newcomer would have changed their mind. Mai had eaten at it many times with her father, so she knew not to judge this book by its cover.

On the street in front of the restaurant were the ubiquitous mopeds and bicycles. By the curb, several cyclos sat idle while their drivers huddled together, smoking cigarettes and arguing over dominos on a makeshift card table. The front of the two-story building was drab and dirty. On the beige, concrete, façade was block letters spelling out Pho Hien Vuong above the entry. Inside, the floor was concrete, not particularly clean, but the smells reminded Mai of her dinners with her father. A mix of aromatic vegetables, hot noodles, spicy sauces, and a few that not even she could describe. The tables were dark wood, splintered from years of use, many carved with dinner knives spelling out two lovers' initials wrapped in a heart. The room was packed. There seemed to be as many waiters as customers, each hustling back and forth through a dark curtain behind the counter.

Scott followed her on his crutches, holding his right leg in the air a few inches, letting it swing. As he tried to keep up with Mai, he glanced at the picture on the wall. It was a black and white photograph with a plastic frame of the current leader President Nguyen Van Thieu. The flavor of the year, Scott thought.

Many of the women were dressed up in deference to the food more than the environment, but Mai stood out in her red dress. Scott liked the way it hugged her, making her look both feminine and athletic. Helping her into her chair, he could see her arms were tight but not muscular from playing tennis. Scott, not as formal, at least, wore the short-sleeve shirt Mai brought to the hospital instead of one of his signature T-shirts. They ordered their food, and hot and steaming Pho was quickly on the table. He had learned from Tai, the driver, that rice was served at virtually every meal, including breakfast. Fish was almost as important, and beef and pork were usually reserved for the wealthy or special occasions. Like this one. He looked at Mai.

Pho Hien Vuong was known for its recipes, tightly held secrets, and many of the dishes were memorable. But Scott was still having trouble with a lot of the food, including the dish that the waiter put in front of Mai. The Bún bò Huế —a stew of pork hooves, beef brisket, and pig's blood—caught his attention. The look on his face brought a smile to Mai's. The smell was bearable, but the visual was evidently too much for him.

Scott tried to avert his eyes as she used her chopsticks to pick from the bowl. He was a southern California boy who loved a good In-n-Out burger and didn't have much experience with more exotic foods. He satisfied himself with a bowl of pan-fried noodles and two egg roll vermicelli. Compared to his diet in southern California, the Vietnamese seemed very smart and health conscious by including many fresh vegetables. And parts of animals he'd never imagine eating were sold at even higher prices than their meat. Scott knew if he stuck to certain dishes, simple food, he wouldn't get any surprises, or at least, that's what he thought. When the waiter put his bowl on the table, he poked at the vermicelli eggroll with a chopstick.

"What are these little brown things in here?" he asked Mai.

Knowing he wouldn't eat his meal if she told him what they were, she smiled and pretended to be busy with her dish.

"Mai, what are these little things?" Scott insisted.

"Oh, those are spices," she answered.

He managed a mouthful from his bowl, saying, "Oh, this is good. Now see, it's okay to keep it simple. No weird stuff."

Scott's crutches were propped against the wall behind him. He needed them to help keep weight off his injured leg because the stitches ran like a zipper from thigh to his knee.

"I have something for you," Mai said, reaching into her purse.

"A present?"

"Yes, considering."

"Considering what? That it's not my birthday?"

"Considering they made it through the explosion, you flying through the air, and landing on me," she said, putting Scott's old green Ray-Ban sunglasses on the table.

"Geeze! That's great!" he said, putting them on immediately. "I got these three years ago in a secondhand shop in Baja, Mexico. The guy had no clue what they were worth. I love them. Thank you! Thank you," he said, still grinning.

"They look good on you—very American," Mai said, smiling at him.

They had eaten in silence for a while when it came to her. "Chua Toi! I know who it was!" she said, nearly dropping her chopsticks on the floor. "Bach Nguyen," she said out loud to herself. "My God!" she gasped.

Not being able to get up to help her, Scott quickly leaned over, putting his hand on her shoulder. "Are you choking?" he asked in a flurry of concern.

"I'm okay. I just realized who that man was, the VC who aimed the gun at you. I can't believe it. It was Bach!"

"Who is he?"

"He has very distinctive eyes. The right one tends to go in almost cross-eyed when he's nervous. I know that was him."

"But how do you know him?"

Mai calmed down for a moment, took a deep breath, and then fanned herself with a napkin. "He's an ex-friend," she said.

For a split-second, Scott's expression went taut, but he quickly recovered. Even though he'd saved this woman's life, he had no claim to her. And despite what had happened they still really didn't know each other that well.

"Ex?"

Before she could answer, the waiter came over and asked, "Is everything all right?"

"Yes, we're okay," Mai dismissed the man.

"Ex?" Scott asked again.

"Yes. Not even an ex, really. Bach was a very idealistic person. He was a political science major. We shared a few classes and went out a couple of times. I didn't have any strong feelings for him except as a friend. But he quickly pushed himself into my life more than I wanted."

"Was that how he became an ex-friend?"

Scott sat waiting, a pair of chopsticks in his right hand, a clump of noodles hanging precariously.

She nodded. "That was part of it. He was very political, very focused. At first, he seemed a Nationalist strictly and then, as time went on, he leaned more to the left. I liked him because he was so smart, but I had no attraction to him other than his brains. He was great to argue with—like you—feisty, brainy, but not nearly as handsome," she added. She dabbed at her mouth with a napkin, waiting for a response, gesture, an expression.

Scott began to feel analytical and even angry. My God, he thought, this is one of the guys who tried to kill us all, almost killed Mai. How is it possible that a terrorist could be enrolled in the University and on top of that, walk into a classroom and murder, innocent students?

"Scott?"

"I believe we have to find this guy. I'm thinking," he paused for a second, "I'm thinking I'm going to cut his testicles off, or maybe burn him at the stake. He almost killed you! He and his gang killed two people."

"Scott, do you know how many VCs are living in the hundreds of villages around here? How would you even begin and, really, why? It's fruitless."

"Tomorrow we have Professor Phan's political science class. He's a walking history book. I'm going to talk with him."

"Scott, I've lived here for nineteen years. I wouldn't search for Bach, not now. He's long gone. Trust me; they are like vapor, that's their nature. There is plenty of danger around us right now; we don't need to go looking for it. Half of them live most of their lives in those damned secret bases or tunnels. You're a journalist, not a soldier."

"I get that, but how did he enroll at the University? How did he just walk into that concert?" Scott asked.

"Because he is one of us, even though he is fighting for the other side."

Mai had hoped to thank Scott for saving her life. Instead, they were now caught up in something she knew would be futile.

Chapter 4

"Students, take your seats, please." Professor Phan, the political science teacher was small, about 60 years old, and had a white mustache and chin beard so wispy Scott wondered why he bothered to keep it.

"Most of this small class is comprised of foreign journalists," he scanned the room. "Ah, but I see a beautiful young Vietnamese lady in the back." His eyes traveled back over the non-Vietnamese. "Some of you already know most of our history. At least for the last decade. Of course, there are a lot of you that are very young and new to Vietnam."

Scott leaned forward on his desk, Mai sitting behind him. He opened a pad of paper and was ready to take detailed notes. The class was just under an hour, and he hoped to understand more about the VC as the class progressed through the semester. He knew the teachers and school were prohibited from discussing the Viet Cong, but he hoped to learn and make some contacts through Professor Phan.

"Someday, scholars will study this as they scrutinize the war in its entirety. Then, maybe they will know the truth," Professor Phan began his lecture. He always tried hard not to be emotional, endeavoring to be a teacher of facts, as far as he was allowed to teach them.

When the class ended, Scott approached Phan and introduced himself. He explained he'd come to Vietnam to observe and to finish the classes he needed for his master's degree in literature. Phan was pleasant, but Scott could tell that the professor knew he had an ulterior motive for introducing himself. The diminutive man stroked his wispy chin hairs. Scott described his experience at the concert, explaining the need for the crutches; wanting to know how such a man could have been a student at the University. As soon as Scott mentioned Bach, the professor closed his book, stacked his notes on top, and put the pile into a valise.

"I cannot talk about such things, young man. I'm sorry."

"Yes, but Professor Phan," Scott began as he followed the small man to the classroom door, "you teach political science and history. How can you do that without telling the entire story, the truth?"

"I'm very pragmatic. I want to live. You're a persistent one, aren't you?" the professor said as he opened the door.

"Yes, I am. Can you help me?"

"No. Personally, I cannot," the professor replied, looking down the empty hall both ways for any potential prying ears. Whispering to Scott, he said, "Givral Café on Tu Do Street. Be there at ten, tomorrow night. He will find you."

"Who will find me?"

"Never mind. Don't write anything down. Just be there if you want to learn. I must go," Phan said, scurrying down the hall and out the back door, peeking over his shoulder until he was gone.

* * *

JANUARY 8, 1968
GIVRAL CAFÉ, SAIGON

Even though Scott was intrigued, he didn't want to tell Mai about his meeting with Professor Phan. Based on the professor's secrecy, for the time being, he would manage on his own until he knew more.

At 9:30 the next evening, Scott was seated in the Givral Café in a booth covered in red plastic. To keep things low key, he hadn't brought his notepad and would just remember everything he could and make notes later. He didn't know what the man looked like, but being a tall, blonde, blue-eyed American civilian sitting by himself in a café late at night would be easy for the man to spot and approach him.

Scott sat in the back of the café sipping tea. There were no other customers near him when a man suddenly appeared from behind a curtain that led to the kitchen and sat down next to him. He was a young Vietnamese, perhaps a student, and nondescript. An attempt at a mustache was a faint shadow over his lips. The man had a cheap green canvas backpack slung over his shoulder, which he immediately put on the floor between his legs and then ordered a cup of tea without giving his name or acknowledging Scott.

Scott was an avid poker player and he knew a tell better than just about anyone. The first thing Scott would look for were any signs that would give him clues: Was the man nervous? How did he feel about Americans? Was he telling the truth? Scott didn't know what the young man would say but thought it better to let the man make the first move.

"Mr. Reynolds?" the young man asked.

"Yes," Scott offered his hand. The man didn't take it. Both arms and hands remained under the table as the man's eyes darted around the room.

He's nervous, Scott realized. He was beginning to feel uncomfortable, too but remained silent.

"Can I call you Scott?"

"Yes. What's your name?"

"That isn't important. You don't need to know anything about me. Professor Phan says you are a correspondent and need some information."

47

"Yes," Scott was keeping his part of the dialog to a minimum until he knew more. He would keep Bach out of this discussion, instead approaching the young man not as a Times' reporter, but as a student trying to get information on his master's degree program.

The man sat silently waiting. Scott took another sip of his cold tea.

"I'm not here to gather news for the media. I'm a student, a serious one. I don't like to feel stupid. I want to get the big picture for myself to better comprehend current events. Do you understand? I didn't study much Vietnamese history before I came here."

The man sat silently as he stirred a teaspoon of sugar into his tea, glancing around the room again. A couple came in and sat down four tables away. He seemed to gauge the distance and if there was still enough privacy to talk quietly. He leaned toward Scott.

"Yes. I understand. I'm a student as well. I have long had an interest in your country. Maybe even more, than you do in mine. Perhaps we could share information from time to time on how our countries have reached a point where we both find ourselves seeking a better understanding of them," the man said, suddenly remembering where he was in 1965.

"You speak English well," Scott said.

"I'm a student, too... and English major." The man flashed the briefest of smiles. "You must be careful. It is not wise to talk politics at this time, understand?"

"Yes, of course; I do now. I'll never repeat a word you tell me, but I'm struggling to understand it all."

"Mr. Reynolds, we are all struggling to see what's going on. The Vietnamese people have suffered greatly from decades of war and upheaval. We are a rural, agrarian culture. Close to eighty percent of our population live in small villages. Most of the people who live in the cities live in small, cramped apartments, sometimes more than one family sharing two rooms. The war has destroyed roads, bridges, harbors, rails, and ports, not to mention the farms and crops that have been defoliated." He shook his head as if the enormity of it was too much to describe to a foreigner.

Scott had good instincts. "You're right. But maybe my understanding begins tonight. I would like to know more about the villages, life outside the city," Scott said, trying not to give away his real intention.

"Let us get another tea," the man said.

As the next hour passed, the café became busier, so the men were nearly whispering to each other, which wasn't a good idea either because it just brought more attention to them.

"Scott, let me summarize for you." The man adjusted his shirt and took on an almost professorial air. "As the scholars study, they will realize that the villages have always been the center of the main political organizations in Vietnam. The people in the villages are uneducated and are the most easily swayed so are fertile ground for propagandists. And this was the principal means of unifying the country before the West ever came in; village by village. To win a war in this country is to control the rural communities, then the provinces, urban areas, and ultimately Vietnam itself.

"Your President Kennedy knew this. That is why he sent in the Green Berets. His was a guerilla war. He knew he had to control the hamlets and villages. When Johnson came into office, all that changed." The man glanced around again and then leaned closer to Scott. "The Cu Chi area is the most heavily bombed, gassed, and defoliated area in the history of combat. Johnson's campaign there, in his Operation Cedar Falls, just started this month, has not managed to eliminate the tunnel complexes entirely. There are fifty square miles of them. The tunnels are like cities, complete with living, dining, and toilet areas. They aren't just holes dug in the ground. The Cu Chi area is the most important base for the Viet Cong."

So far, Scott couldn't find any tells. The man was deliberate and stoic, and he seemed to be genuine. He used no hand gestures; he never brought them from under the table.

"The American people don't understand the players because the media doesn't either. And it doesn't make much difference unless you are a history student or are here fighting a war. The Viet Cong and the National Liberation Front or NLF are the same. It gets confusing because there are so many people from the North in South Vietnam that came here after the Geneva Accords. A Communist is a Communist by any other name. You just can't tell by looking at them."

Scott was enthralled. He was beginning to see some of the pieces to the puzzle he knew he would have to understand. After his forty-minute conversation with this man, he better understood the infrastructure of the Viet Cong. How they lived in those villages and tunnels and moved in and out. Even how they blended in with the Nationalist South Vietnamese. Drawing an imaginary line across the country at the 17th parallel had nothing to do with the color of people's skin, their religion, or their politics. It didn't keep the bad guys from living in the South and, for all intents and purposes, being South Vietnamese.

"I must leave, Mr. Reynolds. We will talk again. I will contact you."

"But how? How will we communicate?"

"You can always talk with Professor Phan, good-bye now."

Chapter 5

Mai sat on the elegant brocade couch in the living room of her parents' house. She was comfortable wearing flip-flops, a loose white cotton top, and bottom. Across from her in the floor-to-ceiling bookcase was jammed an eclectic collection of history texts, Vietnamese novels, poetry, family albums, the Bible, and many books on the Buddhist religion. In Buddhism, there isn't a book like the Bible, Torah, or Koran. There are only Sutras, writings or recordings from the Buddha but oddly, they aren't as revered as the other books. Mai had studied both the Bible and many of the Sutras. She remembered her father's lecture about Buddhism. One of the things the Buddha taught was: Follow my forefinger, you will see the moon. After seeing the moon, forget my finger. No one should just believe what I say. We should all think for ourselves and discover the truth through our own experience.

Mai's mother had been a devout Catholic, but Mai was too young to remember much that faith. For most of her upbringing, she listened to her father's talks about Buddhism. He had always been as spiritual as her mother, just in a different, simpler way. She looked wistfully at the room. It contained several crucifixes her mother had proudly hung on the walls. And a statue of Buddha made of bronze that sat on the black baby grand piano her father had given her when she was only four. This room was where her mother spent so many hours playing concertos that Mai would later play by ear. She remembered her delicate hands and long fingers. As a child, she hoped that was how hers would grow. So much so that she often tugged on her fingers hoping to coax more length from them.

Her father was still stationed in Pleiku and so she lived in the large house by herself, commuting several miles each day to the city or the University. Hang Xanh was more of a suburb, a hybrid between the city structure and the farms and villages. It was the kind of area where career army officers, politicians, and businessmen lived. The neighborhood was typical of the villages outside the city. All the roads were dirt and lined every hundred yards with twenty-foot mini-towers that the American Army had erected to string communication wires. There were wooden or stucco houses of varying sizes and appearances with concrete posts in front of some that didn't seem to support any gates or fences.

Staring out the large front window, she was surrounded by pictures of her mother and several of her parents together. Her father had put his wife's pictures away for the entire year after her death. It wasn't until Mai was almost twelve that they started showing up on tables and on the mantle again. Though she did keep one of her own close to her at all times, in her wallet. She was staring at them now trying to determine who she resembled more—her mother or father.

She said silently, Mom. I miss you so. You know I will never forget you. Mai often talked to her mom as if she was in the room, always sensing her presence, a hand-on-her-shoulder feeling that was a comfort. I know you see all this, Mom. I pray for Father's safety every day. The fighting is fierce. I pray that this war will be over soon though it appears it will go on forever. You were right; it seems we have been fighting for a hundred years. I've met a young American, but then you already know that. I think you would approve. You were always so enlightened and open-minded. He saved my life. Mai softly rubbed her finger across the picture of her mother's face as if to caress her and then returned the black and white photo to her wallet as she sat back quietly.

Bach Nguyen! Mai sat thinking about how they'd met and who the strange man really was. Chopin's Opus 9 No. 2 in E-Flat: That was how they met. Mai clearly remembered the day. She was a freshman, in the music room playing in preparation for her recital. She'd become adept with her favorite composer. The room was seldom used; many students had lost interest in learning to play instruments. The times didn't seem to call for it as much as before the war. The hardwood floors were stained and scratched from many years of moving instruments, especially the piano. Because it was in the basement with a lone window above the piano, the room was cold and musty.

Surrounded by orchestra equipment and instruments, she lightly tickled the keys, limbering her chilled fingers, which were perfect for the instrument, for her exercise, effortlessly combining chords with just the right timing and pressure. She was so engrossed in her practice that she didn't see or hear the young man standing in the doorway. He was a young Vietnamese: athletic, tall, with an unusually long face, but not unattractive, and with an expression of appreciation, as if he were dreaming with his eyes open. She had never seen him on campus, but then there were many people she didn't know on the large, busy University grounds. As he closed his eyes and waved his finger, tapping his foot in time with the sounds, Mai stopped abruptly and looked at him.

"Excuse me," she said. "This is a private practice."

"Oh, I'm sorry," the young man replied, embarrassed. "I was down the hall and heard the most eloquent rendition of Chopin's Opus 9. I just had to see where it was coming from," Bach said, shuffling his feet, like a little boy who'd just been caught stealing a cookie.

Now Mai was embarrassed.

"Oh, that's all right, I suppose. There are going to be many more people at my recital, I hope. I guess I should be used to it by now."

"May I listen a little more?" he asked.

Mai thought for a moment, "No harm I suppose. Come in and sit down if you like."

"Thank you. I would like that. My name is Bach. What is yours?"

"I'm Mai."

"Lovely, as beautiful as your command of the instrument," he said, sitting in a foldout steel chair by the door.

Hmm, he's charming. I'll give him that.

Mai finished playing while the young man sat entranced as if the music was continuing on in his head.

"What is your major?" Mai asked, attempting to make light conversation.

"Oh, sorry. I was in a little trance. Your playing is mesmerizing. I'm a political science major. What about you?"

"History and English."

"Oh, you must be very smart—a double major?"

"I'm just inquisitive about many things, I guess."

As Mai relaxed with the young man, she found herself caught up in a lengthy conversation that included her family. Still sitting on the piano bench when he left half an hour later, her impression was that he was smart, sincere, and passionate, but they'd finished talking before she could pinpoint his political passions. He seemed to be enamored by both sides of the spectrum - right and left - but then most inquisitive students were.

Though she enjoyed his company and their discourse, as she rose and put her sheet music in a valise, she wished she hadn't revealed so much about herself. But Bach was an adept listener and perhaps even an adept interviewer.

Walking to the door, she also wished she hadn't shared any information about her father and his military assignment. But she was proud of him and it seemed so natural as Bach and she had discussed the war.

Chapter 6

The media were housed in various places throughout the city, including what the State Department called 'small' hotels, which were any available buildings that could hold six to eight men. The correspondents referred to them as Officers' Clubs. Often, they contained nothing more than cots with mosquito nets hanging over them and a small locker to secure belongings. Luckier journalists, like Scott, were housed in real hotels, two to a room. He and another correspondent shared a room in the Caravel Hotel. His roommate was a reporter for Reuters News Agency and so his stories reached a range of media outlets; Scott's stories went directly to the L.A. Times.

Scott sat in front of his Remington typewriter. He'd written hundreds of pages while stationed with the 633rd, most of them firsthand accounts of rescue missions or leaflets for propaganda runs, dropping them throughout the country. Now that he was in classes three days a week, his reports were sparse.

Today was no exception. He couldn't write, at least not about the war. He was struggling to remain objective about it because now it was part of his life and grew more so every day. Now more than any other time in the seven months, since he'd, arrived he felt his private world was at war, too. Falling in love with Mai had made it so.

He wanted to find Bach and burn him for almost killing her. He and his gang brought the struggle right to his doorstep, forcing him to rethink the roots of his involvement: why the Americans were here in the first place. During the cold war, America was trying to keep Communism from spreading. The same reason was used to justify the Korean War and now this, the war the American government continued to call a conflict for various political and economic reasons. Were there any other motives and secret agendas? World Wars I and II were different. There were clear-cut needs and purposes. Vietnam seemed more civil war, so far from home, and one we did not need to become involved in.

It was easy for Scott to understand Bach's fervor; he was a zealot. He believed he could help save his country. In a strange way, he also owed the young terrorist – a man he now knew wasn't an insurgent at all. If Bach's gang hadn't tried to kill everyone in the room at the concert, he might never have saved Mai. Now the story was taking on a new perspective. Mai's smile and a wave across campus. An invitation, a brief concert, and then the world nearly broke into horrid fragments, but he was able to save her. Her presence in the hospital, a quiet dinner, and here he was about to slip over the edge of an emotional cliff with this young Vietnamese woman.

Looking at the empty sheet of paper in his typewriter, Scott had so many questions. It was unusual for him to draw a blank. Mostly, he couldn't wait to tell a story, to ask why to use this machine to explore his own thoughts. He pushed back from the table for a moment, crossed the fingers of both hands behind his head. He tried to think clearly, but the only thoughts that kept coming to him were those of Mai— the graceful, beautiful, sassy young woman who was so intriguing to him.

He'd only known her a short time and knew so little about her. As the bright sun streamed through his window and the curtains swayed gently in a rare afternoon breeze, he couldn't get her face out of his mind.

On the busy street below, the honking horns, the shouts of the cyclo drivers, the street people selling their vegetables, and all the ever-present mopeds masked the violence just below the surface. Though neither he nor those people had any idea of what was coming. For now, the fighting throughout South Vietnam was at an impasse, with the Americans rarely gaining ground. However, Saigon was free and safe.

The stores, the hotels, the University, and all the rest of it moved as if daily life were a regular routine and the war was hundreds of miles away.

In fact, that's how Saigon had been since the Americans first arrived. Considering the mayhem surrounding them, the people in Saigon were actually spoiled if one could use that word. To this day in January, their daily lives had been mostly unaffected.

He hadn't seen Mai since they'd had dinner three nights before. Tomorrow they would be in class together. He wasn't sure how much of his investigation he should share with her. He knew that if he pursued her, his story would become even more complicated: a developing love story, a political quandary, war, and his education. But he was, after all, a writer. Sitting upright, Scott put his hands on the typewriter keys. Before he could begin, Arturo, his roommate, walked into the room with his small transistor radio blaring Vietnamese music. He was smiling and moving with the rhythm.

Scott had become accustomed to the very different sound and scale of the indigenous tunes; the sounds of mandolins, zithers, and long-stringed guitars. Once in a while, Arturo (who Scott saw as a romantic), would play the popular love songs, the slow, sad ones that were so loved by the Vietnamese. Scott guessed Arturo liked those most because they were so similar to those from his Latino youth.

As Arturo sat on the edge of his bed, Scott smiled, looked at him, and raised his index finger to his lips, pointing to his typewriter. Arturo nodded, picked up a book, and turned off the radio.

The slow ballad put Scott in just the right mood. His fingers began to peck the keys vaguely at first. And then within a minute, his hands were dancing across the keyboard like a pianist caught in the throes of an extravagant melody. It was an effort at a poem, something that would tell this young girl he had every intention of pursuing her without actually saying so. After an hour, his wastebasket was full of crumpled efforts and, for the time being, he thought better of the idea.

* * *

Mai stared out the window of her living room as she talked, in her mind, with her mother. She often consoled herself by having what her friends said were one-way conversations. I can feel your hand on my shoulder, Mother. I've only known him a very short time, but I'm drawn to him. I'm afraid. For the first time since I lost you, I'm frightened. How can I be afraid of love? I'm not afraid of the war, of the Communists or any of it, but this man is causing me concern. War is no time to be in love. Since your death, and with all the fighting, I ask myself every day, how many mornings are left? I need guidance. I cannot tell him how I feel even though I know he will soon begin to pursue me. I can see it in his eyes and his funny nervous gestures. Mother, please touch me with your wisdom.

Mai finished, not knowing what to do next. She was full of energy directed nowhere in particular and yet, her legs were weak. She had to prepare for the next day's class. That is where she would take her mind for now.

Chapter 7

In the hamlets and villages connected by miles and miles of tunnels, Bach had become more than a physical fighter, a guerilla. He was becoming more of an idealist every waking moment. His father had first been involved with the Viet Minh and then later with the Viet Cong, so he chose that path as well. His father had died in a firefight with the French, but he'd always told his only son that one day he would be a great leader. When his mother died, he was raised by the Viet Cong, moving from one village to another, never settling on land he could call home. Since then, he had known nothing but the struggle for the cause and now, a full-blown war.

Bach sat in a tunnel by a small kerosene lamp. The dampness and the odors of rice cooking, gunpowder, mold, and dirt were so familiar he was comforted by them. Writing in a small journal he kept with him at all times, he made notes. Perhaps they would be used today when he talked with the villagers.

As he continued to scribble with the stub of a pencil, he glanced at a dog-eared page and remembered what he'd written months ago. It was a letter he knew he would never send to Mai. He thought he could make her love him, and he told her that. He thought he could convince her to join him in the cause, but she was too stubborn and brainwashed by the Americans.

It had been almost three weeks since that night at the University. I should've shot that man, he thought. The Americans were little more than cockroaches underfoot, arrogant and stupid. He pressed the stub harder into the paper. I will crush them all.

Through the chain of command, Bach knew that the Party's leadership in Hanoi was planning a surprise for the Americans. It would begin in Khe Sanh and look just like any other battle. For the first time, everything would be integrated, coordinated, and strong. Eighty thousand fighters would descend on cities throughout the country. He, like most from the North, felt they would be welcomed as liberators and heroes. They had visions of being hailed as saviors for those in the South, not as conquerors.

Bach closed his journal and put the pencil stub in his top shirt pocket. His last thought before his talk to his men in the morning—I should've shot him.

* * *

JANUARY 30, 1968
SAIGON

The 30th day of January fell on the first day of the Lunar New Year, the Tet celebration. Classes at the University were out. It was a time for celebration and best wishes for a new beginning. Mai and Scott planned to party at a favorite club called *The Queen Bee* in the central quarter of Saigon. They would celebrate the New Year and Scott's new freedom—his doctors had removed his bandages for good, and he returned the loaner pair of crutches to the hospital. He wouldn't be dancing yet, but he would be walking on his own.

The couple was being drawn together incrementally, so gradually neither of them realized it wholly or at least admitted it to each other. They were seeing each other nearly every day.

It was a warm balmy afternoon, perfect for a stroll in the park without studies, time to relax and try to forget the war. The North, South, and the Americans had agreed to a ceasefire for seven days, from January 27th through February 3rd. Many of the Army of the Republic of Vietnam forces took the opportunity for Tet and for the ceasefire to go on leave. Saigon was quiet and vulnerable.

"I'll pick you up at two o'clock this afternoon," Scott told her. "I have a surprise for you."

Later that afternoon, Mai was inside the house when she heard the shrill sound of a horn—but it wasn't a car horn. She pulled back the curtains and looked out front to see Scott sitting on a motorcycle with a grin on his face from ear to ear.

Smiling, she went to the door and waved to him.

"Come on. Let's go for a ride," he yelled. "A friend of mine loaned me his Triumph. It's a blast."

Filled with excitement, Mai grabbed her purse, a small picnic basket and ran out of the house. The motorcycle looked graceful yet powerful—not anything like the mopeds that zipped in and out of traffic, sometimes almost nearly invisible and without sound.

"Hop on," Scott said, patting the passenger seat behind him, twisting the throttle and revving the engine for effect.

"What is this? It's so big, almost brutish," Mai said, still smiling.

"It's a Triumph Bonneville. My friend, Hank, loaned it to me."

"Who's Hank?"

"He's an MP, a military policeman, I met. He's a good guy. He works base security and has duty today."

"Are you sure you're well enough to be driving a motorcycle?" Mai was concerned.

"I'm all right," he grinned then saw the look on her face. "Seriously, I'm okay... and we'll take it easy."

"Well. Okay, let's go to the park," she said, suddenly without fear, throwing her leg over the backseat and then wrapping her arms around Scott's waist. The two shuffled in and out of traffic until they arrived at the park. Just before Scott put the bike on its stand and they got off, he realized that that ride was the longest time she had held him. He liked it.

They had no other plans, no other agenda. It was going to be a quiet afternoon, maybe even a quick nap in the sun on the grass preparing for what would surely be an evening of celebration. They walked out into the greenest section of Tao Dan, the largest park in the city, that some likened to the Vietnamese version of Paris' Luxembourg Garden though not nearly that large. Many large magnolia trees had been planted by the French years before. They were well over twenty feet tall and provided a shady and inviting spot for the two to sit and talk. The smell of magnolia and the freshly mown grass was a mix of sweet and spice, kind of like his companion, Scott thought.

"What is that?" Mai asked as Scott touched the white envelope in his back pocket.

"It's a homework assignment. I'd like you to read it," Scott said, reaching into his pocket to pull out three folded pages. "It's my translation of a Vietnamese love story, The Boatman's Flute."

"I've heard about it but never read it," Mai said, taking the pages from Scott and unfolding them.

"In my Asian literature class, our assignment was to translate a Vietnamese story into English. I'm not very good at doing that yet, but I do see how much more lyrical your language is than English. There is far more poetry to it, more emotion. Even though it's very simple, the story is beautiful. It's about... well, you'll see."

Mai read but was having trouble with it because the verbs and subjects didn't agree, and the grammar was way off. Returning the pages to him, she said, "Oh yes. You need work, but it's new to you, and Vietnamese is a tough language. You're pretty good already with the questions, though. I guess that's the journalist in you: who, what, when..."

"Yeah. It's important to be able to ask where the bathroom is," Scott laughed. "Anyhow, the first part is about a remarkable man who had just one daughter. His wife had died and his daughter was all he had left. Reminds me a little of you."

"Interesting," Mai said, more interested in Scott's electric blue eyes. "Please go on," she sighed. She still hadn't told him, but she loved his voice as much as what he was saying, which had a strange tug on her. If he had been a salesman, she would have bought a bag of mud from him.

"Since the wealthy man treasured his only daughter so much, he selfishly kept her locked in a room in his mansion, high atop a grassy hill. The only window that the beautiful young girl had in her room faced the river below where she watched sampans drift by every day," Scott stopped reading. "I had to condense the story so I could fit it on three pages."

"What happens next?" Mai shifted toward him.

"Well, one day as the beautiful but lonely young woman sat looking out the window, a small boat drifted by. She couldn't see the man who was piloting it, but she could hear a flute playing lovely, soft tunes. She was mesmerized by the songs. And every day after that, at sunset, she would go to her window to listen to the man who floated by and played the beautiful music on a simple flute."

Mai continued to move closer. She had kicked off her sandals, he had slipped off his deck shoes, and they were running their toes through the grass. When Mai's bare foot brushed his, he didn't know if she had done it on purpose or accidentally.

He cleared his throat and slowly turned to Mai. The two young sets of eyes locked, and neither could turn away. Mai's pulse quickened as Scott dropped the pages on the grass and leaned toward her, smelling the light intermingling fragrance of the magnolias and her lavender perfume. It and Mai were intoxicating. He looked for a sign. He couldn't help himself; he didn't want to make a fool of himself. Is she feeling the same thing I am? He couldn't be sure and finished the story.

Mai sighed. "That was lovely. Even though the boatman was ugly and disfigured, she fell madly in love with him. She saw his heart, not his face?"

"So, my translation wasn't bad after all?" he asked.

In the silence of an awkward moment, both knowing what they wanted to say, each held their thoughts. In the lull Scott rose, picked a bloom from the tree above them, and then sat next to Mai, holding it next to her face. She smiled.

"Your skin puts this to shame." He smiled and put the flower down on the grass, with a nervous laugh. He knew he expressed himself better in writing than in words.

Mai's bare right foot stroked his ankle. This time, he knew it wasn't a mistake. Back home, there would be none of this subtle, slow courting. But this was different. Vietnamese women and everything about this culture was different. Relationships between men and women required specific procedures—even in time of war—complex beyond just male and female. They had to cross cultures, economics, and religion.

"What's in the basket?" Scott finally asked.

"Just some snacks, including a new experience."

"And what might that be?"

"Rượu nếp," she said, pulling out two small bottles and handing one to Scott.

"What is it?"

"It's a traditional Vietnamese rice wine. It's good. To celebrate the New Year," she said, clinking her bottle against his.

When they had finished, Scott picked up Mai's purse and the empty basket and said, "Come on. Let's go ride some more before it starts to get dark. I'll drop you off in time for you to get ready for this evening."

* * *

The Queen Bee, located in the middle quarter on the busy street of Nguyen Hue, was the place to be in Saigon.

The night air was filled with energy, anticipation, and a sense that nothing else in the world mattered. The New Year would bring a fresh start for everyone. The Vietnamese were an optimistic people; it was in their nature to have hope along with a healthy dose of patience. Their struggles had gone on so long that war, civil or otherwise, was a running commentary.

Scott hadn't seen this side of Mai yet. She was excited, almost dancing as she walked into the club. Though it was dark inside, the interior was alive with the strategically placed lighting of multiple colors that swirled and blinked. A giant mirrored ball turned from the ceiling, reflecting the lights, which multiplied their effect. Velour lounges and chairs beckoned. Alcohol was flowing, and the music, provided by the top deejay in Saigon, was already jumping at 9:30.

Scott ordered a beer, and Mai asked for a Mai Tai.

When their drinks arrived, she said, "Mai like Mai Tai." Then she laughed and took a big swallow of the large drink with the umbrella stuck in it and two pieces of fruit floating at the top.

Scott raised his beer in the gesture of a toast.

"Scott like Mai," he was going to say but said instead, "Scott like Mai Tai, too! Happy New Year."

Mai was sharp. She'd caught his shyness. She knew he felt the same way she did, but she also knew she would have to be the one to make the first move.

"Mai like Scott. Mai like Scott very much," she said, tapping her glass against his bottle and taking another healthy swallow.

He suddenly felt like a child. He'd been distancing himself. It was time for him to make a move—perhaps during a dance tonight or sitting in a booth a little bit farther back in the room. He would forget the cultural conventions for at least one night. He was pretty sure she felt the same; he knew he was the reluctant one. He didn't want to admit it, but riding the Triumph reminded him of home. The motor thumping between his legs gave him some balls, and the beer would further help to loosen him up. He'd never felt this giddy before, but then he'd never really

73

been in love so he had nothing to compare it to but his very short-lived relationships at home.

The party came to a crescendo at midnight with confetti, loud horns, firecrackers, and lots of music.

Scott looked at Mai, knowing he should kiss her, but he wanted to save it. He wanted to take Mai down near the river, say something, and then kiss her passionately—he hoped.

"Come on, Mai. Let's go for a ride."

"Are you sure you're okay to drive?"

"Yes, and it isn't driving; it's riding. You drive a car and ride a motorcycle. Let's throw our legs over the Bonnie and rumble around town. It's nice out."

But, before he could grab Mai's hand, a man appeared out of nowhere. Scott immediately recognized him as the stranger he'd met with over tea at the Givral Café. He looked frightened and harried. When their eyes met, he came closer to Scott and whispered in his ear, and then as suddenly as he'd appeared, he was gone, out the door, running into the streets.

Chapter 8

Mai giggled, not understanding, and followed holding Scott's hand as he nearly dragged her out the door. She thought Scott seemed anxious as he told her to quickly jump on the bike and hold on tight in case he had to make a sudden stop or speed up. Maybe we can make it out of the city before it all breaks loose, he thought, keeping it to himself.

At first, he cruised cautiously down one street after another, watching couples kissing and dancing in the streets, the music blaring everywhere. The night was no different than any other Tet celebration. Pop, pop, pop, bang all around them—firecrackers, or so Mai thought as she laughed and hung onto Scott with only one arm.

Scott knew better. This was going to be a catastrophic evening in Saigon. The distant pops and cracks soon became louder, and more frequent. It was gunfire. He knew the sound of an AK-47 very well.

Telling her to squeeze him, he added, "It's not fireworks, it's gunfire. We're getting out of here."

Before he sped off, he stopped the motorcycle, put one leg out to hold them up, and then grabbed a horrified young man running past by the sleeve.

"What's going on?" he asked, wanting to confirm what he thought was happening.

The young man looked as if he was going out of his mind. "The truce is over! They're attacking the U.S. embassy. Get out of here," he said, grabbing his arm back as he kept running.

Scott had to get them to safety. The only place he could think of was Mai's house. It was in the opposite direction of the embassy and probably the safest place if there was such a thing. He also gave a thought to taking her to the army barracks, but then Mai yelled, "Go! Go! They're coming," she said, looking back down the street. Hundreds of VCs were running into the city from all directions, firing automatic weapons, and screaming like banshees.

It was as if someone had poked a vast hive of black wasps. Mai was horrified, confused. "Go! Go!"

Scott jammed the bike into gear and pulled the throttle all the way back. The front wheel stood up a foot off the ground, and Mai was squeezing him so tight, he could hardly breathe. The wheel bounced, spun several times, and then caught and settled. The rear tire bit into the concrete rocketing the two down a narrow side street, leaving a cluster of VC not two hundred yards behind.

The smell of gun smoke, the rattle and crack of all kinds of weapons, and the screams turned the truce and the new beginnings into an old nightmare.

Although it was night, Scott pushed the bike as fast as he could through the confines of the narrow street. There was no moon, but he could still make out people ahead who were falling, being bayonetted. Grenades were exploding everywhere and there seemed to be no place to hide. It was total chaos and except a couple of MP units, there were no American soldiers to intervene or to defend.

Scott jammed on the foot and hand brakes at the same time. He gave the handlebars a quick jerk to the left, narrowly missing running over a body. The young man was lying in a pool of blood, his head a pile of mush.

Scott's survival instincts were the only thing keeping his mind going quickly. Where, where, where? It seemed every street was closed off or besieged by forces in black.

What he hadn't thought about, as he kept the bike going toward Mai's house, was that a lot of the South Vietnamese Army had gone on leave. Since this offensive was a surprise attack, he knew the U.S. forces and his media buddies had been caught off-guard, too. No wonder there was pandemonium. Shit! He thought we're supposed to be in a ceasefire. Saigon is utterly defenseless. Is this it? Is this the end?

Darting around corners, he began to get closer to the edge of the city; his mind was going in a hundred different directions. He envisioned all the American MPs in their barracks, grabbing their weapons. Or in the city trying to find each other to band together and get back to the base. The media guys would all be working to make sense of it, attempting to file the breaking news somehow, or just figuring out how to stay alive.

Turning down the last street, about to race out on the long stretch of highway and thinking ahead, he remembered the weapons Mai's father had displayed in their library. He knew he'd seen a shotgun, an army issue .45 mm 1911 and maybe a Kalashnikov. He wondered where the ammo was hidden.

"Are you okay?" he yelled, turning his head to Mai, her arms still in a death grip around him.

"No!"

"Have you been hit?" he yelled at the same time he glanced back at the road.

"No. Just get out of here—now!"

Suddenly, out of the corner of his eye, Scott saw an oncoming motorcycle from the right. It was closing in on them fast, and he saw there were two riders—both dressed in black. Crack! He felt a bullet whiz by his chest. The passenger was shooting at them. Another bullet hit his gas tank.

Shit! It's two VCs, Scott thought, taking an immediate hard right, directly at them.

"What are you doing?" Mai yelled.

Scott didn't respond. He just gunned it. Now the two bikes were on a collision course only one hundred yards apart.

"They're going to shoot us. What are you doing?" Mai said again, ducking her head behind Scott and clutching him so tightly her nails dug into his gut.

Scott could see the passenger raise his gun again. Instead of turning away or off to the side, he had turned directly into them. It all happened in less than a blink.

It was as if Scott was in a slow-motion scene again, just like he felt the night of the concert. It was almost suicide, but running right at them was their only chance. He didn't have a weapon and he could see the bike was a very fast Italian café racer, probably a Ducati; he'd never outrun it, not with gas dripping out of his tank. The game of chicken had begun and at the last second, he saw the passenger, behind the man gripping the handlebars, was a woman. They had to be VC and both wore a ba-ba.

Their bikes were closing at about 50 mph each and the VC refused to turn. At the last second, as they almost touched, Scott stuck out his left leg and kicked the woman in her thigh. Her gun went off again, aimlessly. He didn't need much force, just enough to tap her at that speed. He'd already braced himself and knew that Mai was a natural rider, leaning ever so slightly only when she had to. The Ducati jerked hard to the right, the front wheel jamming and locking. The two passengers flew off the bike into the bushes alongside the road. Scott and Mai's bike shimmied violently, the front wheel wanting to jackknife, the entire bike wobbling viciously.

Even though he'd already let go of the throttle, Scott was going to crash if he didn't get control. He began to brake halfway, then slowing more as he took them off the road through a row of bushes. He shouted to Mai, "I'm going to lay it down. When I yell, stand on the foot pegs and jump to your right. To your right! Got it?"

"Yes. Yes."

"Okay, now!"

Mai jumped and landed in the reeds and a small creek, breaking her fall. Scott stayed on the bike another twenty yards, slowed it even more and then jumped off himself, letting the Triumph run into a tree. It wasn't going fast, but with the gas trickling out it caught fire and then exploded, throwing rubber and steel into the air.

Scott looked back. Several hundred yards away, he could see the two assailants slowly getting up. Then he ran to Mai. He got one arm under her shoulders and the other behind her knees and picked her up, intending to take her into the thicker wooded area beyond the bushes. She was bruised and dazed but otherwise seemed okay.

As he stood and glanced back, Scott could see the two attackers running toward them. They wouldn't give up. Why are they so persistent about us, two strangers? He thought he knew the answer: He was an American.

With no weapon but his fists and adrenalin, Scott had to decide whether to run or fight. He didn't think Mai would be able to run, but they had no other choice as the man leaped at him tackling and wrestling him to the ground.

Mai was trying to regain her balance and stand up when the woman ran up to her. She was holding the gun at her side until she came close and then began to point it at Mai's face as if she was relishing the moment and wanted to enjoy every second.

Mai was no slouch; she was an athlete and knew she had strength. The woman began to pull the trigger as she continued running at her. Mai slipped to the ground at the last possible second, threw her legs into the woman's ankles, and twisted her violently to the ground. Before the woman could get up, Mai kicked her gun away, picked up a rock and slammed it into the woman's head.

Breathing harder than she'd ever breathed before, her heart pounding almost out of her chest, Mai turned to help Scott. The two men were wrestling at the edge of the creek, and the man was about to overwhelm Scott. Mai looked around for the gun and then suddenly the man turned his head and looked directly at her. Mai was stunned. It was Bach. He had a large rock in his hand and was about to open Scott's head like a ripe cantaloupe when Mai yelled at him, "Bach, why are you doing this?" He didn't answer her and didn't stop. "I'm going to shoot you." Scott fell to the ground as Bach raised the rock to bring it smashing down. Without more talk, Mai cocked the .45, pointed it at Bach, and without hesitation, pulled the trigger. Bach slumped to the grass on his knees and then fell forward into the water, blood oozing out of his back. Scott jumped up, grabbed Mai, and said, "Let's get out of here. Your house is only a couple of miles away."

Mai threw the gun in the woods, grabbed Scott's hand, and they began to run.

* * *

JANUARY 31, 1968, EARLY MORNING
HANG XANH (EAST AND SOUTH OF SAIGON)

When the two neared Mai's house, they stopped on the road and crouched in the bushes. Scott looked around carefully for any VC. "Come on," he said. "Let's go

82

through these bushes to the back of the house. I don't have a good feeling being out here." They darted, crouched slightly, and went in through the kitchen door. It appeared no one was in the area. "Grab some clothes and food and put them in a backpack. We're going to the river." As sure as they were standing there, the VC would be expanding their attack out from the city to include the nearby neighborhoods, and then perhaps further into the villages.

Mai didn't answer, she just ran upstairs. When she was out of sight, Scott went into the library and opened the gun case. Reaching in, he took the .45. He popped the clip out. It was full—seven rounds and no time to look for more. Within a minute, Mai appeared backpack in hand, and the two left by the back door again.

Staying off the main roads, it took almost an hour to reach the river. The closer they got to the city, the more they had to hide. The gunfire and explosions continued, seemingly from every direction. Reaching the edge of the river, there were several sampans tied up to a small dock alongside a powerboat. Scott took Mai's hand and continued out onto the dock.

"We'll jump in this. It's enclosed," he told her as he helped her down and into the small cabin below. Space was cramped, but they would be out of sight. There was a flashlight on a counter, which Scott grabbed. He scanned the dark room and saw a below deck set of dual controls for the starter, throttle, and fuel.

As she followed him down the short set of stairs, she saw the gun in his waistband and under his shirt. She recognized it as her father's for its distinctive ivory handle but didn't say anything.

"It's worth a try," Scott said. Thinking he probably wouldn't be able to start the craft without a key. But when he pushed the red button, the big dual outboard engines roared to life and the dials began to twitch and move. The fuel gauge read half-full.

Mai sat on a small bunk watching, still breathing hard.

"Where are we going?" she asked.

"I don't know just yet, but out of here."

"Do you think he's dead?" Mai said.

"You mean your friend?"

"He's not my friend. I told you, he was—and apparently still is—a nutcase."

Scott didn't answer. He put the throttle in reverse and maneuvered the boat back away from the dock, keeping it very slow and as quiet as the powerful engine would allow. He'd done this many times back home in the Newport Harbor when his friend's father would let them use his outboard.

He could see out the back hatch and forward through a narrow window facing the bow. Once out in the river, he kept the throttle at four miles an hour. It was just dawn and murky out. The two could still smell the gunpowder, but now from their vantage point, they could hear the distant muffled sounds of automatic weapons fire. He didn't know how many VCs were attacking or their concentration of weapons, but he had to assume it was well planned to coincide with the ceasefire and probably involved thousands of VCs.

The exhaust on the speedboat was loud even at idle so Scott kept one eye through the narrow window and the other on the wheel.

"We'll slide down further southeast, anywhere that is away from the city for now," he said, looking out both windows.

Even from this distance, he and Mai could see plumes of smoke coming from several different directions. The city was still under siege—perhaps all of South Vietnam.

"We'll dock somewhere down near Nha Be," Scott said.

Mai's breathing was returning to normal as she began to feel a little safer.

"That was some maneuver back there. You scared the shit out of me," she said.

Scott tried to play the chase down. "It was our only chance. His bike was too fast for us to outrun and it would have been easier for her to aim if they were chasing us instead of dodging. I figured they'd think we were crazy, or maybe we had a gun, too. Either way, it was a better idea than running," he shook his head. "But I thought for sure he would turn."

"Well, you did just enough to make them miss and kicking them as they shot by was brilliant," Mai said. "You saved me again and now I owe you two lives."

* * *

FEBRUARY 1, 1968
NHA BE (SOUTH AND EAST OF SAIGON)

Scott settled down and realized that he now had a reliable source. That the stranger knew about the surprise attack could only mean he was CIA, South Vietnamese Army Intelligence, or a reformed VC. And he had reiterated his desire to talk further, using Professor Phan as the contact.

He and Mai were staying on the boat for now. Seventy-two hours had elapsed since the attack. They remained below deck and fed on the few things they found in the small refrigerator.

"How are you holding up?" Scott asked.

"In which way?"

"I mean, the woman and the shooting." Scott didn't want to stir up her emotions, but he wanted to know if she was okay. The boat remained nearly stationary; the only thing gently moving it was the slow flow of the river.

"I can't believe you actually did it. In all that confusion, you found the gun, cocked it, and shot both of them." Scott marveled.

"I had no choice. She was going to kill me, and he was going to kill you. I've never shot at anyone before. It all makes me sick to my stomach; all of this killing. Will it ever end?" she said in complete frustration and exhaustion, slumping back on the bunk. "It began before I was born. Everyone wants a piece of Vietnam."

Mai put her head into her hands and cried as Scott put his arm around her shoulders.

"It's okay, Mai," he replied, sensing she felt as guilty about the shooting as she was angry about the war. He had never killed anyone either. Journalists, almost like medics, were supposed to be neutral, but he knew better. He would not hesitate if he were confronted.

Mai wiped her eyes and took a deep breath. "I'll be all right. I'm in shock, I guess. By now, I should be used to the killing, the anger, the politics, and the lies!"

Suddenly, as quickly as she'd grown sad, she pulled herself together and stood with her back to the console. The two were only a couple of feet apart. She began to pace in a tight circle, chewing on the fingernail of her right index finger while peering out the window.

Then she stopped chewing on her nail. She'd given whatever she was thinking about enough thought. She turned to Scott, who was now bathed in the early morning sunlight streaming through the small window facing the bow. She guessed it was about 9:00 a.m. The speedboat was still. She could see out the side portal that everything was quiet, belying the violence that wasn't far away. Perhaps the bloodshed was over, or maybe it would just start up again today.

In those few seconds, she thought how fleeting life is. One minute her mother was going to visit a small village outside the city; the next minute she was dead. Her father could be killed at any moment near Pleiku. She and Scott could be dead an hour from now. Everything was always so tenuous. Despite her maudlin feelings, outside herons were pecking at the grubs in the riverbank silt. She saw two doves overhead, most likely looking for food together or heading home.

"Scott, now we owe each other." Scott started to rise and object, but Mai pushed him back down. "There is a bigger story here than you can imagine. You've only been here for eight months. We have been here for hundreds and hundreds of years."

He realized that she was angry and was lashing out aloud more than at Scott.

"You're a journalist. It is your job to report the facts to your people, but do we need body counts and kill ratios every night? You must avoid telling the truth only as you see it. Do the American people even know that over two million of my people have already died—two million!?"

"Mai...," Scott started to interject. He wanted to explain how much they were both on the same wavelength. He knew what she was about to say was what he had been agonizing over since he'd arrived.

Suddenly, the speedboat began to wobble and sway in what was at first calm waters. Scott could hear the sound of an outboard engine approaching. He grabbed Mai and pulled her down to the lower deck.

"Shhh," he whispered, his index finger over his lips. "Don't say a word; someone's coming."

Scott took a deep breath and waited. The sound of a growling exhaust came closer—could be an American river patrol, could be VC.

He stood slowly and inched his face up to the portal only about five inches in diameter. It wasn't American. There were three ordinary Vietnamese men, two standing on the bow with automatic rifles and one piloting the boat.

Scott wondered how much of the city they'd taken, or had they been repelled? Perhaps the area was surrounded, under full control of the North. He had no way of knowing, and he wasn't about to ask questions. Their powerboat was partially hidden near the shore where he had dropped the anchor. He prayed they wouldn't see that and just keep going. It looked like they were patrolling or watching for something.

The exhaust from the VC boat went from a growl to a dribble and then disappeared into the distance, going south downriver.

"It's okay. We can get up now. They're gone. I think they were just patrolling."

Chapter 9

The Colonel stood over Bach, waiting for him to open his eyes. He was an imposing man; tall, strong, stern, eyebrows always seemingly furrowed in introspection.

Colonel Chung hadn't heard the story yet, but he knew the doctors dug a .45 slug out of him. He also knew the wound was the result of some encounter during the offensive, which at this point, wasn't going well. The bullet had shattered Bach's left scapula, careened off his clavicle, and lodged itself in the right side of his neck. He had three broken bones, two severely. But he would survive, perhaps with permanent damage to his left shoulder. But that wouldn't affect his thinking except to make him even more resolved to the cause, which is what Colonel Chung was most interested in.

Chung had been good friends with Bach's father. He'd fought alongside him against the French in 1953, just before he was killed, dying in the then-Lieutenant Chung's arms. Before Bach's father died, he begged

Chung to take care of his only son, to watch over a future leader. That's exactly what Chung had done for the last eighteen years, raising the boy up from the age of three. By the time he was fifteen, Bach already held the rank of Lieutenant. Some of those escalations in rank were the result of his guerilla combat experience; others were attributed to his leadership qualities. He was considered by Hanoi to be among the future pillars of the Party.

Bach finally awakened. Seeing the Colonel, he turned his head in embarrassment.

"Captain Bach, do not feel disconcerted. You did well," the Colonel said, patting Bach's arm. "You have nothing to be ashamed of. The conception of our strategy was brilliant. Five thousand of our comrades descended on Saigon to begin our intensive efforts. You made it possible for them to infiltrate the city in the weeks leading up to our attack. You had the idea to disguise them all as peasants celebrating the holiday. You decided that none of them would be carrying weapons that could betray them. Who else could've thought of smuggling those arms in laundry trucks or even staging those fake funerals for the South Vietnamese soldiers using those empty caskets to bring in the guns—a Trojan horse? The fact that you and your men trained with live fire using the fireworks' celebration as a distraction was brilliant. Comrade Bach, you are a born leader. It makes little difference that you were shot in your quest. If anything, you are a hero. Wear your wound like a badge of honor. I do not want to know the circumstances. It isn't important. What is important is that you are alive and you are going to be given a very special honor. I will tell you more tomorrow. But, for now, rest; I'll be back."

Bach sighed and saluted his mentor, but he wasn't satisfied with the praise. The applause quickly gave way. He still hadn't managed to kill the American, and the woman he loved had not only murdered his companion but shot him as well. He was mortified. He should never have involved himself with Mai. She's never going to change. His efforts were a waste. While his comrades thought he was dating her; he knew that, quietly and secretly, someone higher up was putting a check mark in the negative column of his record.

What did they expect? He was sent to the University in Saigon to infiltrate the South. To him, that meant not just a physical presence. It included making friends, acting like a Nationalist and pretending to hate the Communists—it meant mirroring their thoughts and assimilating their culture to be accepted by them. He'd been so good at it; he'd fallen in love with a beautiful young girl loyal to the South.

All of this is what the Colonel Chung didn't know, or at least, he hoped he didn't because it was the source of his secret shame. Then to be shot by that girl was almost more than he could bear.

What did the Colonel mean? What surprise? Bach could have no way of knowing. For now, the doctors told him, he would remain here in this bed for at least another few days. He couldn't stand lying here all day. He'd even contemplated escaping and returning to his unit in the Cu Chi tunnels. Colonel Chung changed all that.

Bach's trepidation was entirely unfounded, but he wouldn't know that for a few days. Like so many others, he was an evangelist. Even though it was as transparent as thin smoke, he couldn't see through the curtain. He believed the Communist Doctrine Colonel Chung initially imbued in him. Every one of his experiences since his fourth birthday only fortified those beliefs.

Now, the only two things he could think about were getting out of this makeshift hospital and finding out what Colonel Chung meant. Was he being promoted? He received the answer to that question the next afternoon.

Colonel Chung arrived as expected. Bach saluted. His left eye was crossing and he knew it but couldn't do anything about it. The Colonel looked out of place in his starched khaki uniform. The room was only large enough to accommodate six beds, each with a recovering combatant. The smells were rancid and dank, alcohol mixed with the smell of fungus or mildew and urine. The hospital was little more than a series of aluminum Quonset huts hidden in the Cambodian jungle, not far from the border. A POW camp nearby was also holding American soldiers and airmen who received no medical care. This facility was strictly for treating small numbers of VC. There was a momentary silence before Colonel Chung spoke up.

"Do you have any idea why I'm here?"

"Am I going to be promoted?"

The Colonel smiled broadly, almost laughing.

"Yes, I guess in a manner of speaking you are, but not in the way you think, at least not now."

Bach's eyebrows lowered, his expression more inquisitive.

"How then?"

"Young man, you are being sent to Hanoi...," there was another long pause, "...and then on to Russia."

What? Russia? I don't understand, Bach thought, remaining silent, reluctant to express anything until he heard more.

"You will be briefed on Russia when you get to Hanoi. You will be released from here in about three days. All of the arrangements have been made. I will be here to see you off."

Bach was confused, yet honored. He saluted Colonel Chung and gave him a slight smile as the

Colonel turned and walked out of the hut. Reporting to a Commissar meant this wasn't military. It was Party business of some sort. Did they somehow know I was shot by a woman, the South Vietnamese girl? Do they think I'm a failure? Colonel Chung praised me, but then he's like a father to me. I'll find out in due time, he thought. Before I go north, I must reach my contact in Saigon. I need him to find and get rid of that girl and her American.

Chapter 10

The .45 was slipping down, inside, Scott's waistband. The only food the two had eaten in days was the snacks at *The Queen Bee* and the two cans of sardines and some stale crackers in the small refrigerator on the power boat. Scott reached around, pulled the automatic out, and placed it on the counter next to the controls.

"I have a confession to...," he started to say.

"I know. I already saw it. You took my father's gun. With the ivory handle, I'd know it anywhere. How many rounds do we have?" Mai asked, surprising him.

"Just eight—one in the chamber and seven in the clip."

"You mean it's loaded?"

"Of course. What good is it if it isn't loaded?"

"I know, but one in the chamber? And why didn't you grab more ammunition?"

"If you recall, we were in a hurry."

Scott was surprised but shouldn't have been. Her father was an army career officer; she'd been surrounded by war for years, so she had to know something about firearms. He could add that to her growing list of talents. Scott had never been in love, not really. He was finding out for the first time what it felt like to know that someone cared about you and had your back.

Growing up, his family life most definitely did not resemble an episode of *Leave It to Beaver*. His father had been abusive, not physically, but in the way that makes a young boy feel abandoned. He was rarely around and never involved. As he got older, Scott sometimes even wished his father had beaten him once in a while just to show him he knew he was alive, but he wasn't home enough for that. And, the only way to get that kind of attention would have been to act like a jerk, to become a minor delinquent, and that wasn't his style. Scott's mother struggled to raise him and his brother and often drank too much. Though his grandmother was a minor celebrity of sorts, his own family life was mainstream and disjointed, and his mother had little contact with her own mother. Apparently, Scott grew up in a different zip code. His parents didn't seem to care about him or his brother. He'd had a succession of what his friends called girlfriends, but they were all superficial; and, besides, he was too young to be in love. Consequently, he and his brother were often left on their own, which more often than not meant they could be creative. Imagine the elation that a young boy feels when he steps into his house knowing that he is king for two hours. And able to leave and explore the world until five o'clock on his own or with his brother.

Scott chose to study, to discover new neighborhoods, to examine his environment and the people who populated it. Which meant all the characters that inhabited the Newport Beach Pier that hung out at his favorite surfing spot. Those people were a library unto themselves.

There was a lot of difference between Costa Mesa, California, in 1959, and South Vietnam in 1968. And there was a tremendous difference between being sixteen at the beach and twenty-five in a war zone. The one similarity was his appetite for knowledge. He and Mai couldn't have been raised more diametrically differently and on the color wheel, he was yellow, she was blue. But together, they were green and in Vietnamese culture that color's meaning was comfort, quiet, new beginnings, and safety. All things he felt when he was with her.

He was 8,000 miles from California, and there was only this woman. He didn't know if they would make it out of here alive. Life seemed very tenuous at the moment. As the two sat on the bunk, the .45 now at Scott's side, without even thinking, he blurted, "Will this be a love story?" He knew she knew, but was buying a moment to gather her thoughts. Not wanting to repeat himself, he waited patiently. Maybe it was too soon, he thought. Perhaps I should give her time to come up with an excuse, a way to get out of this.

She didn't need any time nor did she clear her throat or chew on her fingernail. She quietly stood up, put her arms around his shoulders, kissed him passionately, pulled back slightly, and said, "Yes, it will."

He felt extraordinarily good, at peace.

She is the first woman I've ever wanted to take care of and protect.

The two lovers gazed into each other's eyes like two deer caught in bright headlights on a lonely forest road. Scott slowly put his hand around the back of Mai's head, pulled her face to his, and kissed her deeply.

Suddenly the tat-tat-tat-tat sound of automatic weapon fire skimmed the water outside the boat and then dunt-dunt-dunt, the bullets made a thudding noise as they found the hull.

Scott pushed Mai down to the deck, grabbed the .45, and carefully peered out the side portal. It was another VC riverboat. One man was piloting the flat-bottomed vessel and two more were on the bow, one of them firing a 50-caliber machine gun that would sink the powerboat in minutes.

This time, he knew he wasn't going to joust with these guys like he had with Bach. The 50-caliber would tear the boat in half and them with it. Mai started to rise, but Scott pushed her down with his foot.

"Stay down. Don't move. They're just sitting there," he said.

He didn't need to cock the .45 with one in the chamber; he only had to pull the trigger, but he was more than outgunned. He didn't have a choice; he'd brought a butter knife to an artillery shootout. The gunboat was about one hundred yards out in the middle of the river. They were keeping their distance. They hadn't dropped anchor or approached. They were just sitting and waiting, he guessed. The shooter was still standing behind the gun, crouched a little with his finger on the trigger.

Scott noticed the current was picking up; the gunboat would have to either drop anchor or approach; otherwise, they would just float away. Maybe they'd just shot to see if they could rouse anyone. Maybe if he and Mai just stayed quiet, the gunboat would leave.

It was the second of February. Scott had no way of knowing how many casualties the friendlies had taken or how the American troops had faired. For all he knew, Saigon had been overrun and was in full control of the VC. Right now, though, the only important thing on his mind was Mai and how to get out of this situation.

"What's happening?" Mai whispered, lying perfectly still.

"Nothing. It's a standoff, I guess. They don't know who's on this boat if anyone, and if there are people on it, how much firepower they might have. With that 50-caliber, I guess they don't care about the arms issue."

Other than the two quietly talking, the area was still, almost peaceful. There were no boats moving or other activity of any kind. Scott felt as vulnerable as he ever had, completely removed from reality, with nowhere to turn.

Tat-tat-tat-tat-tat! The gunner was firing again, but only into the water in front of the boat. Was that a signal?

When the shooting stopped again, Scott looked up. The shooter was reloading; his cohort was pulling up another box of rounds. Scott knew it would take at least thirty seconds to replace the box and then pull the belt out of the box and feed it into the side of the gun. He didn't know why they just didn't come aboard, but he figured his best option was to attack, not sit like a wounded duck at the end of a one-way street.

"Hold on and stay down," he said. He picked up the .45 in his left hand, turned the ignition switch with his right, and then pushed the throttle forward. The engine roared and the boat took off like a dragster on the surface of the water, the nose high in the air, blocking his view.

Mai was slammed against the bench but stayed down, the force too much to get up. The powerboat made up the one hundred yards in less than five seconds. Scott figured he still had time. He guessed at everything: the intentions of the VC, the timing of their reload, and the time it would take to get within about ten yards of their boat.

With his right hand still on the steering wheel and the .45 in his left, he instinctively reached behind him to feel if Mai was there. Just then, the gun went off accidentally. He heard Mai yell. He jerked his arm back and with his right hand, cranked the wheel hard to the right. Just in time to miss the gunboat by three feet, sending a cascading rooster tail of water into the VC boat.

At the same time, he pushed his left arm through the open portal and fired seven rounds at the gunner, who was shot and thrown off the boat as the pilot struggled to maintain control of it. When he'd cleared them, he pushed the wheel back to the left and sped off down the river as he looked over his shoulder for Mai. She wasn't there.

It had all happened in less than two seconds.

Chapter 11

Billy Rietveld was an American, but he didn't give a shit about that. He'd been drafted and sent to Vietnam, but he didn't like it. He didn't care who took over whose country. It didn't matter a damn to him. He was just glad he'd wangled a job that didn't put him out in the bush like those poor grunts. The irony of being a military cop had worn off quick and he became quickly bored and wondered what he'd do when he got out, which wasn't too far off. He didn't have a clue.

That was until a chance meeting led him to some interesting people. The kind of people that pay money for information. There were all sorts of that around the airbase and embassy. He'd passed what he found on and pocketed his cash, building it into a right tidy sum. And he'd been able to up the ante and use them to reach major heroin suppliers based in Cambodia—the kind of providers he could take to his old buddies back in Chicago. Then he'd be set for life. They wouldn't be calling him 'Carrot-top' after that. He'd get some goddamned respect.

But those who had helped him had their hooks in him too. And one of them was digging hard right now.

"I can't just walk up and shoot them, Bach. I have to wait for something to happen so it looks like they got caught at the wrong place and wrong time. Collateral damage or insurgents from outside Saigon. I'm close to going home with a bag full of money and those drug contacts in Cambodia your people set me up with." He was getting red in the face. A private walking by the pay phone glanced at him. He lowered his voice. "Send a message when you have the timing of something definite I can use as cover and I'll take care of this. But then I'm done, Bach. I'm done." He hung up the phone and wondered if he really would be.

Chapter 12

"Mai!" Scott yelled as he slowed the powerboat down and then shut off the motor. He looked down to the deck where she'd been crouched and saw several spots of blood. Quickly turning, he noticed that the door to the head was open and Mai's leg was sticking out.

Space was narrow and the head was at the end, just beyond the control panel. She had been slammed by the force of the boat speeding off, slid across the shiny hardwood floor, and then through the open door to the bathroom. She lay unconscious, a rivulet of blood running down her forehead.

"Oh my God! I thought I'd shot you," he said aloud. He patted her face, but she was out. He stood up, grabbed some toilet paper, moistened it with water, and then used it to wipe her neck and brow and remove the blood from her face.

"Mai, wake up. You hit your head. Wake up," he said, gently shaking her.

106

Mai slowly came around, shook her head, and said, "Where are we?"

"We're okay. We made it. I think we're downriver about three miles near Ben Tre."

Mai shook her head again and then began to push herself up. Scott put his arm around her and helped her back to the bunk. "Here, lie down for a minute. You took a nasty hit."

Mai touched the walnut-size lump on her forehead. "Wow! That was something else. What happened?"

"I didn't have any choice. When they went to reload, I charged them, just like I did on the motorcycle. I shot the gunner and then made a hard right turn, and here we are."

"Maybe you should've gone into the Green Berets instead of journalism," she said. "What do we do now?"

"I'm not sure; I only have one round left in the .45. I have no idea what's going on in Saigon or anywhere else for that matter. And that reminds me: My friend, Hank, is going to be furious when he finds out we destroyed his prized Triumph," he said with a forced laugh intended to soften the moment.

"What do you mean, we?" she returned with a smile. "I'm serious. What are we going to do?"

"I am, too. I just have to think…" he paused. "Oh my God, I forgot. This boat has to have a radio somewhere. I haven't had time to think about that until now."

Scott stood, almost hitting his head on the bulkhead. He looked below the controls where a radio would normally be. Nothing there but an empty drawer.

"It must be topside," he said, climbing the four steps to the deck.

"Be careful. Someone might see you," Mai cautioned.

Neither of them had been out of the lower space since they stole the boat. The sun was setting and the mosquitoes were out in full force. There was no sign of life on the riverbank or the river. He estimated they were about three to four miles south of Saigon.

On the deck, there was a duplicate set of controls, a large panel...and radio! He turned the volume control until it was nearly off and then pushed the power button.

The radio immediately came to life with the voice of a Vietnamese newscaster.

"Mai, I found it. It's clear. Come up so you can translate. We have to see if it's safe to go back."

Mai felt her head again, sat up slowly, was a little dizzy, but she steadied herself on the counter and then climbed up the stairs. Peering around the river first, she crouched down and kneeled at Scott's side.

"It's okay. We're clear," he said.

"Well, I prefer it here. Go ahead, turn it on. Let's see what we get."

Scott pushed the power button again and immediately the voice began.

"What is he saying?"

"He is saying that the VC's attack has been a failure."

"That means Saigon is still under our control."

"Yes... wait," Mai said, trying to listen to what the man was saying.

"He says that none of Hanoi's objectives was achieved. There is sporadic fighting on the outskirts and some sections of the city are severely damaged—mostly by American retaliatory airstrikes. As a result, maybe hundreds of civilians are dead, but many more VCs. The city is littered with bodies."

"Jesus," Scott said, holding his forehead.

"Wait. He is saying that VCs overran portions of the airfield at Tan Son Nhut but were beaten back. It's closed now."

Scott was thinking. His friend, Hank, the one he'd borrowed the Triumph from, was with the 716th Military Police Battalion. They were perhaps among the real armed fighting U.S. Forces in Saigon.

Hank was a First Sergeant with the unit. Somehow Scott had to find him; the only way out of here wasn't away from Saigon—it was straight up the river—running the gantlet, maybe jousting once again.

A major problem was he only had one round left. They would have to get within a mile or so of the city and then go the rest of the way on foot.

The headquarters for the 716th was near Tan Son Nhut. He knew the base was closed, but it was also secured.

Scott turned the radio off.

"Come on," he said, holding Mai's arm. "Let's go downside. We're going to make our way back home."

Home, she thought. Hmm, now Scott is calling it home. That's a good thing.

Chapter 13

For a man who had lived for months in underground tunnels like a rat, Bach shouldn't have found the University dorm nearly unbearable, but he did. The heat was generated by a large coal-burning furnace located somewhere in the basement. That is if anyone had ever bothered to put coal in it. The room was musty smelling of an odd mixture of wet wood and maple syrup. He had no idea what caused the sweet smell but taken together, it reminded him of a dank cellar too close to a river.

The University buildings were enormous. The dorm building appeared to be older than the central administrative offices or classrooms, and they were at the back of the campus, which was about a twenty-minute walk to the front. It was like a small city.

He was by himself. His satchel of clothes and toiletries sat on the end of the bed. The floors, walls, and ceiling were all painted concrete. The paint was peeling away, almost as he looked at it. One small window illuminated the room. There was a single desk, with a solitary light on it, which he surmised he and his six roommates would share. There were three bunk beds in the room. Each had a wafer-thin mattress laid across stiff horizontal springs with one soiled sheet and a wool army blanket stretched tightly over it. A single six-drawer dresser sat next to the desk. Bach glanced around for the bathroom. There was none. He learned there were two communal rooms down the hall. Each with a line of rust- stained sinks; four toilets sitting together, about a foot apart; and a line of showerheads on the other side of the room. The entire area had a yellowish-white tile-from-floor-to-ceiling appearance. There were two large drains about six inches in diameter. He could imagine the whole room dutifully hosed down once a week. This was to be home for the next year. He sat dejectedly, watching the fog billow out of his mouth every time he exhaled.

Bach was strong, though. He'd been raised all his life by Party members or guerrillas, most of the time in tunnels and small dusty villages, usually near a riverbank. The only change from that life in the last five years was when he attended the University in Saigon for a year—a respite that began to turn the wheels in his head.

To some extent, during those first times, he'd seen how the other half lived. He liked it, but it made him feel guilty. He liked being with Mai, even if it only meant having a political argument. He enjoyed the music that always seemed to be everywhere in Saigon. The food was better and there was more of it. The beds were more comfortable. Hell, before going to Saigon, half the time he'd spent his nights on straw mats, the same ones the feral village dogs slept on.

In Saigon, he was forever astonished by what the stores in the city sold and what people felt they needed to have. All the trinkets, the accessories one would wear or buy for their homes, most of it meaningless stuff. But things he sometimes found even he wanted, especially things from the West.

When he thought of America beyond the ideology, removed from politics, he always thought of their culture. He'd only seen a few television clips on an old Emerson black and white, once in a café, and several times at the University. The cars, the palatial homes, the fine clothes, and all the money—how could that not tug on you? He thought, lying on his scratchy worn out wool blanket.

He closed his eyes and all he could see was a picture of Mai and her American boyfriend and the attack on the concert. He hadn't known she was going to be there or he never would have approved the grenade attack. But then, when he saw she was with that tall, blue-eyed American, he became enraged and wanted to kill him and her. He would remember that night for the rest of his life. The scene with Mai and her boyfriend would replace the one of the first time he'd seen Mai playing the piano in the gymnasium.

Chapter 14

Scott stayed as close as possible to the western bank of the river. There were still no other boats on the waterway and when they had reached a point near Ben Bach Dang, he found a small private dock, tied up the powerboat and helped Mai off.

"Where are we going now?" she asked.

"We need to find an American military man who can tell us what's happening."

They tiptoed; alert to their surroundings. As they reached the city, there was no movement except by the MPs and soldiers. The constant chaos of all the vehicles fighting each other, the never-ending horn honking, and the loud voices of the vendors were all gone. The sandbags were piled even higher than normal. There were bodies everywhere, some were locals, but most were VCs dressed in their black ba-ba. Everything seemed to be covered in blood that had sprayed, splattered, and run. The carnage started at the city limits, with vehicles burning, buildings on fire, even some bodies smoldering. The stench got stronger the closer they got to the center of the city. However, it looked like the VCs had been pushed back and the South Vietnamese soldiers and American MPs were in control.

Eyes darting from side to side, as they walked, Scott pulled his media credentials out of his shirt pocket. If needed, he hoped it would serve as their pass. The two large laminated badges hung from a steel chain around his neck, much like dog tags. An MP Jeep came around a corner suddenly; the two soldiers inside drew their guns and told them to halt.

"I'm an American journalist," Scott showed them his press badges. "This is my friend; she's a National."

"Let's see some ID," one of them told Scott and eyeing Mai carefully.

"Hey, fellas, it's okay. I'm a friend of Hank Palmer with the 716th," Scott said as he slowly pulled his wallet out. "We hope you can help us to meet him. I work for the Los Angeles Times."

"A correspondent," one of the MPs said in a condescending voice.

"Yes, that's right," Scott shot back, repeating "I'm a friend of Hank Palmer. Do you know him?"

The red-headed MP checked Scott's ID card and credentials. Reading the name, he looked up at him then at Mai, a hard stare on his face. He nodded at the other MP and then said, "Yeah, we know him. Who's she?" he jabbed his rifle at Mai.

"I told you. She's a National. She's a friend and a student at the University."

"Yeah, where's she live? I need to see some ID on her."

Mai put a hand on Scott's arm and took her identification card from her purse and gave it to him. "I live in Hang Xanh."

He took it from her carefully reading. "This your current address?"

"Yes."

The MP cocked a thumb at Scott. "He living with you?"

Scott stepped closer and took the ID card from him handing it back to Mai. "You ask a lot of questions. Yeah, she's my girlfriend. Is that a problem?"

"Well, we can't always be sure. Bad gook or good gook... ya know, if ya've seen one gook, ya've seen 'em all."

Without saying a word, Scott swung a quick hard uppercut to the man's jaw, sending him sprawling into the street. The other MP jumped in Scott's face, holding his rifle across Scott's chest.

"Calm down, fella. Take it easy," he said to Scott. "Billy here lost his manners, is all. You two go on."

Billy picked himself up, reached for his rifle and glowered at Scott. "Better keep a low profile on my beat," he said, "Hank or no Hank. I don't give a shit who you know." The look in his eye held a promise of something more than just payback.

They turned and walked away. Out of the corner of his eye, Scott could see the red-headed MP use his radio and make a call. He took Mai's hand. "I want to apologize for that idiot." But he knew no amount of apology would take back what the man had said.

"It's okay. I've heard it before, plenty. It's all right, really," Mai said, putting her hand on his forearm.

Halfway down the street, a camouflaged Jeep made a turn and moved slowly toward them. He could see the heads of two men through the windshield as it came to a stop. The driver emerged, gun in hand. Hank recognized his friend immediately and holstered his automatic.

"Shit!" he said, approaching Scott. "First, you get blowed up and then I feel sorry for you when you get out of the hospital and loan my motorcycle to you. What in the hell happened to my Bonneville?" he asked, giving Scott a bear hug.

"That old piece of crap?" Scott replied. "It needed a major overhaul and you know it. You needed to get a new one... right?"

"It didn't need an overhaul. Do you know how much time I spent putting that gold-leaf on the tank?

"Well, I'm sorry, really; it couldn't be avoided. We were being chased and... well, we had a little accident."

"What kind of accident?" Hank stopped smiling.

"Your motorcycle got kind of... smashed." Scott hurried to add. "That night, New Years, this VC and his girlfriend chased us out of town shooting at us. I couldn't outrun him on the Bonneville so..." He spread his hands. "I'm sorry Hank."

"You owe me big time," Hank said, pointing a finger at Scott. "There wasn't another one like it and you know the saying, if you break it, you own it." He looked around and his eyes followed a trail of smoke into the sky. "We'll let it go, for now, more important stuff to tend to." He turned and asked, "Who's this lovely lady?"

"This is Mai," Scott said, putting his arm around her shoulders.

"Glad to make your acquaintance, ma'am," Hank said with his Texas drawl. "I've heard a lot of good things about you." He leaned in close to Scott's ear and whispered, "This is the one, right?"

"That's affirmative," Scott answered. "What in the hell is going on? We had to hightail it when the fighting started."

Hank said: "Well, the VCs really shot this town up. They took the embassy for about four hours, but when the cavalry showed, that's it, it was all over for 'em. But, I guess you know that."

"So where is it safe?"

"Nowhere; not right now. We have the city on lockdown. They're still fighting in the villages and on the outskirts, but that's minimal now. We pushed 'em out of the city yesterday. The Air Force came in and bombed the hell out of a few spots so we finally got some cover. I'd say the safest place for both of you is with us at the barracks. There are other media guys holed up there, too, and they've set up a communications post. Word is going out everywhere. It's still pretty chaotic. Nobody knows how long it'll last. As you can see that with all these bodies, there's still a lot of cleanin' up to do."

Mai broke in. "What about the area outside the city. Is it safe to go there?"

Scott looked at Mai, knowing what she was thinking. Hang Xanh was three miles outside the city.

"Ma'am, as far as we are aware, that area is clear...for now," Hank answered.

"Scott, we must go to my home. I have to see if it's still intact. There are things I need to get."

"I don't know, Mai," Scott responded hesitantly. She walked back and grabbed the first bicycle she saw. Sitting on it, she said to Scott, "Are you coming or not?"

Hank looked at Scott with raised eyebrows. "You've got a livewire there. I'd do as she says. Looks to me like she's goin' with or without. Here, take these," he continued, pulling four ammo clips for a .45 caliber automatic out of the Jeep. "I see what you're carrying now. Nice 1911A; I like the ivory handle."

Mai pointed at another bike propped up against the building. Scott jumped on and the two pedaled away from the city.

"Talk to you soon," Scott yelled back at Hank.

"Be careful!" He waved and got back in his Jeep turning it around to head into the city.

* * *

MAI'S HOUSE

After a long ride down several dusty roads, Mai said, "Go left here... down that path." A few minutes later, "here we are." They had pulled up in front of Mai's house from a different direction than when Scott had picked her up for New Year's. They saw a man riding a bike nearby and a couple of chickens crossed the road in front of them as they rode up; other than that, everything was quiet. Hiding the bikes in the bushes, they went to the back door.

"Ahh," Mai sighed as she walked into the kitchen. "Everything is still here. It's untouched. We are very lucky." Scott followed behind as Mai ran into the living room. She noted the bookshelves were still stocked and the piano still sat in the corner. Nothing seemed to be touched. The half-empty cup of tea was still sitting on the side table where she'd left it.

Scott had the .45 in his hand, the clips stuffed in his two front pockets. He quickly looked around the room and into the den. "Everything looks okay down here, Mai. I'm going upstairs to check it out."

Mai smiled. For the first time in days, she felt almost normal. She sat at the piano as Scott climbed the hardwood staircase and disappeared into the hall. Pulling up the cover that exposed the keys, Mai touched the white rectangles lightly, enjoying the polished enamel feel under her fingers. She looked over her shoulder and then sat down on the black bench and immediately began to play her favorite piece of Chopin, her fingers gliding across the keyboard effortlessly.

Like a sweet smell, the sound wafted lightly up the staircase. The subtleties and rhythms of the notes brought Scott downstairs. He went to the front window and looked down the street, and then stepped out the front door for a better look.

"Back in a second. Going to check the road," he said and then began walking along the hedges, surveying the homes and the street in both directions. Everything was still. Since there weren't any tire tracks on the dirt road, it seemed safe. Closing the front door, he slid the deadbolt as he heard Mai still playing. "That's unbelievable. You really are good. What is it?"

he asked, giving a small sigh as he returned the .45 to his waistband.

"It's Chopin's Opus 9 No. 2 in E-Flat."

"Opus: one of a series of musical works. Especially one of a numbered series by the same composer arranged to show the order in which they were written or cataloged," Scott quoted as he walked to the front window.

"Quit showing off. Why don't you sit down and play instead?" Mai offered.

Looking out onto the dusty road, the chickens walked freely as if they were shared by all the neighbors. Scott thought Mai is probably the only person in these suburbs that has a piano and who can play one.

"I think I'll stick to my own kind of keys," Scott finally answered.

"How did you know what an Opus is?" Mai asked.

Scott turned with the hint of a smile, "Well, I was about to earn my master's and even though it's in journalism, I do know other things. Besides, my brother plays. I've tried a few times but only by ear." Scott glanced over at the bookshelves and saw an older Remington typewriter, similar to his own, whose ribbon was nearly worn in half. "Is that your typewriter?"

Duyen Nguyen

She shook her head. "My father used it to write poetry and short stories. It was his way of unwinding."

"Do you mind if I use it?"

"No, go ahead. There's some paper in the drawer in that table next to the couch."

Scott walked over, grabbed the heavy machine with both hands, and took it to the coffee table in front of the sofa. Reaching into the small table's drawer, he picked out a sheet of writing paper and fed it through the roller. Cracking his knuckles, he took a breath, pushed the carriage back to the start, and began to type. He loved the way the keys felt under his fingertips. He marveled at how someone ever thought to make such a thing. How they took such a complicated jumble of armatures, springs, screws, gears, and steel and turned it into a piano for thinkers. He limbered his fingers by typing, how now brown cow, four score and seven, over and over again and thought about how good it felt when he was creating something. And at the same time could be entirely lost in the tempo of his fingers and thoughts.

Mai turned to him. It sounded almost like a percussion instrument in his hands.

"You know, there is harmony to this, isn't there?" Scott said as he kept typing.

"Great minds think alike. What are you writing; are you telling our story about the attack?"

"Yes, in a manner of speaking."

"Can I read it?" Mai said.

"In a moment," he continued typing.

"I'll get us some tea." In a few minutes, she returned with two cups on a tray and put them down on the table next to Scott. He stopped.

"Ah, a little formality, eh? Nice to be back to civilization." He picked up one of the cups in a dainty mock gesture, using just the tip of his index finger and thumb, and presented it to Mai for a toast. Mai picked up her cup and held it to his.

"To love is to admire with the heart. To admire is to love with the mind," she said.

They tapped each other's cup and took a sip.

Scott smiled. "That's how I feel about you, Mai. You're beautiful, smart, and I love you with my heart and with my mind."

Mai put her cup down and gently knitted her fingers together behind Scott's neck, pulling him closer.

"You're incredible," Mai said with no further explanation. She placed her lips softly on his and then opened them. Their long kiss was a tender embrace. She slowly pulled away and gazed into Scott's eyes, looking for a response.

He sighed, smiled, and reclined as if still savoring her lips.

"What have you written?" Mai asked, breaking the quiet.

"I was thinking about war. About what we just went through, about the river, about...." He was going to say, "About you killing that woman and about Bach," but didn't want to remind her. She'd been through enough. "Just about how stupid all this really is."

"War is always stupid," Mai agreed. "Senseless." As she spoke, they both realized they had gone from love to war in the blink of a few neurons scattering about in their brains; the holy to the horrific. Perhaps it was an intuitive way of keeping them from going too far too quickly. Were they falling in love because they were surrounded by war and time was so precious? Because they'd saved each other's lives? Or was she truly in love with this American? A few seconds had passed before Mai broke the reverie. "Let me see what you wrote."

She turned the typewriter toward her, rolled back the sheet of paper to the beginning, and read:

> Fourscore and seven years ago, our forefathers brought forth on this continent a new nation; conceived in liberty and dedicated to the proposition that all men are created equal. Now we are engaged in a great civil war, testing whether that nation or any nation so conceived and so dedicated, can long endure.

"Lincoln," she said.

"Fits, wouldn't you agree?"

"Yes, two sides; both think theirs is the right way, the only way. One nation divided; brother against brother, cousin against cousin—the definition of futility. History just keeps repeating itself, doesn't it?" Mai said.

"Sadly, yes."

The two had sat silent for a moment before Scott spoke again. "You know, sitting here at this Remington reminds me that I need to be writing. The first thing you did, when you came in, was to play your piano. I need to tap the keys, too. I don't know what the media pool has written, or what they know back home, but it's only been four days since this attack. We don't know how organized it was or how extensive. Hank said we'd pushed them back but still, you can't stay here alone, so either we remain together or we go to Hank's barracks temporarily so I can start doing my job. I don't know how long it will be before classes start again, or even if I'll be able to continue at the University. Which should we do?"

"We should stay here. You should write. Let's get in touch with your friend Hank. Maybe get a two-way radio from him so we can stay in contact and figure out where to go, but from here."

"I like it. I'll take one of the bikes tomorrow and catch up with him. Will you finish the Opus for me?"

Mai took a last sip of tea, stood, walked over to the piano, and began where she'd left off. The music filled the house. For the first time in weeks, Scott felt a little bit of security. He knew this was the safest and happiest place for Mai and for now, those things would suffice.

The war would continue. There was no end in sight to the fighting. Now that the North had invaded, they would be emboldened to much larger offensives, more organized attacks. What would the U.S. do? Would they change their strategy at all? In four years of fighting, there had been nothing more than one stalemate after another.

Though he didn't have much information, Scott could feel the credibility of the U.S. position beginning to wither. Not more than two weeks ago, General Westmoreland had stated, "The war is being won rapidly." However, the media asked Lyndon Johnson, "If we are winning the war, how come the Communists are still active in downtown Saigon?" Johnson didn't have an answer. And then the Tet attack came out of nowhere, further eroding the credibility gap between the people back home, the military, and the administration, not to mention the media. That was the only thing that was crumbling rapidly, not the resolve of the North.

Mai finished the last soft notes and sighed. The music had warmed her soul. She turned to Scott and the two gazed into each other's eyes, knowing exactly what the other was thinking—we need to decompress, if only for a couple of days. There is plenty of food in the house so we can avoid going outside. Keep all the doors and windows shut. Hold each other.

"Would you like some wine?" Mai offered. "My father keeps a very nice French Bordeaux."

"That sounds great," he responded.

"One of our famous Kings said that wine was the nectar of the gods. It helped to make people happy."

"Are you making that up?"

Mai smiled and walked toward a cabinet. "Not quite. In fact, common sense tells us that a little morning wine wouldn't hurt our cause. And it's good for digestion

"You're funny. Bring on the Bordeaux."

Mai took a bottle from a recessed rack, selected two large crystal glasses and returned with them nearly filled to the brim.

"Sit here," Scott said, patting the couch next to him. "Let me make a toast."

The two raised their glasses.

"Here's to good Kings. May they rest in peace."

Mai giggled, clinked her glass with his, and took a swallow. Then without hesitation or saying a word Scott drank, set his glass on the table, turned and put his arms around her. He could feel her heart pounding under the thin gauzy top she wore. He looked into her eyes and then down. Her skin was as smooth as the magnolia petal he'd held up to her face the day in the park. Her breasts were perfect, the color of coffee with a lot of cream in it. He tried not to stare. Her nipples were erect and it seemed her breasts quivered and danced, wanting to escape the blouse. They were the size of large oranges, but formed in the shape of teardrops, absolutely perfect, he thought.

Stroking her neck, running the tips of his fingers down to her hands, he felt the goosebumps running along her forearms. Her breathing became as heavy as his. He could feel the tingling in his groin and thighs. He pushed her back slowly so that her head was resting on a cushion. He pulled off her sandals, stroked her feet and ran his hand over her calf to the edge of her dress. He paused with his hand just under the hem. Her body trembled as she closed her eyes and let out a small gasp of air.

"Mai, I love you. I truly do."

She ran her fingers through Scott's thick, wavy, blonde hair, stroking his cheek and neck. She felt her back arching involuntarily under him, and she said, "I love you, too."

Very gently, Scott kissed her. She teased his tongue with hers and held his face as they kissed ever so gently and tenderly. She loved to brush the tip of her moist tongue on the edge of his brilliant white teeth and then across his bottom lip. She wanted Scott to take his time, to bring her to the edge until the tension he created in her body was almost unbearable for both of them. He could feel himself fully erect and pulsing. He felt the hard nipples and firmness of her breasts heaving against his chest with her breath. He felt her warm wetness as he entered her. Her hips rose to meet him as they moved to the rhythm of the music that played in their hearts. She crested and it seemed it... it seemed she... would never end.

Chapter 15

FEBRUARY 5, 1968
SAIGON

Professor Phan sat in the study in his home. It was uncertain when and if classes would resume. The city was quiet and according to the U.S. embassy, many American combat troops were being deployed. Not only in and around Saigon, having pushed the VC out, but they were also mounting defenses in all the major cities under siege.

The Vietnamese and American military personnel were carting off hundreds of bodies from the city streets, mostly VCs, but many locals as well. Even if you didn't venture out, it was a horrific scene, the pungent odor of death mixed with all the smoke from the smoldering fires a constant reminder.

Across from Professor Phan sat a young man in a large leather chair; the wall was lined with books and texts. The man sat silent and listened attentively.

"The American journalist wants to meet you again. I have a message I want you to deliver to him at your next rendezvous," the professor paused, "I cannot afford for the government, for anyone, to know about this. My entire future is at stake," the professor said sternly, "Even my life... you know this!"

"I wouldn't have come if I hadn't thought it was important," the young man finally said.

Professor Phan nodded and moved closer to his counterpart. They whispered their conversation as if the walls had ears. Professor Phan handed several pages to the man. Finally, the professor stood up and said:

"I never wanted to get caught up in this anyway. After today, do not come to this house. If you need to talk to me, use the usual channels. Do you understand?"

"Yes, Father."

* * *

TAN SON NHUT AIR BASE

The radio crackled in Hank's barracks. Eight MPs gathered around it in the Quonset hut and listened intently. It was a shortwave radio capable of picking up signals all the way to Europe and beyond. The news announcer sounded nervous and was apparently reading from a prepared script.

"On U.S. national news tonight, Walter Cronkite said, and I quote:"

"I'm certain that the bloody experience of Vietnam is to end in a stalemate...

... another standoff may be coming in the big battles expected south of the Demilitarized Zone. Khe Sanh could well fall with a terrible loss of American lives, prestige, and morale, and this is a tragedy of our stubbornness there...

We have been too often disappointed by the optimism of the American leaders, both in Vietnam and in Washington, to have faith any longer in the silver linings they find in the darkest clouds.

They may be right that Hanoi's winter-spring offensive has been forced by the communist realization that they couldn't win a longer war of attrition and that the Communists hope that any success in the offensive will improve their position for eventual negotiations. This is Walter Cronkite. Goodnight."

The announcer continued.

"Further, Joint Chiefs Chairman, General Wheeler, at the behest of General Westmoreland, asked

President Johnson for an additional 206,000 soldiers and to mobilize reserve units in the U.S. Speaking purely subjectively, this reporter says we are really beginning to scrape the barrel. I don't mean that in any derogatory way, but if Westmoreland gets his requested 206,000 men and we start sending reserves and the state militias, we will have half a million men in Vietnam. Half a million!

As far as the Tet Offensive goes, Hanoi hoped to achieve one or both of two goals: first, to force the Americans to the negotiating table; second, to stop the bombing of the North. One or both would be a victory; but, of course, the real goal was an enormous offensive that would ultimately lead to the Americans leaving Vietnam entirely and unifying the North and the South.

The problem for General Westmoreland wasn't only the number of men involved, it was American opinion. Nothing, no matter how decisive or victorious at this point, would be acceptable to most people in the U.S. On the other side of the ledger, the Viet Cong had hoped their liberation of the towns, cities, and villages would lead to an uprising against the Americans.

This is William Stafford, signing off for tonight."

FEBRUARY 7, 1968
MAI'S HOUSE

Scott awakened on the couch, covered by a blanket, wearing only his jeans. His shirt hung over a chair and his sandals were sitting on the floor. He rubbed his eyes and looking out the window, guessed it was about six-thirty.

He still remembered the meeting he had with the stranger the night before. At first, the information he received appeared to be beyond any perceivable logic. But the more he thought about it, it became more and more believable. It proved Washington had realized that this war couldn't be won by mere superior military power and that the U.S. had begun seeking to withdraw in the least shameful way. There were two major concerns before he could write anything about the news. First, the authenticity of the documents he got and second, the legal consequences involved with the release of classified information about national security. He could be charged with treason or espionage and face severe punishment.

Mai was still asleep upstairs. He saw this as an opportunity to write her a letter, a love letter. Maybe he would give it to her today, or maybe he would wait—but he knew what he wanted to tell her. Slipping a fresh sheet of paper behind the roller of the old Remington, he peeked upstairs one more time and hoped his typing wouldn't wake her. He sat back down and began:

'Dear Mai,

Even though we haven't been together long, I feel as if I've known you a lifetime. Perhaps the fighting has only increased our awareness of how fleeting life can be. I want you to know that I adore you. I want you to marry me, and I want us to go to America when this is over. For whatever reason, if I do not make it out of this, there is something important I have to tell you. If the war ends and we have not won, you must somehow leave and go to California to my brother.'

He stopped to think and then continued on another page that ended with a secret he could only share with her and how he felt about her. 'I love you more than life.'

When he was finished, he pulled the last page out of the typewriter, folded the two-page letter together with some other pages, wrote Mai's name on the front, and put them in his pocket. By then, he could hear her stirring. He glanced up to see her coming down the stairs wearing an odd pair of slippers and a thin gauzy, long shirt that came to the middle of her thighs.

"Good morning, Sunshine," he said with a huge smile.

"Hey, sailor. You look like you've been up to something."

"No. Just thinking about you. Let's get something to eat, something simple."

"Okay. How about eggs?"

"Perfect."

Scott remained in the living room thinking about his love, the war, and the message he got last night. He could see from the window it was beginning to rain. The clouds outside were joining into large billowy forms. There was a breeze giving force to the drops and Scott could see the chickens across the street scurrying for cover.

Mai soon returned with a tray, two eggs and a piece of bread on each plate, a small pot of coffee, and two cups. She placed the tray on the table and walked over to the bookshelf. There was a row of eight-track cassette tapes and a player sitting on a lower shelf. She pulled one out, turned on the player, and pushed the tape in. A piece by Mozart began to play. She came over to Scott, sat next to him, and took a sip of coffee. "Oh wow! That's strong," she said, paused then looked at him, adding, "I have a plan."

"I figured you would," Scott answered. "What is it?"

* * *

FEBRUARY 7, 1968
MOSCOW

Three thousand miles away, in a different century it seemed, Bach sat up in his bunk after a fitful night of sleep to find that he wasn't dreaming anymore. He really was alone in Russia. He wondered when the other students were due to arrive. He hated the silence. He hated the cold.

He had dreamed all night of Mai and the American, part dimly-lit nightmare, part wistful planning. He'd awakened angrier than when he had dropped off to sleep, wanting to kill every American in the world with his bare hands. He knew if he could liberate Mai from her friend, he could convince her to be with him. With the audacity of Tet, he knew he had a fresh chance. He'd been told that with the invasion, the South would join the North and Vietnam would be whole. He would be an important Party official with influence. After the defeat, she and the South would realize his way was the only way that made sense, and he would be like a god to her. He threw his legs over the nappy wool blanket and walked to the window. It looked colder than ever outside. Without any sun peeking through the overcast, a few people, probably teachers, passed far below carrying stacks of books. Sitting with his book at the small table facing the window, he thought: How can I pull it off? Where will I have them taken? His only regret was that he wouldn't be the one to shoot, or better yet, to torture the American slowly. The thought made him smile.

Chapter 16

"Scott, we have to get back to the city and talk to Hank. I want to know about my father and what's going on in Pleiku. I'll come with you."

"No, no you won't. Please stay here. You'll be safer. The Beretta is loaded. You know where it is and how to use it, just pump and pull the trigger. You have six shells in it. I mean it. I'll be in and out in less than twenty-four hours," Scott said, giving Mai a serious look she couldn't misinterpret.

"All right. But find out all you can about my father. We talked about this."

"I know how important it is. I'll do what I can."

Scott took one of the bicycles they had stashed in the bushes and looked down both ends of the empty dirt road. Except for the three chickens pecking at the ground in front of the house, there wasn't a soul-stirring.

* * *

SAIGON
U.S. EMBASSY

Less than 15 minutes later, he peddled through Saigon and saw that nothing had changed, with the exception that the bodies that remained were either covered with blankets or in army body bags. The MPs were still cruising every other street, some in Jeeps with .50 caliber machine guns mounted on the back.

First, Scott went to the U.S. embassy on Thong Nhut Boulevard. The main part of the compound comprised the Chancery offices, a six- story white concrete building, one of the tallest in Saigon, built with a unique concrete lattice façade designed to deflect rockets.

However, as Scott could readily see, the VCs had not used rockets in their attack. They had blown a hole in the side of the perimeter wall facing Thong Nhut. Though that the nineteen fighters had entered to take over the building.

Hank had told him that eighteen of the VCs were killed within less than two hours; the other one wounded and captured. He'd also said that General Westmoreland had ordered his unit to clear the embassy as their first priority. They were supposed to be augmented by troops from the 101st Airborne Division by landing on the rooftop helipad, but they had been driven off by several Viet Cong, so it was up to his unit alone.

Scott figured if he could talk to one of the ambassador's assistants or, at least, an attaché, he could get part of what he needed to know. Then, he would go to the Marine guards' living quarters five blocks from the embassy and talk with Captain Napoliello, a pilot he'd gotten to know when he was dropping leaflets with the 633rd.

From there, he'd go to the 716th MP barracks on the other side of town and see if he could find Hank. Between those three, he'd have a better idea of what the overall situation was and what was happening in Pleiku.

But more importantly, he hoped that the talks with those people could reveal some truth to the news that he got last night.

"Well, it could've been worse, young man," Donald Archer, one of the ambassador's staff, told Scott. "We've been here for almost three years. Despite the presence now of half a million troops, the Viet Cong still managed to penetrate this embassy, sovereign U.S. territory. And they did it without tanks, artillery, or rockets. By God, this is the symbol of American power, and they just blew a hole in the wall and walked in," Archer said, disgusted and angry.

"Mr. Archer, what can you tell me about the overall situation," Scott asked, reaching for his notepad and pen out of his back pocket and waggling his press credentials hanging from his neck. "I've been out of the loop now for several days."

"Son, it's a mess, but not as bad as you might think. All the VCs have been routed from Saigon, but the outlying villages sustained a lot of damages; unfortunately, mostly from our own bombs.

"The VC attacked eighty cities all on the first, except for Khe Sanh, which was hit days before. Those goddamned cockroaches. They signed the ceasefire but had to have been planning this for months, just like Pearl."

Scott was writing as fast as he could take notes.

"We think Khe Sanh was a diversion. There are five combat divisions now on the ground opposing and, from all we've heard, they're pushing the VC back. They have a lot of them on the run. It's an hour-by-hour thing, but everything here in the city is stabilized now.

"You might be better off talking to someone at Army Staff Headquarters. I don't know how much they'll tell you, though. That's it in a nutshell. Sorry, I can't offer more right now. I've got to run."

Scott turned and kept writing as he worked his way back to the front door. Archer pulled out a notepad of his own and jotted down Scott's name and then saw something like a letter out of the corner of his eye on the floor. He bent down and picked it up. It was folded but not in an envelope so he opened it, reading only the first sentence:

'Dear Mai, Even though we haven't been together long, I feel as if I've known you for a lifetime.'

Archer folded the letter the way it had been. It was personal. It evidently belonged to the young journalist. He opened his notepad and read the name one more time, Scott Reynolds. He wouldn't be hard to find, but he didn't have time now. The ambassador had called a staff meeting; all hands on deck.

* * *

Outside the embassy, Scott got back on his bike and began cycling to the Marine headquarters. There he managed to talk to a captain, who pretty much repeated what Archer had told him, but he seemed oddly tight-lipped and Scott had no luck getting any more information out of him.

The captain finished by saying, "I'm not at liberty to tell you anything further right now."

Scott sensed the captain thought he was just another one of those so- called naïve reporters. What he'd read just after he came into the country rang in his ears. "These so-called writers are mere messengers, translators, cameramen, or backup staff. But not true journalists and not legitimate. Most of them are here for less than a week, just long enough to give their work at home some semblance of cachet, but hardly enough for them to learn much about the war."

He'd memorized that report by the General, and it angered him all over again. He had to talk to Hank, the only one who would be straight with him. Besides, he owed him an explanation about his beloved Triumph Bonneville.

As Scott came coasting up to the gate of the 716th, he got off the bike, leaning it against the barbed wire, reaching for his notepad again. He wanted to make sure he'd written Archer's name down. Then he panicked; the letter was gone. Oh God, no one can read that, he thought and sat on the seat of the bicycle for a moment, trying to catch his breath, reaching back one more time to his empty pocket.

* * *

716TH MILITARY POLICE BATTALION

"Howdy, Scott. You're back and where's that beautiful lady?" Hank asked.

"I left her at her father's house. She's safe there."

"Hey, not to get off on the subject, but the night my Bonny got shredded, what exactly happened?"

"Well, Hank. First, I'm sorry, really sorry again about your motorcycle, but that was an extraordinary circumstance and besides, who knew the VC were going to attack?"

"All right, I get your drift; don't worry about it. Tell me what happened."

Scott could hear the former state trooper coming out in Hank. "Mai and I were leaving *The Queen Bee* around midnight. Just as we were walking out, this guy, which is a whole other story, came up to me and whispered in my ear."

"What did he say?"

"I'm getting to it. This Vietnamese guy whispers for me to get my girl and get out of the city immediately. He said, 'There's going to be a surprise attack.'"

"Well, how in the hell did he know that and who was he? Ya know, believe it or not, I'm a cop—and a good one. This is my job."

"I knew that he knew what he was talking about. I still don't know how or who he really is, ofbut a professor at the University introduced us several days before New Years. I was trying to get information for one of my stories and somehow, this guy knew what I needed to know."

"And you don't know who he is?"

"No." Scott paused.

"Go on."

"Well, after this guy clued me in, I grabbed Mai and we ran to the Triumph parked in front. I practically threw her on the back and took off like a bat outta Hell. No sooner had I turned the corner headed out of town than the shit hit the fan. VCs were coming from every direction, shooting, lobbing grenades, the whole nine yards...well, you know."

"Yeah. Westmoreland designated us to be the lead in fighting them back at the embassy. No combat troops here."

"But these two VCs were on a bike, too; they were chasing us and we couldn't outrun them. I had to make a split-second decision. And when they started shooting at us, coming out of a blind curve, we bailed off the bike, the bike kept going, crashed into a tree, and exploded."

"Oh, maaaannn... maybe I don't wanna know any details... it hurts."

"Yeah, I know. An army truck was headed into the city and slowed to check out what was on fire. The guys on the other bike just kept going."

"Well, you two are alive. That's all that matters. I can always get another bike," he said sadly. "Now, tell me about this Vietnamese guy at *The Queen Bee*... you sure there's nothin' else?"

Scott knew Hank wouldn't let it go but in reality, he didn't know anything about the kid other than what he looked like and what he knew so far. Scott didn't want to tie the young man to Professor Phan because he knew how tenacious Hank was. He'd go out and interrogate him and then that would be the end of a crucial relationship. And he needed all the information he could get. Scott also didn't want to get into the fact that he knew the VC, Bach, and his relationship to Mai, so he changed the subject.

"I don't know who that guy is, Hank. Look I've got to start filing some stories, which means I have to have some information. I promise you I'll make the bike up to you. I'll give you money when I get back Stateside. Can you help me with some information?"

"Don't worry about it now, pardner. Everything always comes out in the wash. Whaddya need to know?" Hank asked.

"Mostly the extent of the attack. A guy at the embassy told me they hit eighty cities all at once, but I'm interested in Pleiku. Was it overrun? What's their status?"

"Why Pleiku?"

"That's where Mai's father is. He's a Lieutenant Colonel. He's also the Deputy Province Chief."

"Pleiku. Yeah, they hit a lot of cities, but we've got 'em on the run, that's for sure. Pleiku, huh? I know, yeah. I'd forgotten because compared to here and other places, they had it good if you can call a single night assault that. I've got a friend up there in security. He told me they sustained a massive attack that first night, New Year's Eve, but fought them off until they got tank reinforcements. The M-60s did the job. By morning, he said, the entire perimeter was protected by the 60s. They didn't take any casualties, probably because it's a small base and wasn't as important to Charlie. So, if your gal's dad is there, he's probably okay."

"Oh God, thanks, Hank. I owe you big time."

"Hey, you spent some time up there, too, didn't ya?"

"Yeah, that was my first assignment. Glad I'm here instead. By the way, have you heard anything about the upcoming Peace Talks?"

"What? How did you know about it?" Hank asked surprised.

Scott sensed immediately that he couldn't help him with anything relating to what he wanted to know. "Never mind!" He said.

Scott was about to leave when he remembered one more question. Standing, he said, "One more thing, Hank. There's an MP, who was on patrol the other night when we met you. I don't know what his name is, but he was a real hothead—a redhead, in fact. Something about him struck me as being odd and not just his racism. Do you know him?"

"Yeah. Everybody knows him. He's a real pain in the ass. There's somethin' off about him but I've never been able to put my finger on it. Probably nothin', just another burnout or nutcase to start with. His name is Billy Rietveld. I think that's his last name."

Chapter 17

MAI'S HOUSE

Scott pedaled back to Mai's, brought the bike around to the back of the house, and opened the kitchen door.

"Good news, baby," he yelled to alert Mai it was him. Suddenly, he realized he'd never called her baby.

"Mai, I'm back," he yelled again.

Mai came briskly into the kitchen, her hair wet, wearing a pair of loose drawstring pants and a t-shirt.

"Oh, Scott, I'm so glad you're okay," she said, throwing her arms around his neck and kissing him, a bath towel in one hand.

"Tell me my father is okay," she said with a look of trepidation.

Scott grabbed the towel, put it on the counter, and embraced Mai again as he slowly talked into her ear.

"Baby, Pleiku is okay; they weren't overrun and they had zero casualties. Hank told me the cavalry saved them. A tank brigade set up a perimeter around the airport and base. I don't know specifically about your father, but like I said, there were no casualties.

The VC attacked eighty cities and bases all on the same day. We are beating them back in nearly every location. Hank didn't have specifics other than that."

"Oh, baby," Mai said, mimicking Scott's greeting, "Thank God!"

She looked into Scott's eyes as if he were a savior and then she threw her arms around him again, this time kissing him passionately. They embraced for several minutes, both thankful to be alive and to know Mai's father wasn't hurt.

"You're my hero."

"Don't say that. I'm no hero. You and your family and every family like yours and our guys on the lines are the heroes."

Mai broke out of Scott's embrace and began twirling around in the room, her arms above her head, making funny humming sounds.

"I feel wonderful," she laughed.

"I can see that," Scott said, smiling and watching this beautiful, vivacious woman dance.

"Come and sit at the counter. I'll make you my father's favorite noodle dish and we'll talk while I play chef."

Mai kissed Scott on the cheek, whirled in a circle, and wound up in front of the pantry door where she began pulling out ingredients and piling them next to the sink.

From the drawer of utensils, she pulled out two pairs of chopsticks, looked at them intently for a moment and then turned to Scott. Holding them in one hand, she said as if she'd just thought it up, "It is important that there are always two chopsticks."

Scott looked puzzled with her seemingly obvious observation.

"And, it's important that the chopsticks are matched in color and aren't stained or chipped."

Scott, waiting for the payoff sat quiet, nodded and said, "Why is that?"

"Like people, chopsticks must have partners. They're a symbol for couples and, of course, one chopstick is practically useless. In folklore, broken or stained chopsticks were an omen of bad things to come for a couple. My father made these two for him and my mother. That is why he painted them with red lacquer so no matter what, they would never be stained.

"Now, they are for us."

Mai smiled and whirled around again, not waiting for a comment from Scott.

Scott grinned, enjoying Mai's happiness. As she continued to prepare the meal, Scott looked around the house, the floors of which were beautiful dark teak. Looking down, Scott could see the imprints of Mai's feet in the glossy sheen as they immediately began to fade one after the other, almost like a ghost was walking. He watched her intently as she hummed, opened packages, and retrieved bottles of spices.

"So, tell me about your family, about California," she said abruptly.

"Um," he murmured, fidgeting because he had been taken off-guard by Mai's sudden change of conversation.

"Oh come on, can't be that bad. Tell me about your family. When I really think about it, I don't know that much about you, other than you like saving my life. Tell me about sunny California. I've never been out of Vietnam except for one visit to Cambodia with my mother. I don't remember much, though. I was only five."

Scott began slowly and a bit somberly. "I'll give you the Cliffs Notes' version. I adore my brother. He's in the army in Germany and due to muster out in about eight months. We grew up in a city in southern California called Costa Mesa about three miles from the beach. I became interested in surfing when I was about thirteen because all my friends were into it."

"What about your parents? Tell me about them."

"The short version is my mother was married seven times, twice to my real father, but I didn't know that until last year."

"Wow, she was busy," Mai said, trying not to sound judgmental.

"Yeah, each stepfather was a jerk, including this last one, but hey, I've been outta there since I was sixteen."

Not wanting to give up her expression, Mai didn't turn around. She continued to chop onions and encouraged him to continue.

"So, where was your father when you were growing up?"

"My brother and I used to visit him each summer when school was out. I loved him but hated where he lived in the south. Every time I got out of school for summer, all my friends would head to the beach and my brother and I would climb on a plane to Atlanta, Georgia."

The large wok on the stove began to heat up, and the smell of oils drifted through the room. Scott could smell coriander and green onions sizzling. He watched Mai as she moved like a cat from one preparation to the next, but he knew she was listening intently.

"You left home when you were sixteen?" Mai asked. "Where did you go? Other than having so many stepfathers, why did you leave?"

"Oh that's all a long story better told some other time," Scott answered, getting off his stool and walking to the window. It was evident to Mai that this was a sore subject.

"Okay, so tell me about southern California and your surfing. Is it scary?"

"California or surfing?"

Mai giggled. "Surfing, silly."

"I could talk about that for hours. I was only thirteen when two of my friends asked me to go to a place called 23rd Street in Newport Beach, the city next door. That was the hotspot and it was in late August when the chubascos were going."

"What are the chubascos?"

"Those are storms that start out in the South Pacific in late summer. Hell, they probably start somewhere around here. They're big storms that really churn the ocean so when they get closer to the West Coast, the waves become enormous, sometimes as high as twenty feet. So, yeah, I was scared."

Becoming more comfortable with the subject, Scott sat down again.

"What's it like to ride a wave, a really big one like that?"

"It's hard to describe, but it's a thrill you'll never forget. Surfing is like a drug; you become addicted to the ride and, in some cases, to the danger.

"Are the onions burning?" Scott asked as dark smoke began to rise off the wok.

"Almost. Forgot what I was doing," Mai said, turning the heat off and moving the pan. "Go on. Tell me more," she said, grabbing two bowls and putting them on the counter. "Would you prefer chopsticks or a fork?" she asked.

Scott looked at the sizzling bowl of noodles with small pieces of fresh vegetables swimming in a red sauce, "Uh, I think I'll go with the fork. On second thought, make it a spoon."

Mai sat down at the counter with Scott, placed a set of chopsticks and a spoon next to the bowls, and then leaned over and kissed him lightly on the cheek.

"Bon appetit! Now continue with your story."

"Well, it isn't so much a story as it is of my experiences. I had three things I loved early on—surfing, writing, and photography. Mostly, I wrote about the water, the ocean, riding waves, sometimes girls, and I took pictures of the same things. I have boxes of photos of waves at home. Some of the best are in black and white."

Mai took a mouthful of noodles and began to chew, but her eyes were glued on Scott. She was trying to read between the lines, wanting to see his gestures, his expressions. She realized that she did not know that much about him, other than that she'd fallen in love. Isn't it odd that we can fall so hard for someone we only know outwardly, she thought?

Scott was caught up in his own story. He could see that one of Mai's talents was her ability to listen with her heart as well as her ears.

"You didn't finish telling me about how it feels. It's like a drug..."

"Oh yeah. I remember the first morning we went out in August. We got to 23rd Street and the waves were as big as buildings. It scared the shit out of me merely looking at them.

"The sun had just come up. It was only about five-thirty and it was actually cold out even though it was August. We only had on shorts and T-shirts and the fog was still thick. In those days, no one wore wetsuits. The surfers were nuts. They'd run out into anything frigid or otherwise if the waves were good. The scary thing was getting out to the waves. They were so big and breaking so far out, we had to paddle forever. But getting over some of them was like jumping off a black diamond run in the snow that was straight down and you had nothing but two poles and your skis under you. In this case, no poles and no paddles. There is nothing quite as powerful as the ocean, especially an angry one. After falling a few times and getting my bearings, I finally got onto one of the waves. I rode for a few seconds on my belly and then threw myself up, like I'd seen the others do, and got balanced. Once I got going to the right and was sliding down the face of this monster, I felt like I was moving at about sixty miles an hour. It was exhilarating. It's hard to describe, but I knew even though I was okay and moving well, I had no control. I was at the mercy of millions of gallons of surging water that just wanted to crush me. And if that's what she wanted, I had no say in the matter."

"She?" Mai asked.

"Yes. Waves are like women, like cars. Men like to refer to them as women as they do with their cars. But that's as far as I'm going with that."

Mai smiled and finished her noodles as Scott continued. She was listening, but she was also watching him, now enthralled with his story, so different than talking about his home life. He was there. He was in the water and he was scared. I love this man, she thought. He has that fire, that inquisitiveness that you can't learn. Maybe that came from his home situation.

"My favorite surfing spot was the Huntington Beach Pier. It's where they have the World Championships every year. Waves aren't big, but they have a great shape.

"Whenever we went surfing there, we'd always finish up by having hamburgers at a place called Ruby's at the end of the pier. It sits over the water, so while we're all talking and eating and grease is running down our faces, we can look out and see the next set coming. That was a special place for me."

"It's a set... like in tennis?"

"No. It's too long to explain and I'm talking too much. Tell me about you now. I know who your father is and you said your mother died when you were young. Give me the rest."

"Let's save it for another time. I'm in too good a mood. I'd rather snuggle instead."

Scott smiled, then laughed and said, "What are we waiting for? After you," he said, gesturing with his hand toward the living room.

To Scott, that was a tell, not a visual one, but a clue nonetheless. He wondered if her childhood had been unhappy. Based on her empathy, intellect, and "talks" with her mother—and this house with all its ghosts—he wanted to believe she was more interested in him at the moment.

She was.

Chapter 18

It was late in the evening. Assistant Ambassador Donald Archer had had enough for the day. Like all the others at the embassy in the past two weeks, the days had been rough and nonstop. Archer was one of the several employees that lived within the compound. He had retired to his apartment and as he took his jacket off to hang on a hook on the back of the door, he felt some paper in the inside breast pocket. Pulling it out, he remembered it was the envelope he'd picked up from the floor of his office as he left. Holding it in one hand, he poured himself a full glass of Macallan 12-year-old scotch. There was one window in the apartment, a floor lamp, and a large chair next to it, the perfect spot to sip his drink and stretch out his legs on the ottoman. He turned on the lamp, sat down, and looked at the paper. He took a large swallow of his scotch.

'Dear Mai, it began. Even though we haven't been together long, I feel as if I've known you a lifetime...' Archer continued. The letter was two, full, typewritten pages, with some memoranda attached. The last page made him stop and take a bigger drink from his glass. The kid was just a young reporter if he recalled correctly, with the L.A. Times and was looking for some information for a story. Jesus, Archer, thought. I have to find him. How could he have this? Archer put his glass down, reached into his pocket and pulled out his small notepad. Scott Reynolds, U.S. Correspondent... was all he'd written. Even a seasoned war correspondent wouldn't have access to anything top secret. Besides, the young man wouldn't have that kind of clearance anyway. How in the hell did he get this? He folded the letter and the additional pages and put them back in the envelope. It was late and he'd have to deal with it in the morning.

* * *

Archer had a fitful night's sleep. When his alarm went off at 5:30 a.m., he jumped out of bed and scrambled to shave and get dressed. His plan was to go early to the Caravel Hotel where some of the media pool were residing on the chance of finding this Scott Reynolds quickly. There were several other places the reporters, correspondents, and television people lived, but he could start there. It would only take him a few minutes to get there, and he might still get back in time for the call he'd have to make to the ambassador... and then to the Secretary of State—if he had to.

Archer put Scott's envelope in his jacket and went to the motor pool to requisition a Jeep. Within minutes, he was shifting gears and weaving in and out of traffic on his way to Nguyen Hue. As he crossed the intersection, he realized he'd almost run over the traffic cop who was waving for him to stop.

It happened so fast, Archer never knew what hit him. A bus that had the right-of-way, but was going far too fast, slammed into the side of his Jeep, which had no doors and no top. Archer was thrown sixty feet and died instantly, his blood mingling with the many other bloodstains on the pavement, and seeping into his breast pocket.

Chapter 19

Scott was elated. The beginnings of negotiations and North Vietnam's willingness to talk were a huge positive. He knew if he were to have an impact, to learn anything, to write stories with substance and break through all the drivel and smoke, he'd have to start now.

While Mai was cooking dinner, he sat at the coffee table in front of the antique Remington, staring. He only had Hank and the stranger as potential leads along with two minor contacts at Army Headquarters, but whatever they could lend would be old news by the time it left their lips.

The stranger offered up the best opportunity for Scott, but he knew close to nothing about the young man: How did he get his information? Who was he? What were his motives? He would have to create a plan out of thin air but, for now, he had decided on voice. He had to stand out from all the media clutter. There were two ways to do that—get the true stories and get them first, and develop his own voice to set him apart from all the other reporters, columns, opinions, and bluster.

Establishing his own voice would be the easiest place to start. He'd always been most comfortable as the troublemaker. The muckraker, a writer with a stinging wit mixed with irreverent humor, like a New Yorker political cartoonist who could make the reader cringe with a few words, a minimum of pen strokes, and the unavoidable and often embarrassing truth of any situation.

He didn't think he'd ever reconfigure the map of Vietnam, be a part of bringing the country back together. Or win a Pulitzer. But he would satisfy himself with an unforgettable flair for revealing deliberate deceptions and for giving the people the information they weren't getting.

He'd always been a great "complaint letter writer." He hated injustices. Things as simple as being overcharged on his electric bill to blatant lies by major American corporations. And he reveled in writing letters to the CEOs, Board Chairmen, even the President of the United States. It didn't matter who they were or how high up they sat with their ears muffled, he would write scathing letters that more often than not garnered him a personal response and his desired action. Sometimes he'd even use humor in his relentless campaigns.

He hadn't had a chance to use that energy for his reporting, which had to follow standard rules of journalism and decorum. And, of course, he'd been stationed in Saigon where until Tet, meaningful war stories were few and far between—at least those he was privy to before the rest of the press corps.

A young comedian and social commentator back home, George Carlin, was gaining a rapid following for his biting views and opinions on every sacred cow imaginable, from politics to religion to the media.

Scott saw Carlin's critical eye, satire, and anger as a refreshing voice in a sea of vanilla imitators. No one cut to the bone of the matter like Carlin; no stupidity, idiocy, or lie was ever left unturned.

Scott had the same voice but had never had the opportunity to use it—until now. He would stand out like a giant red hot boil ready to burst on the cheek of the U.S. and North Vietnamese governments. A sore that couldn't be overlooked or explained away. Maybe he couldn't provide all the answers but his air-raid siren would be heard.

Scott continued to sit in front of the Remington, staring at the keys, when Mai walked in wearing an oil-stained white apron over her gauzy cotton pants, a pair of wooden tongs in her hand.

"Writer's block?" she said. "What are you working on?"

"No block, just formulating a plan, a voice," Scott answered and then as if to dismiss her for a moment, he said, "I think I have an idea. Give me a few minutes."

"No problem. Dinner's going to take half an hour. I'd love to read what you come up with."

Suddenly, Scott's fingers were dancing across the keyboard, enthusiastic and full of bite. He'd heard from his Marine Corps connection that one of the two major stumbling blocks to the yet-to-be-decided start of the Paris Peace Talks was the shape of the table to be used at the conference. He couldn't believe what he'd heard. The fate of Vietnam and America and a good part of Southeast Asia was going to depend on whether the conference table was round or rectangular? It was the most asinine thing he could imagine! How would these two powers, which had fought so bitterly for so long, ever come to an agreement of such monumental proportions as lasting peace. If they couldn't agree on the size and shape of a table?

It was beyond ludicrous and just confirmed Scott's sense of the futility of this war, a war that had claimed hundreds of thousands of lives. What could be more dangerous in the grand scheme of life? And yet, these so- called intelligent, well-meaning politicians, who were supposed to be protecting the American people, were quibbling like four-year-olds. Fighting over who got the chocolate in the carton of Neopolitan ice cream and who would be left with the strawberry.

Scott couldn't wait. He put a piece of fresh white paper in the roller and twisted the knob, bringing it up to the top. He placed his index fingers on the F and the J and began to type furiously.

Mai could hear the clackety-clack from the kitchen and from the sound of it, it was a Rumba, not an opus. She smiled. Her man was back in his element. As she stirred the onions over the hot flame, she began to hum a song.

Added to his lack of sources was the fact that reporters in Vietnam had few official statements on which to base their reports. The army was just now getting back to their nightly-sponsored briefings near Tan Son Nhut that was dubbed by the reporters as "the five o'clock follies" because of the questionable amount of real information disseminated.

Scott would have to enlist the help of lower-ranking officers and move away from trying to use official government sources for information. Donald Archer at the embassy was a case in point; his four-sentence assessment was hardly the stuff of news. That left him with a basket full of Captains and the stranger.

It was also a time of skepticism and disdain, with many at home accusing the media of negatively reporting the war and eroding public support for the military. They were even blamed for losing the war one day at a time. In many ways, it was a true Catch-22 for the correspondents.

Scott would worry about all that a day at a time. For now, there was no disputing the world-class absurdity of bickering over a table. This would be the beginning of his voice and the byline of Scott Reynolds if he could get one.

Scratch that, he thought, make it Scott J. Reynolds. His parents hadn't given him a middle name, but he liked the way it looked and sounded.

* * *

Scott wrote his commentary in twenty-eight minutes, just in time to sit down with Mai to eat. He pulled the single sheet out of the typewriter with that familiar spinning sound of the platen.

The aroma of spices made Scott's mouth water, enough heat but not too much. Mai dished up the noodles and vegetables, saying, "Sorry, sir, we have no fish today."

"What? No fresh fish! What kind of joint is this?" Scott played along. "It smells delicious."

"It's rau muống xào tỏi, Vietnamese spinach sautéed with garlic and soy; very vegetarian."

Scott tucked the linen napkin Mai had put next to his bowl into the collar of his t-shirt and picked up the chopsticks.

"Don't want to get your good shirt dirty, now do we?" she said.

"Hey, if I have to use these two branches to eat with, I need some armor to deflect the sauce."

Mai laughed and picked up the sheet of paper.

"Can I?" she asked, not sure he wanted her to read it yet.

"Oh, by all means. It's done, ready to hit the presses if it ever gets that far. I was on a roll. I love this stuff. Tell me what you think?"

Mai decided to read the piece out loud. She began and then stopped to read to herself only. About half way through the piece, she paused and said, "Oh Scott, this is fantastic! Is that right?"

"Yes, it is. I know it's hard to believe, but it's true."

She cleared her throat and decided to read aloud, starting at the beginning.

```
Dear America:
     "Ring around the rosy, a
pocketful of posies, ashes,
ashes, we all fall down."
     Remember this from
childhood? We played it in
kindergarten.
     Soon, in Paris, the
Americans, the South
```

Vietnamese, and the North will hopefully be sitting down at the negotiating table, but just like the kindergarten ditty, they will all fall down. How could this be, you ask?

The Paris Peace Talks will not have any effect on the war, at least not anytime soon. These high-ranking, supposedly knowledgeable government representatives are barely able to tie their shoes, let alone determine the fate of millions of people.

I know that's not what you wanted to hear. You wanted to believe that what the administration is shoveling is something other than fertilizer. If you're like me, the smell matches the bad taste they've been putting in our mouth with their always uplifting,

positive status reports of
how well the war is going.

How can any war go well?

Now, here's the best
part about the hope the Peace
Talks will amount to
something. The folks up North
wanted a big circular table
so that everyone would be
equally important. The
Americans wanted a
rectangular table, which
would metaphorically show the
distinct two sides of the
conflict.

This is important stuff,
so keep following me.

Do you know what they
have finally settled on? A
pocketful of posies? Ashes?
Nope.
They settled on, "We all fall
down." After much bickering
among the preschoolers, they
have somehow come to an
agreement on this vital
issue. All the muckety-mucks
from the North and South get

to sit at a big round table
and presumably refrain from
throwing notepads at one
another. The other
inconsequential players, the
Americans and the Allies, all
get to sit at little square
tables on the outside of the
big round table.

I'm not kidding you!
This is entirely accurate.

And if you research the
origins of the song and the
game where the kids walked
around in a circle while
reciting the ditty. You'll
find it dates back to the
Great Plague of London in
1665 when people knew even
less than these folks. The
primary symptom of the plague
was a red rash on the skin in
the shape of a ring. People
filled their pockets and
pouches with sweet-smelling
herbs or posies in the belief
that the disease was
transmitted by bad smells.

The term "ashes, ashes" referred to the cremation of the dead bodies.

I say tonight, we all fill our pockets full of posies to ward off these bad smells. Ashes, ashes, we all continue to fall down. This is our plague. It belongs to everyone who believes this farce.

Don't forget, these are your leaders. You've put them in charge of finding peace and yet, I doubt any of them will be able to find the light switch. Let alone figure out which table to sit at—and they certainly won't find a solution to the war anytime soon.

Scott J. Reynolds,
for the Los Angeles Times

Mai put the paper down, jumped out of her chair, and hugged Scott, talking right into his ear. "Baby, that is great. I'm not kidding. I didn't know you could write with that kind of bite. I love the sarcasm, and I can hear the disgust loud and clear. My only question is, do you think they'll let it go to print? Will it even get out of Saigon?"

"I don't know and frankly, Mai, I don't give a damn. I just had to get it off my chest."

"Scott, you have to give a damn. I hear your voice. It's defiant. It screams, 'Pay attention!'"

"Well then, tomorrow, I'm going to go to the embassy and see the guy I met there the other day. His expression should give me some good feedback."

* * *

The following day, Scott pedaled into the city, down Thong Nhut, and up to the Marine guards at the front gate. As he approached, he remembered the letter. As important as it was, it had slipped his mind. He retraced his steps of that day. Somewhere between the embassy and Hank's quarters, it had slipped out of his pocket. It could easily have wiggled out of his jeans as he pedaled the bike and his legs churned up and down, or he might have lost it while he was talking to Archer. He hoped that was going to be the case. Perhaps Archer had even picked it up.

He showed the guards his press pass, left the bike just inside the gates, and walked up to the front door. More guards stood inside, just in front of a reception desk where a female Marine sat filling out forms.

"Hello ma'am," he paused for a second, reading her name tag, "Ms. Edelson. I'm here to see Assistant Ambassador Archer."

The woman gave him a strange look without answering. He'd expected her to ask if he had an appointment.

"Oh, I'm sorry. I guess you haven't heard."

"Heard what?"

"Mr. Archer was killed two days ago. It was an auto accident only a few blocks from here. I'm terribly sorry. Did you have an appointment with him?"

Oh God, now I'll never find the letter. No one can read that except Mai.

Scott stood still for a few seconds, not knowing what to do or say now.

"Are you okay, sir? Was he a relative?"

"No. I'd just met him. I was doing a story and he was giving me some information. I'm sorry he was killed, but I'm not sure how to finish the story now. Is there anyone else I could talk with?" he asked, showing her his pass.

As she was looking through a directory on her desk, Scott glanced around and then stopped. The janitors would have swept it up already!

"I think Mr. Jacobs might be able to help you. He's an attaché who does some work with the media."

"Perfect. Is he in?"

"Yes, but I don't know if he can see you right now. I'll give him a ring."

"Thank you."

Scott sat down and waited. Within a few minutes a tall, dark-haired man, much younger than Scott expected, came across the foyer and held out his hand.

"You must be the reporter," he said.

Inside, Scott cringed. "Yes. I'm with the Los Angeles Times. I'm here because I was starting on a story with Mr. Archer just before his death," he lied.

"Yes, that was a terrible accident. He was a good man. God, you come here to serve in a war zone, the embassy is attacked, people die, and yet all of us were unscathed. Then he's driving to work and whammo, he's hit by a bus. Sad, very sad indeed."

Scott didn't like the guy already.

"Yes, it is. I'm sorry I have to even bring this up at a time like this, but we started on a story and I was hoping you could help me finish it."

"Perhaps. I guess it depends on the story. What were you working on?"

Scott cleared his throat, hopefully not in a nervous manner, but he had to lie for two reasons. First, he now realized, he had to find out about Archer's personal effects and that would take time. Second, he had to get information on the story he'd already started, his new assignment, the Peace Talks. If he could get Jacobs to verify the story, even obliquely, he would feel comfortable enough to file it.

"We were conversing about the Paris Peace Talks, how everyone has his hackles up about the seating arrangements," Scott answered, waiting for a tell. Although the story hadn't broken anywhere yet, he figured Jacobs probably knew something.

The subject seemed to irritate the bureaucrat as Jacobs rubbed his chin, buying time to think about his response. Scott could see he was about to lie.

"Well. Yes, that is a bit uncomfortable, isn't it? But, I don't really see that as a story, at least, not a big one."

"Mr. Jacobs, can we sit down someplace?"

"I only have a few minutes, but yes, we can sit over here by the window."

They walked across the marble floor to a small table with two chairs. Following behind, Scott could see that Jacobs' shoulders were coiled.

"What kind of story are you going after?" Jacobs asked.

"The truth," Scott said, waiting calmly for a reply.

"What does that mean? It is what it is. The delegates are playing a game of one-upmanship, par for the course. You know, they all walk around spreading their wings, fluffing up their feathers, staking out turf—

no big thing. So where do you think you're going with this?"

Scott was already learning to know the answer to any question before Jacobs even asked it. What he did know just from instincts was the fake-it-'til-you-make-it attitude that all reporters had to use occasionally. Sometimes they had to draw the stories out of reluctant interviewees, stories they evidently didn't know because if they did, they wouldn't be investigating.

"I'm going to my paper with this, the insanity of our leaders, supposedly intelligent men who can't even decide what shape of the table they want to sit at." He paused. "You know the old saying," Scott added.

"Uh no. I don't think I know the 'old saying.' Why don't you refresh my memory," Jacobs said tersely.

"That which is left unexamined eventually becomes invisible," Scott said with a wry smile.

Jacobs didn't share the expression, "I don't know where you're getting your material, and I hope you haven't divulged privileged information. You better explain yourself."

"My sources are reliable, Mr. Jacobs. And thank you for helping verify them," Scott said, closing his notepad and then. Then as if it were an afterthought, he stood, turned back, and said, "Oh, by the way. Mr. Archer had something of mine that he was going to return. Does he have any family here? Do you know what they did with his personal effects?"

Jacobs stood, looking a little puzzled before he said, "No, he didn't have any family. The embassy people took the things out of his apartment and what he had on him, and put it all in boxes. They're in storage in the basement for now until someone figures out what to do with them, but no one's allowed to go through them yet. I would have no idea if he had what you want."

With that, Jacobs didn't speak again or even say good-bye; he just turned and walked to the elevator.

Scott put his pad in his satchel and in a loud voice said, "Thank you for your time, Mr. Jacobs. We'll talk again soon."

Jacobs didn't turn; he just waved over his shoulder.

Scott had effectively confirmed his story. Now he did actually have a source aside from the stranger, who he was beginning to believe could be trusted.

As Scott walked out the door and toward the front gate, he thought, I don't really care where my guy gets his info. As long as I can confirm it until I know more, I'm good.

Now, he just had to figure out how to get into that box in the basement.

In the elevator, Jacobs was grinding his teeth a little. He had his own set of instincts, and he knew this young man was going to be trouble. He'd be back, he knew that for sure. He also knew he'd have to maintain some civility with this Scott Reynolds to help ensure he didn't totally alienate him. He might be useful. On the other hand, he might end up being a genuine problem. Some things are best left unsaid. While others should not even be considered, at least regarding national security. That old ace in the hole, national security, always good for just about anything that ails your career.

Chapter 20

Scott sat on the couch listening to Mai play Mozart. When she finished, she turned to face him.

"How did it go today? Any leads?"

Scott quickly related Archer's death and then fast forwarded to Jacobs.

"They introduced me to an attaché named Jacobs, a real jerk I could tell, but he's my only contact now. I got him to confirm the 'Ring around the roses' story; he didn't even know what hit him. Now, I can file it early tomorrow. Technically, I could use him as a source, but I won't since he didn't actually initiate it."

"What do you mean?"

"I pulled him along until he got angry and demanded to know what I might do with the story. Then he defended the status quo and played it down as if it were all a bunch of men puffing themselves up like roosters in the chicken coop. At any rate, he definitely knew what I was talking about."

"That's great, a productive day. As soon as I finish this piece of Mozart, we can play house," Mai said with a coy smile.

The sun was setting and the orange light poured in the front window, spilling across the hardwood floor. As Mai played, she was apparently lost in her music as the gnats of dust flicked around her shoulders in the bright sunlight.

Scott didn't have a clue how he was going to find his letter. It could've blown all the way to the river by now, picked up by an embassy janitor or—or, he thought, maybe Archer had it with him when he was killed. Scott had never put it in an envelope; it would have been easy for the bureaucrat to read it and, of course, know what had happened—what might still occur.

His trance-like state was broken when Mai finished the final two cords, turned on the bench, and smiled at him.

"Well, did you like it?"

Not missing a beat, Scott said, "Absolutely. It was wonderful. You're wonderful. We make a good pair, don't we? You, the piano prodigy, and me, the Pulitzer Prize winner," he laughed. "Just kidding, Mai. You play like an angel. It makes me drift off–almost like meditation."

"Thank you."

"Come over here and sit with me. I want to talk to you about something."

Mai went over, curling up to Scott's leg, and put her arm around him. "What is it, baby?"

"About playing house; I'd like to go into the city tomorrow, to the Caravel and get my things. All I have is a suitcase of clothes and my Remington. I'd like us to stay here together from now on. There's no need for me to remain in the city in a hotel. We're close, and I could just use the bicycle. Maybe I'll buy one of those little mopeds the next time I'm in."

"Or maybe you could purchase a cyclo and earn a little extra money on the side while you're digging up more dirt. That is what you like to do, isn't it?"

"Well, yes. I guess so though I wouldn't put it like that. I just think there's plenty of hypocrisies flying around and a lot of lies and pure idiocy with it. I don't like to be treated like a sheep in the flock, blindly following the butt of the sheep in front of me."

"Baby, you know what's going to happen? The Times is going to love your story. It's unique and a breath of fresh air. They will love it so much they'll give you your own column. They'll call it 'Dear America,' by Scott J. Reynolds, War Correspondent. That sounds good, doesn't it? By the way, what does the J stand for?"

For a split-second, Scott was going to make something up, maybe even something silly, but then he thought better of it. He gazed into Mai's dense brown eyes, set into her creamy, flawless skin. She was stunning even in a t-shirt and baggy pants. She could have been wearing a parka and he wouldn't care.

He had already decided she was the one, and he wanted the cleanest slate possible with her. He vowed in his mind, and would tell her tonight, that he would never, ever lie to her about anything—anything. Even something as trivial as making up a false initial and adding it to his name.

"I don't have a middle name. I just added it to the commentary because I thought it looked cool."

"That's cool. I think a lot of writers have done that. Adds cache," she said before kissing him softly. "Let's have some more of that Bordeaux. My father had three bottles of it saved."

"Great! Let's celebrate."

Mai jumped up and bounced out of the room. Scott glanced over at the large bookcase behind the piano where the eight-track player sat.

"Where are your tapes?" he yelled as he walked over to the shelves.

"In the piano bench."

Scott pulled open the top of the seat. Inside were ten tapes, everything from Mozart to Count Basie. He chose Nina Simone and pushed it into the player. The sultry French singer's voice poured, like honey, out of the speakers.

Mai came back in with the bottle of Bordeaux in one hand and two wine glasses between the fingers of the other.

"Good choice, surfer boy," she said, putting the bottle on the coffee table.

"So?"

"So what?" she asked.

"Do you want to live here together?"

Mai smiled at him, waiting a few seconds to make him squirm before she said, "Positively, without a doubt. You're my man."

"Will you pour?" she asked.

"Absolutely."

Sipping her wine, she gazed into his eyes, feeling her skin begin to tingle. She ran her fingers through Scott's hair and unknowingly made a sound like a cat purring.

Scott turned his head slightly; a light blush came over his face. He could feel the moment; he could see it in her subtle smile.

Tension filled the room, begging Mai to speak and hoping Scott would absorb her signals.

"Hmm, I think you ought to make it J. Scott. You know, like F. Scott," she said, looking up at the ceiling as if engrossed in an important thought.

Heat came over Scott like a giddy 5-year-old that still believed in Santa Claus and was about to open his presents on Christmas morning. Just say it. Just do something. He took Mai's wine and placed it on the side table with his. As he led her upstairs, holding her hand gently, they ascended Jazz continued to play softly downstairs. A light breeze blew the gauzy bedroom curtains away from the open window. There was no further need for conversation. Mai had accomplished what she wanted with only a purr and a smile. It would be unseemly to do otherwise—and far too obvious for a beautiful, educated Vietnamese girl.

The two embraced at the bed's edge as Scott pulled her t-shirt over her head and gently untied the drawstrings of her pants as she unzipped his jeans at the same time. They slowly sat and then lay back on the large soft pillows, embracing and kissing each other. Surfing the wave of growing passion. She stroked and could feel him shudder and make an "awwnnh" sound, a little primitive utterance of expectation, wanting to prolong this forever and yet wanting the wave to crash onto the shore and never retreat.

She moved slowly, still kissing him, arching her back, pushing hips against him, teasing with her thrusting my pelvis. Again, that "awwnnh" sound and his member stood rigid, pulsing, and bobbing, as she lowered her lips onto it. After a while, she rolled over astride him and pushed down gently. He placed his hands on her bottom and pulled her closer onto him. She felt like a morning flower opening and then embracing the new day's sun and caught her breath as he slowly slid inside her. He didn't move. Her body quivered and shook, wanting him more than anything in Heaven or on Earth.

He held her breasts gently, using his thumbs to lightly tease each hard nipple. She nearly exploded trying to push down on him to get all of him inside. The ocean acquiescing to the surfer skimming along its surface. Nerve endings began to twitch and jerk.

He held her hips, pushing himself in another inch, moving slightly in and out, ever so slightly. She was aching, begging and yet at this moment, he was as much within her soul as physical; two incredibly powerful feelings intertwined, the spiritual and the physical—beyond sublime and almost impossible to describe here.

Then, without warning, he pushed himself up and full into her. The throbbing of a thing unleashed inside her. His "annh" became a soft, slow moan, a release direct from Heaven. She groaned and twitched; her breathing heavy as her thighs and arms clasped him tightly, never wanting to let go. She was the wave holding on for dear life. They rode to shore together pushing, pushing everything in front of them out of the way; a total surrender of power to absolute resignation, a moment without one iota of tension or force, a complete giving into the universe.

Mai nestled her head in the crook of his neck. They fell fast asleep as the mosquitoes buzzed outside the net, wanting to come in. She knew in that instant she wanted him in her life in every conceivable way—forever.

* * *

The next morning, Scott woke up with the sunrise as the light dappled across the blanket. Next to him, the pillow was empty with the impression of Mai's head still perfectly shaped. He decided to get up slowly, waiting perhaps for the smell of breakfast crackling in a pan to drift up the stairway.

Downstairs, Mai was sitting in her father's leather chair, her legs pulled up under her, her worn brown leather journal in her lap, a pen in her hand. She'd risen early, around 5:00 a.m., and left Scott to sleep. The lovemaking from the night before left both lovers filled with the release endorphins bring.

Waking up, she had walked downstairs; she could've been in Paris with Nina Simone still repeating on the eight-track. She almost forgot she was in the middle of war, feeling as if her feet weren't even touching the stairs.

Now, enjoying her memory with a cup of tea beside her, she heard Scott coming and closed her journal. He appeared in the archway, a soft smile on his face.

"Hi, baby. Did you sleep well?" she asked.

"Like hibernating," he said, smiling. "You're unbelievable. When I drifted off with you in the crook of my arm, I had the most fantastic dream," he said, walking over to the chair and kissing her.

"What was it? Sit on the ottoman. Tell me what you dreamed about."

"I was back in Newport, riding one of those giant chubasco waves—only I wasn't scared, not in the least. I just kept sliding down the face of it forever. It seemed like it was never going to end like it reached all the way to San Diego. It was so scary and yet so incredible. I felt like I was in total control but knew I wasn't. It was amazing, hard to describe."

Mai smiled all the way down to her toes.

"No, I think I understand. And to answer your earlier question: Yes, I believe we should stay here together."

Chapter 21

A satchel slung over his shoulder, Scott rode up to the house on an old white moped that was popping and spitting brown smoke. Mai came out from the side of the house.

"You got it. Must've been cheap."

"It was. Needs a little work, but it'll do the trick for now.

"I have a surprise," he said, swinging his leg over the two-wheeler. He was grinning from ear to ear as he pulled the satchel over his head and reached in, pulling out a piece of paper.

"What is it?"

Scott stopped walking and unfolded the paper, reading it to Mai:

```
Dear Mr. Scott J. Reynolds:

We love your piece on Paris.
Send more. Keep it in the same
```

191

```
tone. Thinking of giving you a
byline and maybe even a column,
if they stand up like this one.
        Keep up the good work.
        Samuel   Rawlins,   Bureau
Chief
```

"Wow! That's fantastic, absolutely fantastic, baby! Now you've got a forum. God, you must be ecstatic."

"You bet. I've got an audience and I can write the way I want to about what I want to. Now all I have to do is find the stories."

"You know, I have a feeling that once these talks get going, you're going to have more to write about than the time to do it. Just promise me one thing."

"Of course; what?"

"Do it from here in Saigon. Don't start going out in the field. I know you guys have free rein to go anywhere anytime, but I want you alive and here with me."

"You got it. I promise. That means I have to go to work tomorrow, have to go back to the embassy and see if I can talk with that new attaché."

As he put his arm around Mai's shoulders, he not only thought about stories, he knew he had to get into that basement. Then, he had to get in touch with Professor Phan. They were going into the kitchen when

Scott said, "They're starting classes at the University again next week on a limited basis. I don't know which ones will be scheduled, but I think I'm going to take a hiatus this semester."

"You're not going to quit?"

"No, I'll keep Professor Phan's class just to stay in the system. But I have to use this time now to start digging. You know, this is the biggest story of our generation. It's the largest in the world. I have to be a part of it."

"You're right, but do it here. You promised."

"Yes, and I meant it," he said, adding, "I love you."

That night, in Mai's father's den, Scott set up his base of operations. Mai had cleared out her father's storage cabinet, which Scott was using to file his leads and research

Following on the success of his article on the arguments at the Peace Talks over the shape of the table, Scott was ready to continue. He hadn't put together the team he needed yet, but his plan had to start somewhere. His friend Hank was more connected than he'd ever let on to Scott so he would be one of his sources, one way or another.

The stranger, though his sources were a mystery, and, therefore, dubious, did seem to be almost clairvoyant, so he would be a major gear in his new machine. Professor Phan was a possibility, but his reluctance and his fear of reprisals made him a dark horse, Scott noted in his ever-present worn, brown leather journal.

Finally, he had Jacobs. It was only a start. But he had his attention and knew if he helped him and didn't step on his toes, kept him apprised before he filed any stories, he could begin to establish a relationship, a symbiotic one. As W.C. Fields once said, "From the lowly acorn grows the mighty oak."

Scott sat in the large leather swivel chair in the den, thinking before he composed his next column. He wanted the same voice, the same tone that would eventually identify his writing without even needing a byline. This time, however, he was taking a chance, something he really didn't want to do. Without viable sources, his commentary would always be suspect and was only an opinion if he used euphemisms for actual source names. It could even be dangerous if his story exposed someone or something that wasn't true. It could cost careers, even lives, but if it could be verified beyond a doubt, and it was actually necessary for the people back home and here to know. Then it was fair game.

At this point, Scott had not yet given a thought to the fact that there might be some who would actually want him dead if his story touched the wrong nerve. Being new to it, he certainly never considered being accused of treason.

At the moment, he felt untouchable. After all, he had one entire Amendment to the U.S. Constitution in his favor, the very first one: the freedom of speech and the freedom of the press.

Scott felt comfortable and more in control of his destiny than at any other time since he'd left home. Mai was in the other room reading. He was working in her father's study, which he had quickly made his own. He had his own column, albeit with just one commentary, and he was in love beyond his wildest imaginings.

Don't fuck this up, he thought as he fingered the keys of the old Remington. With the singular exception of Mai, this was all he'd asked for, all he'd dreamed of.

Before him on the desk were several notes and pieces of resource materials. He swiveled in the chair and surveyed his lair. Floor-to-ceiling bookshelves stuffed to overflowing lined the walls. Thick, ancient, woven carpet on the floor. On the desk a pipe rack next to the other chair; and the cedar box full of cigars. It was warm and inviting. He could envision Hung Trinh, Mai's father, sitting here in this very spot, contemplating some battle strategy or writing about politics.

He felt Trinh's presence as a ghost lingering, watching him and ensuring he didn't disturb anything, but also smiling at the relationship he'd developed with his daughter. Mostly, Scott hoped that Trinh would approve of him.

The dark paneling, the books, and the smells set the mood for Scott so perfectly at the moment. There was something noble about what he was doing and where he was going. He picked up a piece of paper on the desk, adjusted the light, and then, with a smile on his face, his fingers began to dance across the keys:

March 1, 1968

Dear America:

You can only read it here, at least until the New York Times picks up the story tomorrow. General William Westmoreland has requested yet another 206,000 troops! He wants more American boys to join in this insanity. Can you believe it?

    As you read this, Dean Rusk isn't even aware of this, and the White House will surely deny it tomorrow—but it's true. Furthermore, Clark Clifford is going to convince President Johnson to turn him down. Good for Clark.

Was this why Walter Cronkite went on national television and told the nation that the war was destined to become a stalemate?

Is this why Johnson will deny the request, and why he feels he's lost the country if he's lost, Cronkite?

When I first arrived here more than 18 months ago. General Westmoreland questioned the quality, and professionalism, of the media. I wonder what he's thinking now?

Better yet, I wonder what the President is thinking. I know, but I can't tell you yet. You'll have to read next week's column.

Scott J. Reynolds

In his mind, Scott was firing on all eight cylinders, but he was treading on dangerous ground. He knew he would have to confirm with the Times Bureau Chief. He'd have to convince him that his sources were reliable but, for obvious reasons, he couldn't reveal their names. It would be a precedent in American journalism to run a story this explosive without proof, but Scott was ready to roll the dice. His source for this one was as solid as you can get. His machine was starting to mesh, and he could invoke reporter's privilege, similar to the attorney and client privilege.

He would submit his story in the morning and then wait. In the meantime, he would use it as a starting point at the embassy with Jacobs. This was one he wasn't going to share beforehand.

Chapter 22

MID-APRIL 1968
SAIGON

Scott read everything he could get his hands on about the news events in the States and whatever he could find out about the trajectory of the war. In the States, Martin Luther King's assassination dominated the news. In Vietnam, the siege of Khe Sanh, which had lasted seventy-six days, came to an end.

For the first time he could ever remember, the start of professional baseball was delayed because of MLK's memorial services. Khe Sanh was officially relieved after seventy-seven days by the South Vietnam Armed Forces and the U.S. 2nd Cavalry. To that point, it had been the biggest single battle of the Vietnam War. The official assessment of the North Vietnamese Army dead was just over 1,600, with two divisions all but annihilated. Thousands more were probably killed by American bombing.

Scott had developed a tenuous relationship with Attaché Jacobs who was surprisingly feeding him the news though most of it was commonly available with a little more work.

Scott's Dear America column had already become a hit at home in the Los Angeles Times, after only two stories—or rather, one commentary and one real story. The story about Westmoreland's troop request was stunning; it even took Jacobs by surprise. He had pretended to be pissed for not having been included, but he thought it better to give the young man a little more rope. He didn't say it to Scott yet, but he was most anxious to know his source or sources.

The story about President Johnson telling the nation he wasn't going to run for reelection was the kicker, though. How in the hell did the kid know that, and just two days prior? This was becoming interesting, Jacobs thought.

As far as news went, in 1968, most of it was in the States. The MLK and RFK assassinations. Nixon running hard as an antiwar candidate. The Civil Rights Act signed by Johnson. And the Paris Peace Talks, which enthralled both sides of the globe and continued to be mired in squabbles over seemingly inconsequential circumstances. By November, Nixon would be elected by the smallest margin in history.

However, Scott was still working on his trifecta of sources, comprised of Jacobs, Hank, and the stranger. His almost daily routine included riding into the city on his moped, spending the day talking to leads, and then riding back to Mai's house in the evenings.

And, Mai was attending classes at the University again.

Chapter 23

At the Givral Café, Bao finally broke down and gave Scott his name, but that was the extent of his résumé. If the two discussed the subtle use of words in the announcements, he also told Scott he thought the Café was getting to be too dangerous.

"Bao, I found it interesting that they used the word 'token,' as if Westmoreland was a young child who could only have one lollipop a day. But, it does tell you what they think about American lives–that they are tokens to be used as chattel between the politicians and the military," Scott said.

"They're tokens between our two countries. Johnson wants President Thieu to know he's still holding the line, even if he's beginning to chip away at the half million men, in a manner of speaking. Westmoreland asks for a quarter million more live bodies and Johnson doles out 13,500. They don't want to lose my people."

Scott suddenly saw an opening. Bao, the stranger, was beginning to let down his guard. Scott nonchalantly took a sip of his tea. The room was nearly vacant as it always was at this time of night, but they still kept their voices low.

"Who are your people?" Scott asked, putting his cup back down as if he was just making small talk and could care less if Bao answered or not.

But Bao was very sharp and dedicated to his countries—both of them. He knew where Scott was going. He'd read his first two columns though they never discussed them. Scott was doing just what Bao wanted him to do. He was shoveling up the truth right into the faces of the American government. So far, there was nothing that was going to change the course of the war, but it was a start; the rock was starting to roll down the hill.

Bao took a sip of his tea as well but didn't answer directly. He thought once again about his own motives. He loved his father but despised what he saw as a rubbery spine. He felt that a professor held an esteemed position, one of trust and that that position should, if not exploited, at least, be used to inform, to tell the truth.

As zealous as the VCs were, Bao was an equal in the opposite direction. He'd spent enough time in his native San Francisco to know how critical democracy was and how capitalism played into that form of thinking, He knew that democracy couldn't survive without a free market society, not to mention a free thinking, free speaking society. It is all that his people ever wanted or, at least, some form of it.

He could never reveal that, but he could feed information to this young man who he had now begun to trust. Sooner or later, he would still have to endure the crucible, but for now, their relationship was performing exactly as he wanted.

"Uh, Bao, hello, anyone in there?" Scott said, waving his hand in front of the young man.

"Oh, sorry. I drifted off there," Bao said, still not addressing who his "people" were.

Scott thought he'd give it one more reference and then leave it alone.

"Your people?" he said, with just a bit of inquisitiveness.

"Oh yes. I was born here in Saigon. Went to the University. My father and mother were killed by the VC two years ago. Not much else to tell."

Scott leaned back in his chair. He knew Bao was lying, but also knew he couldn't say anything, either.

"Oh, I'm very sorry to hear that," Scott said in his most sympathetic voice.

Bao took one final sip of his tea, grabbed his backpack, and stood. "Listen, Scott, I've gotta go. Let's not meet here anymore. It's beginning to be a routine, and we don't want any regular contact. You never know who's listening."

"You're right. Where then?"

"Don't know yet. I'll be in touch. Sorry, I didn't have anything, but I've got some real deep stuff stirring. I'll let you know when I'm ready."

With that last tantalizing statement, Bao had the hook back in Scott's mouth and then he disappeared as fast as he'd entered.

* * *

Nearing 10:00 p.m., the restaurant was busy. Professor Phan sat down maintaining a safe distance from Bao, his son and ordered a cup of tea, his eyes darting back and forth across the faces of the customers.

Oddly, neither the younger nor older man, even with all their connections and understanding, realized that the Pho Binh Noodle Café had served as a hideout for the F100 Viet Cong cell. Or that they had planned and helped carry out Saigon's part in the Tet Offensive. They were Bach's group.

However, not many in the seven table eatery, who sopped up the ladles of steaming soup made with strips of beef and piles of rice noodles, fresh basil, and cilantro, knew either. Most of the satisfied customers were oblivious that a very unpeaceful plot that unfolded just four months prior had been hatched in the family rooms upstairs.

"Father, why are you so suspicious?"

"Don't call me 'Father.' I've told you a hundred times, no one can know we are related, or that we even know each other. And, I'm naturally suspicious - nothing new."

"No, nothing new."

The two men picked up their cups in unison and took a sip of the lukewarm tea then looked at each other silently. Bao's green backpack rested at his feet. He wore a baggy white shirt and cotton pants. Phan could see his fingernails were filthy and his hair looked like it hadn't been washed in a week.

"Since when do you perform manual labor?" Phan asked with a smirk.

"Since you stopped helping me; I have no money, professor," Bao began as he leaned in closer, stage whispering.

"I thought the ambassador was paying you."

"Archer is dead. He was killed two weeks ago. A bus slammed into his Jeep."

Phan put his head into his hands. He sighed and sat back. "Shit. I wonder why that cousin of yours didn't tell you about it."

"Perhaps my cousin has better things to do—like the Paris Peace Talks, maybe?"

"The Peace Talks are going nowhere; they never will. The Americans don't understand how it all works."

"Professor Phan," Bao said with exaggerated respect, "why have you blessed me with your presence this evening. This is not like you. You must want something."

"Yes, in a manner of speaking. You know everyone and seemingly everything. Have you heard from our friend, the American?" Phan asked, his eyes darting around the room again.

"Yes, earlier this week. I've given him what I'll call some starter stories. That first one about the fight over the shape of the table was the one that earned him the column. I'm making progress. Johnson, not running - now that was a coup. He did well. I will also tell him about our cousin's plan, but that one has to wait. Imagine the indignation when the press finds out that Nixon is in cahoots with President Thieu. Our cousin thinks Thieu can wait and get a better deal with Nixon if he helps him win the election. All hell will break loose."

"He's your cousin, not mine."

Bao whispered, "Sir that is but a technicality."

"No, that's a fact. Your mother divorced me, left San Francisco, and remarried; that doesn't make her new relatives mine or even yours. They aren't your blood."

"Like I said, a technicality; we're all Vietnamese. What does it matter, as long as I can get the information we both want? More importantly, we can affect events—maybe."

"Let's not forget Bao, that your genes are Vietnamese, but you are still an American citizen."

"You don't need to remind me. I know who and what I am," Bao said sternly.

"I know, but I'm worried, and I don't trust that guy Jacobs at the embassy. I can't figure out if he's on our side or not...I mean your side," Phan corrected, turning for the final time to glance around the room. Finding nothing suspicious, he took the last swallow of his tea and stood to leave.

"Professor Phan, don't forget you are in this as deep as I am," Bao said.

Without expression, Phan replied, "We will talk again in a few days. See if you can ingratiate yourself somehow with Jacobs."

"Already thought of that. But we have to be careful to play one against the other. It's a delicate line—a balancing act right now."

Chapter 24

For now, things were quiet. Scott sat on the couch reading while Mai played the piano. His mind wandered away from the mystery novel and like an out-of-body experience, he felt himself hovering over the scene. It was almost like what he had envisioned his own family life could have been: Dad sitting with his pipe, reading; Mom playing the piano or baking cookies—the perfect setting for a simple life where everyone was good to everyone else and parents actually loved each other.

Scott watched Mai make love to her piano keys and realized that, other than a family photo on the wall-type of description, he'd never actually asked her much about her parents. He knew about how her mother had died and that she had been smart, beautiful, and encouraged Mai to think for herself. Her father was a Lieutenant Colonel, a hero, who had been fighting wars for more than ten years. He had built her a basketball court (of sorts) in the backyard.

Scott dog-eared the page of his book and put it down.

"Mai."

She stopped playing and turned. "Yes. What's up?"

"Will you sit by me?" he answered, gesturing to the leather couch.

"Sure. Got something to tell me?"

"No, not really," he said, thinking how her mind worked as she walked over to him in house slippers and wearing his baggy boxer shorts. She lives on a different planet that includes a sort of ongoing awareness and even mild concern about everything, all the time. Example? I ask her to sit by me, she automatically thinks I have something important to tell her, that I have news—maybe even bad news.

She nestled next to him, curled her legs up on the couch, and put her arm around his neck. "Are you going to tell me a story? Hope it's a good one."

"Hi, Smokey." He called her that because she once actually put on makeup just before they made love, something he'd never before seen her do. It floored him. He had always been attracted to her natural beauty, but after she had applied the gray and lavender highlights to her eyes, he was stunned. He'd never forgotten it and hoped he could someday nudge her to do it again. Secretly, he, of course, hoped it had nothing to do with his lovemaking prowess. As it turned out, it hadn't.

"I'm not going to tell you a story. I did that all day, or at least, I tried to. The news is slow now. I just thought maybe, if you wanted, you could tell me some more about your parents. I told you my story, so you owe me one."

"That's sweet, baby. Well, let me see," Mai said, snuggling in closer, looking into Scott's eyes, and stroking the side of his face. "My mother is here," she said, pausing for effect.

"What?"

"Yes. I talk to her all the time, although we haven't conversed much since we started living here together."

"What do you say?"

"I thank her for everything she did for me. I ask her for guidance. I ask her to keep my father safe. Mostly, the conversations are one-sided, but occasionally she talks, too."

Scott smiled, leaned over, and gave Mai the glass of Bordeaux she'd left on the table. She took a sip and then gave it back to him.

"What does she say?"

"Oh, I get little pearls of wisdom."

"Come on. What?"

"Most of them are secrets," she said, pausing, "like the things you write in that journal in Father's office, or rather yours now," she corrected.

"I didn't know you knew."

"I would never breach that trust. I don't look. I just see you intently writing in your journal from time to time. I know they're your secrets. We all have them."

Scott instinctively did a mental rundown of what he'd written, but there was nothing he wouldn't share at some point with her. They were his dreams, some angry moments, a few good ideas.

"So give me a pearl. What does your mother tell you?"

"Well, when I first met you, I prayed for guidance. I remember it like it was yesterday. It was after you'd gotten out of the hospital and we were eating dinner; you were disgusted with the pig's hoof in my soup."

They both laughed.

"That night, I was alone. I was worried about you living in that hotel, about your leg, about the war. I was already trying to figure you out, how much of that passion was real, you know? I sat here and spoke with my mother. In fact, I wrote it down in my journal."

Mai jumped up suddenly and walked to a cabinet in the room, pulling out her worn, brown, leather journal, flipping through several pages. At first,

Scott thought she was going to read through his journal but then quickly realized hers was identical to his.

"I would never have shared this with you until recently, but you asked." She read the open page.

January 1968

I can feel your hand on my shoulder, Mother. I've only known him a very short time, but I'm drawn to him.

I'm afraid. For the first time since I lost you, I'm frightened. How can I be afraid of love? I'm not afraid of the war, of the Communists or any of it—but this man is causing me concern. War is no time to be in love. Since your death, and with all the fighting, I ask myself every day: How many mornings are left?

I need guidance. I cannot tell him how I feel, and I know he will soon begin to pursue me. I can see it in his eyes and his funny nervous gestures. Mother, please share your wisdom with me.

Scott was touched. He felt closer to Mai than ever. She was baring herself to him. She was vulnerable, which he didn't often see. He looked at her and saw that she was crying, wiping her eyes as she put the journal back.

With a lump in his throat, Scott stood. He couldn't explain it, but his soul was attached to this woman.

"Baby," he said, wrapping his arms around her, "it's okay. I'm here. Your mother must've given you some good advice," he said and then changing to a lighter side, added, "Oh, and you 'knew' I was going to pursue you?"

She gave a quick laugh and wiped her eyes again.

"Yep. And you did...and I'm glad."

She put her arms around Scott and hugged him until he had trouble breathing. Then she let go, put her hands on both sides of his face, pulled him toward her, and kissed him passionately.

"Come on, baby," Scott said after disengaging. "We can talk about your parents later. Let's go upstairs where you can do that thing with your eyes again."

Chapter 25

AUGUST 1969

Several months had passed with little change and Scott had continued to send in his weekly column, which began to play a part in gaining the Times increased circulation. His latest effort included a reference to Nixon's late July visit with Thieu–his only visit to Vietnam during his entire presidency. That tidbit was a minor coup only because it was published four days before an official White House press conference.

Behind the now opaque curtain, however, in early August Kissinger made his first stealthy meeting in Paris with representatives from Hanoi. This would be the beginning of a long string of clandestine meetings. The following week, the Viet Cong began a new offensive, attacking 150 targets throughout the South.

Until August, Scott was still unable to figure out where Bao was getting his information, and he was growing increasingly concerned. The young man had been 100% correct so far, but Scott had been hanging on a thin string with his exposés that sometimes had no

215

trustworthy sources. He was able to maintain a tenuous relationship with Jacobs, getting him to verify some of the stories. But it was time to dig deeper, time to get Jacobs off the pot and, more importantly, time to find out who Bao's source was.

Except for the Paris Peace Talks, that summer through November things were heating up everywhere. Scott's breakthrough came in August when he and Bao met for the fifth time. This time, the spot was a downtown nightclub and bar. Outside, it was stifling, with temperatures in the high 90s and the humidity nearly the same. Inside wasn't that much better as Scott tried to adjust his eyes as he entered through the back door. The interior, as he guessed it would be, was dark and quiet. It was early in the morning. The bartender was cleaning up and getting the club ready for the day.

In the background, Rolling Stones' *Sympathy for the Devil*, played loudly. It was one of Scott's favorites. The deejay's crystal ball was still spinning, but there were no lights focused on it. There were about twenty circular tables near the dance floor toward the front. In the back, a row of faux-leather booths were all empty, some with empty beer bottles and half-full cocktail glasses from the night before. It smelled wet and sour, the odor of frenzied bodies dancing, and spilled alcohol. Apparently, the Stones were the bartender's, or this song, were his favorite as well because he turned up the volume.

Scott didn't want to call out because he knew Bao wouldn't want his name revealed, and he wasn't sure if he'd gotten there first. As his eyes adjusted to the dim light, he could see the bartender spot him and was pointing to a far corner of the room. He nodded and made his way back.

A minute later, Bao emerged from the shadows and said, "Good morning, Scott. Please, sit down. I can have my friend at the bar bring you a soda sữa hột gà."

"What's that?"

"It's a traditional egg soda," Bao replied.

"Uh, no thank you. I don't need anything," Scott said, thinking, eggs and soda together?

Scott slid into the booth and could see Bao's constant companion, his cheap green, canvas backpack sitting between them.

"So, what's interesting?" Scott asked, knowing this would be the time and place where he would broach the subject of Bao's source or sources. At the moment, he didn't know how he would segue into that, but he was always eager to hear any news.

"Well, you'll love this. My cousin--" Suddenly, Bao's hands jerked up from under the table as he covered his mouth as if to suppress a cough. He hoped Scott hadn't heard his blunder. "Uh, I, uh...," Bao stammered and took a drink of his soda sữa hột gà as if to wash the choke out of his throat.

Scott decided not to pursue Bao's mistake yet. He'd apparently just given up his source but then again, maybe he was about to relate some story about his cousin. If he'd let it go and continued on with a trivial thing, he might have gotten away with it.

"Are you okay?" Scott asked as if concerned about Bao choking.

"Yes, thank you; I just swallowed some soda the wrong way. As I was saying, my cause for concern," he said, trying to come up with something sounding like a cousin, "is that things are really getting sticky and maybe even dangerous now."

"Why is it more dangerous now than before?"

"Because now everyone is cheating, not just the North."

"What do you mean?"

"Nixon and Kissinger are meeting representatives from the North behind President Thieu's back. As you know, and you promised not to write about yet, Nixon told the North that America would not participate in ousting Thieu in any way, shape, or form. However, they did arrive at a secret agreement.

"Now, Thieu finds out that Nixon is going behind his back and that scares the shit out of him; but, more importantly, it makes him, shall I say, outraged."

"Oh my God," Scott sighed. "This is huge. It could screw up everything."

"Don't get too excited. I'm not finished, and I'm not so sure now is the time anyway."

"Then why did you want me to meet with you today?"

"I'm brainstorming with you. We know each other well enough now that I can think of you as a collaborator. I have given you much information the past few months and now I need a favor."

"A favor?" Scott said, thinking how it had taken Bao so long to come out with his own wants. He knew this would happen eventually and he wasn't above working a deal; but, of course, it would have to make sense.

"Yes, favor, but not right now. I just wanted to ease you into it. I will be able to tell you in a few weeks what I need. For now, just know that everyone is cheating and everyone is angry. Thieu is furious, and when he makes his speech this week, the North will go ballistic and claim that they were duped into a propaganda ploy by Kissinger. Thieu will refuse to accept such an agreement, saying it's worse than it actually is."

Scott now had what he needed and if Bao did not share his source, he knew how he could find it himself.

"Bao, you know I won't write anything until you give the okay; I never have. I trust you and I know you believe me as well. Isn't it about time that you told me who your source is? I will not divulge anything, I swear it."

"Not yet, but soon. This is all I have now. Feel free to use it in your next column, but don't hesitate, because Thieu is going to make his speech in three days."

With that, the two men dispersed, Bao walking out the back door and Scott about to head to the front when he noticed Bao's backpack still sitting in the booth. He looked both ways and saw that the bartender was still drying glasses, so he decided to stall for a few moments to see if Bao would come back for it. If not, he would take it and tell Bao later that he'd only taken it for safekeeping.

As he approached the bar, he kept looking over his shoulder. His heart was pounding through his shirt as he made casual conversation with the bartender and asked where the bathroom was.

He decided to use the bathroom and give Bao even more time but when he returned, the bag was still there. He quietly headed to the back exit and on the way, quickly grabbed the backpack and disappeared into the alley.

He wouldn't open it until he returned to Mai's house and had a chance to let it all sink in. He didn't think Bao knew where he was living, but he couldn't be sure, seeing what the young man was capable of discovering.

* * *

Scott gave himself a full day. He left the pack sitting in the den untouched just in case Bao showed up. He didn't open the strap, even though Mai could hardly stand it and kept encouraging him to go ahead.

"What are you going to do?" Mai asked as the two sat drinking Bordeaux. The sun had set and the heat was beginning to dissipate a little. They'd left the back door open and several of the kitchen windows that faced the basketball court. The front was always left locked tighter than a bank after business hours.

Still visibly excited as he took a big gulp of the special edition of the collector's wine, he said, "I have a plan. I'm going to go and see Jacobs tomorrow at the embassy to find out if he wants to talk about some family relationships."

"I don't understand."

"While I was talking to Bao, he inadvertently began to say the word 'cousin.' I'm pretty sure he was going to refer to his source but just screwed up and changed his sentence by coughing and pretending to wash it down with his soda.

"If his source is his cousin, then I've got a great lead—not that I could use his name, of course, but it would be invaluable, could lead to others. The problem is, I don't know if Bao was his family name, an acronym, nickname, made up, or what. He's been pretty damned secretive, so I have a feeling it isn't his real name."

Scott paused and took another swallow of his wine.

"Wow. So why don't you check his bag? Maybe he's got ID in there, or notes or something."

"Exactly what I was thinking, but until I can get something out of Jacobs, I'd rather just leave it alone. He might know where I am and if he shows up, I want him to know I didn't rifle through it."

"How would he know?"

"He's a very difficult kind of guy. He's just the type to have it booby trapped."

"You mean like a bomb?" Mai said, now warily eyeing the bag in the corner.

"No, no, but whatever he's got in there, he's probably organized, and the type that would notice if anything had been moved. At any rate, it's only for tonight. After I meet with Jacobs, we'll open it together."

Chapter 26

In September, Ho Chi Minh died and the U.S. Army finally brought Lieutenant William Calley up on charges concerning the My Lai Massacre of March 1968. That month Nixon ordered the withdrawal of 35,000 soldiers and a reduction in draft calls. Then two weeks later, an American opinion poll indicated that 71% of Americans fully approved of the President's Vietnam policies.

Scott remained among the few who had no ax to grind, other than to get at the truth and to divulge it. Most of the other journalists did their jobs, but they were always a day late and a dollar short on stories. Anything of eye-opening, air-gasping news came from his column every Friday just in time for Americans to enjoy their weekends, barbecues with friends and have plenty of fodder for discussions and arguments. And, of course, whatever the American and European media put out, the Vietnamese read or watched intently as well, above and below the 17th parallel.

Scott's Dear America column had become the thing to look forward to in every Friday afternoon edition of the L.A. Times. The New York Times, the television media, radio and The Chicago Sun-Times were forever wringing their hands over his scoops and their many missed opportunities.

Even Jacobs was jealous and as it turned out, had more of a vested interest in Scott than Scott could ever have predicted - and not in a good way.

* * *

"Let's go to church this morning."

"What? Why?"

"Just because," Mai said as she got dressed.

"You mean the Catholic church or the Buddhist temple?"

"You're funny. Ritually, Buddhists aren't required to go to temple on Sundays."

"Oh. I didn't know that. The Catholics worship all the time, don't they?"

"Yes, pretty much whenever they want, but Mass is always held on Sundays. It's a big deal. Will you come with me?"

"I guess so, but why now?"

"I don't know, really. I was just talking to my mother last night and she said I ought to go, that there would be a sign for me."

Scott pulled his shirt over his head and let out what he thought was a nearly inaudible sigh, but Mai had the hearing of a hunting dog.

"I heard that," she said with a small smile. "You know I don't actually hear her, don't you?"

"Yes. I wasn't saying anything."

"No, but you let out one of those sighs. I know what that means."

Scott walked over to Mai and put his arms around her. Looking intently and earnestly into her eyes, he could feel her tense muscles go weak as they almost always did when he held her.

"Sweetie, you know I understand. I see what you mean when you say you talk to your mother. For all I know, she watches us all the time."

They both paused and looked toward the ceiling, thinking the same thing.

"Uh, I mean spiritually, I know what you mean. No one around me has ever died so I've never had that feeling. No one in my family or any of my friends. But I have had a weird feeling once in a while with some dogs."

"Are you making fun of me now?" she said, pulling away.

"No, absolutely not. When I lost my dog, I was despondent for months. I couldn't eat or really concentrate on anything. About a year afterward, just before I came over here. I began to run into people walking their Australian shepherds, same as mine, and I would stop and pet them. And several times, I could've sworn they were talking to me, as if it was him, reincarnated."

"Well, actually, that's really more of a Buddhist thing. But if you consider the resurrection, then I guess it's a Christian thing, too."

"Okay. Let's go to church. Where is it?"

"It's near the city on the way in from the north road. Wear something nice and not your flip-flops."

"All right. Are deck shoes okay?"

"It's the only pair you have...so, yes."

When the service was over, the enormous, heavy wooden doors of the church swung open to a bright hot day. The first person out was the priest followed by the parishioners. One by one, the priest greeted them by shaking their hands and addressing them by their names.

When Mai approached, the priest's face lit up with a smile as he reached out to her.

"Mai, so glad to see you again. It's been far too long. How is your father? And who is this young man? Are you a Catholic?" he asked, shooting a sharp look at Scott.

Scott thought it odd that one of the first questions from the priest was a worried tone about him being or not being a Catholic. He wanted to say, does it matter? But he didn't.

Scott hadn't been raised with organized religion. He'd come to know God through his own devices. But was never interested in the different beliefs other than to learn from them. When he did learn, he realized they were all essentially the same anyway, with only minor variations. But that was just him and his always questioning attitude.

Mai jumped in, "Hello, Father Cao. My father is okay. He is still in Pleiku. This is Scott...Scott Reynolds. He's a journalist and my friend."

"Well, well. How do you do?" Father Cao said, offering his hand to Scott. "And so, are you a Catholic?"

"No, Father. I'm not. I guess I'm an agnostic. The jury is still out on me," he said, trying to be polite.

"Oh? Well, that's okay. Jesus isn't afraid of a little skepticism," Father Cao said and then paused. "But don't drag it out too long," he added, laughing at his own humor.

The young couple left on Scott's moped to return home. They were silent for the five-minute ride. When they came through the back door, Scott turned to Mai and said, "Do you believe that Jesus died for all of mankind?"

"Well, I'm really the wrong person to ask. My Buddhist father was a big influence on me, as was my mother. To a certain extent, I guess I'm still as open as you. I think that God sent many messengers, all in different cultures—speaking different languages, wearing different clothes—so that they would blend in with the local populace and be more receptive to his message. That's why we have Buddha, Jesus, and all the other prophets."

"Hmm, I never thought of it like that," Scott said, stroking his chin.

"When you come down to it, in their essences all the great prophets gave us the same message: love, courage, and forgiveness. But Jesus ended up sacrificing himself for mankind."

Mai could see the wheels turning in Scott's head. He didn't comment or answer, he just put his arm around her waist as they walked further into the house.

"But I'm still not sure about the redemption. How is man redeemed?" Scott wondered.

"Through forgiveness. Jesus died for the sins of all men and women."

"I don't know. I don't think I agree, but perhaps that's why there are so many different religions."

"I'm not talking about religion, Scott; I'm talking about redemption. Would you die for something you believed in more than anything in the world? Of course, you would; you offered your life for mine. Twice. What about truth?"

Scott had come to know Mai's expressions. This one wasn't quite one of disgust as much as resignation.

"Oh, never mind. This is not the day to resolve this with you," Mai said. "I'm famished. Let's cook something. What're you in the mood for?"

"Anything that doesn't have mystery brown bits floating in it," he said with a hint of a chuckle, helping to change the subject.

She laughed, the calm expression on her face giving way to a smile.

"It's Sunday. The custom after church is to share a meal of chicken testicles stewed in pig's blood topped with a heaping helping of sticky white rice, the kind you love," Mai announced way too loud.

Scott had been studying Vietnamese culture, but he couldn't remember that particular tradition.

Mai kept a straight face, waiting for Scott's over-animated revulsion to spill out as it always did with food.

"Oh God! Save me from the sticky rice. Rescue me from the chicken balls. Give me some wine."

Acting serious, as if she was paying no attention, Mai walked over to the cabinet, pulled out a large pan and a bottle of wine and placed them on the kitchen table. She was having fun. She felt as light as fairy dust with the prospect that she had found the man she would share her life with, perhaps one day even she'd go to America with him. The farthest she'd ever been was one short trip with her mother to Cambodia as a child.

"Oh, we have one other Sunday tradition," she said. Giving Scott a coy smile as she rubbed her hands up and down lightly on her forearms. Her signal that her skin was beginning to tingle. Scott was now starting to realize what she meant; she was ready for him, but she would never initiate lovemaking in any other outward fashion.

"Well, I'm not going to go against thousands of years of tradition. Let's just have the sticky rice later; skip the eggs." He walked around the table, held her wrist in his hand and asked her to put the pan on the table. Then he thrust his right arm under her shoulders, his left under her legs and scooped her up.

She giggled. "Wait, grab our wine."

"I love you," he said.

"I love you more."

Mai stayed upstairs and changed her clothes while Scott went downstairs. There were another couple of hours of sunlight left. He was in a good mood, poured himself a glass of wine, and decided to see if he could still bang out a tune on the piano. He hadn't played since high school and he couldn't read music, but he played a few songs by ear, and he played them well.

The original ivory keys were beginning to turn the color of an old man's teeth, but they were sturdy and amazingly still in tune. He had been born with perfect pitch, which was what allowed him to pick songs up just by listening, but he'd never had the patience to stick with the early lessons his mother had paid for.

Mai was still upstairs as he began to tinker, using just his two index fingers. After he had plucked out the main notes of the melody, he started in earnest to play an old Jerry Lee Lewis favorite. 'If this house is a rockin', don't bother knockin', a raw boogie-woogie song that made his feet want to dance. Within a moment, he was banging out the chorus and it sounded pretty good when Mai appeared at the foot of the stairs applauding and smiling.

He finished the last two chords with a flourish and turned, smiling himself.

"Wow! Is there anything you can't do?" she said, going over to him.

"Funny, I was just about to ask you the same thing," he returned.

"You didn't tell me you actually played. I'm impressed, very impressed."

"Naw, I don't really play, not like you. I hear the notes and then somehow find them and just add some chords. Certainly couldn't make a living at it, even in a dive bar full of drunks."

"No, I'm serious, that was good. Do you think we could play something together?" she asked, slipping in next to him on the black bench.

"I don't know. I really don't know how to play," he said.

"Let's try it for fun," Mai said, placing her graceful fingers alongside his large hands. "Come on, let's do this," she urged. "You play the beginning of that in C. After I hear it, I'll add my own touches at this end of the keyboard."

Scott smiled. God, he thought, I love this woman. It's funny how little things can grab you; a look, a smile, a gesture or a laugh, and you find yourself just head over heels again.

Scott began in the key of C, the notes growing closer together, faster and louder. After he'd finished the melody and the first chorus, he stopped.

"Got it?" he asked, looking at her eager twitching hands.

"Yep. Let's go."

Scott started in the bluesy rock-n-roll tempo and Mai played along, only she wasn't following his notes, she was making up her own notes and chords, which complemented his perfectly. His pace was fast, hers was slower. They were having a blast when suddenly someone knocked on the front door and the music stopped abruptly.

No one had come near the house since they'd returned. They looked at each other for an answer. Mai shrugged as if to say, "I don't have a clue."

Scott got up, dashed into the den, pulled out the ivory-handled .45, and peeked out the curtains, motioning for Mai to stay where she was. There was only one window in the living room and that was covered by a curtain. The door was solid hardwood and it was locked.

Scott came back into the living room, his finger up to his lips.

"It's some old woman. Never seen her before."

Mai thought for a moment. Maybe it was a neighbor.

"I should answer it," Scott said, checking to make sure he had a round chambered.

"No, you stand behind the door. I'll get it," Mai said emphatically.

She tiptoed up and turned the deadbolt as Scott went behind the door. Opening it just a few inches so she could peek out, the weathered old woman on the other side was beaming with a smile from ear to ear. Her cracked teeth and deeply lined face couldn't be mistaken.

"Mai, girl. Is that you in there?" she asked. "It's Bà già," she said, still grinning.

"Oh my Lord, it's you, di Sang," Mai said, suddenly perking up. She opened the door as Scott walked around from behind.

"Come in. Come in. I've told you not to use that name. You're not an old woman. No Bà già," Mai admonished, wagging her finger. "Come in. This is Scott," she said, motioning to him as he slid the gun into his belt and under the back of his shirt.

The old woman shuffled in and, seeing that she wasn't moving well, Mai showed her to a chair.

Sang sat, the smile not yet leaving her face. The couple stood in front of her, Scott slightly behind Mai.

Though the woman was full of good spirit, she looked tired. Mai turned to Scott and explained as she gestured to the woman.

"This is Sang, my nanny. I call her Di Sang or Aunt Sang. She took care of me from the time I was about five."

The woman interrupted, "Four."

"Yes, four. She was my mother's best friend and when my mom passed away, she came over all the time to help my father. She practically raised me."

"I did raise you," Sang corrected again. "Your father was gone an awful lot, little girl. I know this house like the back of my hand. I'll bet you never got around to painting that horrible pink bedroom you had."

Mai laughed and blushed a little.

"Nope. You're right. Never did, but I haven't used it in years, either."

"Bet your dad also never fixed that big crack in the court out back," the old woman continued.

Mai laughed again.

"Come and sit down on the couch. It's more comfortable. Let me get you some tea," Mai offered.

"I'd like that," Sang said, taking the hand that Scott offered so she could stand and he could guide her over to the couch. Since she was wearing house slippers, Scott knew she lived close. He watched her put her veined and rough hands that matched her face on her lap. He wondered just how old she was. He guessed if she had been taking care of Mai since she was four and Mai was twenty-one now; she could be as young as forty. But her appearance made her closer to seventy. Not important, he thought.

"I'm not as feeble as I look, nor as old," she told Scott with an almost psychic response. "It's just that when the VC came to the city, I was living in an old apartment not far from the embassy. I was out front and caught a little shrapnel in my knee."

That set off a full conversation between the two as Mai prepared the tea. The old woman got so comfortable with Scott she proudly shared her war wound, a large scar across the side of her knee that was obviously never treated.

Scott couldn't help himself as he pulled up the left leg of his jeans past his knee to show Sang the beginning of one of his scars. The one that ran all the way up past his navel.

"Did it hurt really badly like mine?" she asked.

"Well, I don't think it hurt as bad as yours, but it did keep me in bed for a few days."

"Oh, you sissy. I never went to bed. Just wrapped it in some cloth and went on about my business."

Scott was thinking, what an interesting old woman. The tales she could tell.

"I know you won't believe me, but I used to shoot hoops with that little one. Wasn't too bad either," Sang offered.

"I'll bet you were an ace," Scott said as Mai walked back into the room. She had three cups of tea on a tray and placed them on the coffee table in front of where they were sitting. Their conversation lasted two hours until the sun was finally down. Scott mostly listened to what he knew would be a wealth of background on Mai and her family. When the old woman said she had to leave, Mai asked what had brought her over.

"We've been living here for quite a while and no one has ever come over," Mai said. "After Tet and a lot of other adventures, Scott and I decided to keep a very low profile. My father is still in Pleiku and Scott is working with the embassy," she explained, shortening her description.

"Everyone is already going back to the way it was and life will go on as it always does in Saigon, no matter how fierce the fighting is on the battlefield. The rich will still party on their boats and dance the nights away. They've all let down their guard, even after Tet. Half the American Navy is parked in the harbor, why worry?" Mai said sarcastically. The old woman nodded in silent agreement.

When Scott offered to walk Sang home, she said, "No, thank you. I can get along myself." Then she added, "The answer to your question, Mai, is that I was walking by as I have done several times over the last three months. There were never any lights on, the curtains were always pulled, and I didn't see any sign of life. But today, after church, as I was walking by I heard some excellent American rock-n-roll coming out of this old house, and I couldn't help myself."

Scott and Mai laughed as the old woman began to cross the dirt and grass in front of the house. She turned with the same smile she'd come with and said to Mai, "Don't let that one go, little girl. He's a keeper."

Mai returned, "Oh, believe me, Aunt Sang, I won't."

"You know how I know?" the woman said and before Mai could answer, Sang said, "He's cute. Being cute means you have a good heart. You can't be mean and be cute. And—he plays some great piano. See you soon."

Chapter 27

When Scott was at the embassy, which was increasingly more frequent, he would talk with Jacobs and, if possible, catch the news on one of the televisions in the lobby.

It was a drizzly, gray day in November. He sat in the downstairs waiting room chair. People came out to the lobby area from several directions to stand and watch Nixon's press conference on the black and white TVs that were sitting on metal shelves above the receptionist's desk.

It was billed as an address to "The Great Silent Majority of Americans," but, of course, it would eventually be seen around the world. Both the civilian and government employees were gathered in small clusters, their eyes glued to the stoic Nixon, seated in front of an enormous American flag as a backdrop in the Oval Office.

"The more divided we are at home, the less likely the enemy is to negotiate in Paris. North Vietnam

238

cannot defeat or humiliate the United States. Only Americans can do that," was part of what he said and what made Scott fume.

He quickly pulled out his memo pad and scribbled Nixon's words down. He wanted to strangle someone. For all the self-sacrificing Vietnamese people who had given their lives in this struggle. For the thousands upon thousands of American boys and men who died or were injured. For all the people back home who were courageous enough to go into the streets and fight the system, even going to jail or worse, being shot at Kent State. He was livid. In fact, he was beyond furious. How dare that pompous, self-serving ass say such a thing? Only Americans can defeat the United States?

Now that Scott knew about the secret talks and deals, he wondered how deep it all went, how far Nixon, Kissinger, and McNamara had gone.

He couldn't wait to chat with Jacobs and then race back out to Mai's to open that bag. He had to find out who Bao's source was. The floodgates were about to open, and he wanted to be one of the first to have the keys.

"Good morning, Scott," Jacobs said, not rising from his chair. His office was a depressing place. One small window, a gray steel desk, with an old black phone, that looked like something a warehouse clerk would use. It was tucked back between some musty rows of inventory and stacks of files that probably hadn't been touched in years. Scott wondered how a man with so much power could've settled for this.

"Good morning, Henry," Scott said, sitting. "Did you watch that?" he asked.

"Yep. He's right. All those hippies back there have been smoking too much weed. If they just understood what we're trying to do for these people, they wouldn't be causing so much trouble. Don't you agree?"

"No. I don't agree. Don't get me started on the First Amendment, okay? Just don't."

Scott was in no mood to banter about war protesters and the Constitution. This guy had always been an idiot, and he was proving it yet again this morning.

"Look, I'm not here to discuss protesters. I need your help."

"What else is new? You know, sometimes I don't think you understand much."

"How so?" Scott wanted to know.

"I help you with your stories and you give me crumbs. Hell, half the time, I don't even find out what you're writing until Nixon comes on TV and apologizes. O Agnew throws a tizzy fit or Westmoreland pulls out what little hair he has left."

"Well, Henry, that's why I'm here. It's your lucky day," Scott said, his hackles up and his demeanor far stronger than the novice he was just one year ago.

"Yeah, I've heard that before. You know, some of this stuff borders on...."

Scott cut him off. "Don't say something you'll regret," he jabbed. "You know what, Henry? I'm so sick of people telling me that we're all traitors, always under the guise of 'national security.'

"Do you know what national security is? It's a safety blanket for the government, a smoke curtain they can hide behind, tell their lies, promote their own agendas as they sit there sucking their thumbs, clinging to it.

"But that's not what I'm here for. I know you don't agree. I've grabbed onto the hottest story I've had so far, and I need you to help me with it.

"Journalism should not simply be the 'first draft' of history. Shouldn't it be the most accurate, the most truthful account, the only one that goes on the permanent record?

"Aren't we obligated to get it right before the Monday morning quarterbacks do their rewrites, their opinion pieces, and their outright obfuscations? Aren't we the eyewitnesses to the train wreck? Do we not know just exactly who was asleep at the switch; who caused the collision?"

Jacobs had to admit, Scott had a point, but still...

"What is it? What do you need now?" he asked nonetheless.

"I need you to do your magic with your system, your files, your informers, whatever and whomever. I need to track down the current lineage of the name Bao."

"Are you nuts? Do you know how prolific that name is?"

"I don't care. If I can find out what I need to know, I'll be deep in the heart of Dixie."

"Pardon me?"

"I mean, I'll be at the source, the heart of it all. Listen, Henry, I know that beneath it all, behind that title plaque sitting on your desk, you want the truth, too. Or are you another sheep with your nose in the ass of the sheep in front of you? Are you one who doesn't like to be fucked with, lied to, and cheated? I think under that suit, you want pretty much the same things I do."

"All right. Give me a couple of days."

"I can't. I've got to have this tomorrow morning. And, I need one more favor. How can I get into the basement?"

"Why would you want to get into the cellar?"

"Your predecessor, Archer, had something of mine when he was killed in that accident. I think it was put in with his personal effects, which you told me quite a while ago were under lock and key."

"That's true. I don't have a key and to tell you the truth, I don't know who does. Maybe one of the MP's. Mostly, there are just old records down there, and they control security here. Let me see what I can do about Bao and the basement."

Chapter 28

"Is it too soon?"

"For what?"

"To name her."

"How do you know it's a girl?"

"I can feel it. I can tell," Mai answered, looking very self-assured as she felt a glow come over her. Scott rubbed her stomach, too soon to show. He was beaming. The couple sat in an embrace on the couch, both dreaming. Marriage would come up soon. Staying here or going to America would come after that.

"I think we should name her Kim-Phung, the golden phoenix; like you, she will certainly be radiant," Mai said, smiling.

"I like it. Kim-Phung it is. But what if it turns out to be a boy?"

"Then he will be Khói, a handsome young man, like his father," Mai said with a loving smile.

"I like that, too."

They sat, reveling in a feeling of total contentment. For the moment, nothing else in the world mattered but their silence. Suddenly, Mai turned and faced Scott. "When will we be married? It is critical to me. I might be progressive, but I'm still old school in many ways. My father's family and our traditions go back hundreds of years here."

Scott shouldn't have been surprised, but he didn't answer right away, which gave Mai pause. She waited...and waited, the corners of her mouth slowly beginning to turn down.

Scott turned, still not talking and then suddenly said, "Tomorrow, next week, whenever you want. Baby, I love you more than anything. I know some of your traditions. I don't spend all day searching for stories. I've actually spent a fair amount of time at the University library."

"Yeah? What have you discovered?"

"Well, for one, I know marriages are usually arranged by the parents, which obviously isn't our case. Likewise, neither Le Hoi nor Le Cuoi would apply," Scott said, self-satisfied with his knowledge and hoping he'd pronounced them correctly. "My family and yours aren't going to exchange lacquered boxes, nuts, teas, cakes, or money. Nor will they be coming to your house to ask permission for me to marry you. In America, we have a word for what we need to do."

"What is that?"

"Eloping."
Mai laughed, turning to kiss Scott.

Chapter 29

LATE NOVEMBER 1969
SAIGON

Scott had put the word out that he was looking for additional sources. An anonymous note had asked for a meeting. He had just put the kickstand down in front of the restaurant. Like a beacon, the man's red hair caught his eye. He remembered their encounter the night he and Mai went into the city to talk to Hank and he'd punched the man for his slur. Now, he wished he'd paid more attention to the two Jeeps that appeared to be following him. He still didn't know who was in the other vehicle. Something crashed into his head from behind and he never found out.

He came to and though still groggy the familiar motion told him he was in a helicopter in flight. Blood poured down into his right eye, running over his chin and dripping off in great globs onto his vest. He didn't know how long he'd been out. The last thing he remembered was someone, maybe another MP, hitting him in the alley behind the restaurant. His wrists were clamped so tightly with handcuffs, he thought he'd lose his hands because of the loss of circulation. And his head was pounding to the point that he saw small flashes like miniature lightning bolts racing through his vision.

Mai was slumped over, unconscious on the seat next to him. This Huey B-1 chopper belonged to a Colonel and was used to ferry embassy Attachés around, he knew that from the officer and State Department insignias on the dash. He'd seen them plenty of times before. Like some Hueys, if it wasn't being used as transport for troops or the wounded, it had a bench seat behind the cockpit.

Further back was a cargo bay that was empty, except for an M-16 leaning on a duffle bag stenciled with RIETVELD. Apparently, wherever he was taking them, they'd be staying awhile.

Scott nudged Mai, but she was out cold. Billy had knocked her out with a single punch to the jaw; he surmised, in retaliation. Scott could see part of her face. It was already turning purple like her hands. Her position had contorted her wrists, which were wrenched at 45- degree angles to her arms.

He had no idea why this idiot had taken them. He remembered him immediately when he saw his face in the rearview mirror of his moped.

Billy was still in his MP's uniform, complete with badge and insignias. He even had his stiff, black baton in its sheath at his side as he maneuvered the chopper at about 4,000 feet. Apparently, he knew how to fly, but had he stolen the Huey?

The bench seat sat facing the cockpit with the right side door wide open so Scott had a good view of the terrain. So far, in the last 10 minutes, he didn't recognize any identifying ground features other than jungle and small rivers.

He felt his stomach begin to betray him as he stared at Mai. He was getting sick thinking about her safety—she was in her first trimester of pregnancy, a crucial time. He could tell from the slight rise in her blouse that she was breathing, but she was definitely out. There were no other wounds, no scrapes or bruises that he could see, so that was good, for now.

Scott's mind began to race as he leaned forward toward the pilot and yelled, "Hey motherfucker! Where are you taking us? What the fuck are you doing?"

Suddenly, Billy jerked his head around, "You, writer boy, shut your mouth! You'll find out soon enough," he said, jabbing his finger at Scott.

"Fuck you!" Scott yelled straining at the safety harness, pulling and twisting his wrists futilely as hard as he could against the handcuffs. The veins in his neck were as thick as ropes.

"When I get my hands on you, you're a dead man, you motherfucker! I will strangle your ass with my bare hands!"

All Scott could think was Mai and the baby. He had never felt such unbridled anger in his life, but he also knew he was helpless for the moment.

Before Billy turned his head back, Scott coughed up a wad of saliva and spit in Billy's face the only reprisal he had available.

Billy quickly wiped the spit from his eyes and calmly smiled at Scott, loving the fact that Scott could do nothing and that he, Billy, was in complete control. He kept the satisfaction of his smile as he turned his head back and took a turn about twenty degrees north. All Billy could think about was turning these two over to Bach's men. He wasn't sure why Bach wanted these two, but he did know that the girl was a student, the guy was a reporter, and both were going to the University. Just as Bach had ordered, he'd tailed them every day for two weeks until he figured out a pattern. Then, knowing they'd be eating dinner at that restaurant, he plotted the rest of his scheme from there. This would be his last favor for Bach and he'd be done. He'd be on an airplane to the States in a month, free from all this crap. Free from Vietnam.

Since Scott had been in and around Pleiku and a little outside Saigon, those were the only two areas he was familiar with. He thought that if he could keep track of the elapsed time from when he woke up their air speed and the sun, he might get his bearings. Which he could use to escape if the opportunity presented itself.

The Huey was flying at about seventy-five knots due north. If they'd left from Saigon, that would take them toward the central part of the country, perhaps the Highlands area around Pleiku and Kontum, or further. He wouldn't be taking them to anyplace that was secured by American troops; that didn't make any sense, but then neither did Billy kidnapping them. But why would they be going into any enemy stronghold? That just didn't make any sense, either.

Scott's head was whirling; the pain was excruciating, but he had to think about every detail. The first priority was to make sure Mai was okay. The second was to identify his location by the time they landed. Third was to escape—the sooner, the better. He knew that the longer they were captive, the less chance they'd have to get out, either by escaping or being rescued—and who would even know they were gone?

They had been flying for about a half hour. Pleiku was about 200 miles from Saigon as the crow flies. At seventy-five knots and a guess at about forty-five minutes of flight time so far, that would put them about sixty miles north of Saigon.

Scott nudged Mai again and she finally began to stir, moaning softly.

"Mai," he whispered. "Mai, wake up." He knew Billy couldn't hear him over the whir of the engine and the blades. Without a headset, it was difficult to even hear someone yell. He also knew Billy couldn't see him unless he turned around. They were too far back toward the cargo area. Mai sat up slowly. Scott wanted to help her but could barely move strapped into the harness. He glanced back again at the M-16 and then back to Mai.

She opened her eyes slowly coming out of a fog, "Where are we? What's going on?" she mumbled, and then Scott saw her face. The entire left side was the color of an eggplant and her eye was swollen shut. She looked so vulnerable; his stomach churned inside at not being able to reach out and hold her.

Scott could feel the heat coming up from his gut and around his neck. Somehow, he would get his hands around that son-of-a-bitch.

He pushed himself as far over to her as his harness would allow.

"Mai, how do you feel?" Scott asked, his eyebrows furrowed in concern. She looked at him like a puppy dog that had just been kicked to the curb, her head rocking on her neck.

"I hurt everywhere. What happened? What's going on?" she asked again.

"I don't know. This is that same MP that insulted you when we went to see Hank. You can't see his face, but you might recognize his red hair. I have no idea what he's doing, where he's taking us, or why."

"Did you get the license of that truck?" she asked with the slightest turn at the corner of her mouth. He had to smile. That was the same thing he had said to her when he woke up in the hospital.

By her attitude, he could tell she'd be all right. Mai was tough, one of the things he admired and loved about her. She didn't take any crap from anyone, including him, but her face looked terrible and her eye was worse, and, of course, there was the baby, which Scott did not bring up.

"My God, Scott," she said, now seeing the gash on the right side of his face. "Oh, baby, what has he done to you? That cut is a quarter-inch deep." She slid over closer to him to look at the damage and jerked at her arms, realizing she was going nowhere.

Scott leaned closer and kissed her on the cheek. The left side of her mouth was swollen to the size of a walnut.

"Baby, don't worry. I'm going to get you out of this, no matter what. I will keep you safe."

Suddenly, the pilot took a hard right turn on a heading of 20 degrees, an eastern direction. There was still nothing outside he could identify but a thick jungle. Scott and Mai sat quietly as the Huey's blades chopped the air and the engine continued to buzz.

* * *

Two hours had elapsed. Scott and Mai remained alert but silent. As the chopper began to descend to 3,000 feet, Scott thought he recognized the terrain. It was similar to the area where he'd flown so many times with the 633rd.

If he was right, they were probably about 60 miles east of Pleiku, the ocean off to their right though too far to see, and the 17th parallel dead ahead several hundred miles.

Now the chopper was coming in lower to land somewhere. Though the area was dense with trees and foliage, there were plenty of clearings. The Americans had used them as Tac sights for staging their runs, either for wounded or to ferry troops in and out of battles.

Slowly, the Huey came down to 1,000 feet, 750, then 500, and then finally a bumpy landing. Engine shut off the massive blades slowed and drooped.

Scott and Mai sat, looking first at Billy and then outside. The area appeared to be a VC camp with several temporary huts and tents set up in a rough circle in a zone about fifty yards in circumference. As far as Scott could see, trees and bushes backed up the area with one narrow path leading in and out.

"I know this area," Mai said. "My father brought me up here when I was a young girl. This is the Central Highlands, Fulro tribal areas. They call them the Montagnards now and they definitely hate the North."

Scott shushed Mai as Billy came around to the open side of the cargo bay.

"All right you two, end of the line," he said, pulling on Scott's shirt.

"Hey freak, you don't have to pull me, I can walk," Scott said. "And if you undo these cuffs, I'll show you how my fists can dance," he added, his mouth crimped, his brows turned down like a pit bull about to enter the ring.

Scott jumped out and turned to watch Mai jump out behind him. She seemed to have her bearings but stumbled as Billy pushed both of them toward one of the huts.

It was as humid as Scott could remember, and the gnats and mosquitoes were as thick as blankets in the air. They swarmed into every open orifice—his nose, eyes, and ears—and he could do nothing to swat them. He felt like a sad horse in a stall with flies crawling over its eyelids, powerless to do more than blink.

In front of the hut, there were two large rocks and what looked like a leftover fire in a ring of smaller rocks. There was no other sign of life except the three of them as Billy shoved Scott down on the rock and Mai followed on her own.

"Okay, you two, just sit there and behave yourselves. We're going to wait a bit until I have to leave."

Scott took that to mean someone was going to take his place but whom: Americans, CIA, VC? He had no idea.

The two captives sat on a rock side by side, watched Billy pace, and glanced down a path leading out of the area.

"Can we have some water?" Scott asked. There was no answer. "Why are we here?" No, answer. Mai looked at Scott and shrugged. Scott had heard firsthand accounts from combat soldiers of the horrific treatment prisoners received at the hands of the VC from scalping, peeling the skin off their bones to setting them on fire. He was terrified of what they would do to Mai, but then he and Mai weren't combatants.

The sun was beginning to set. Mai's wrists were bleeding and she was sure they were fractured. They'd been sitting on the rock for hours without water, managing to create a simple code with facial expressions when Billy wasn't looking. One blink, yes; two, no; and a shrug of the shoulders meant, I'm okay. A nod of the head from Scott said don't worry. I'll get you out of this, which he used repeatedly.

Billy had retreated to the front of a tent. Sitting on a crude bench made from part of a tree trunk he chain-smoked as he silently pulled the .45 automatic out of its holster and played with it as if to remind his captives.

Suddenly, it dawned on Scott: Billy was still wearing his MP uniform! He'd be shot instantly if this were VC territory. Nothing added up. Were they in an American-controlled area?

"You two just sit tight. I'm going to take a piss. If you move, I'll shoot both of you."

For a few seconds, Billy disappeared into the bushes. Scott could hear him rustling in the branches and suspected he was relieving himself of more than urine, so he took the chance to whisper to Mai, "I think we must be in friendly territory. He's still wearing his uniform. If this were VC, he'd be shot. I don't get it."

Mai peeked over her shoulder to make sure Billy was still occupied and then whispered, "I think we are in the Highlands, probably near Kontum. Most of this area is where the Fulro tribes live. They're very sympathetic to Americans—don't like the North... or the South, for that matter."

She stopped abruptly; the crackle of twigs and underbrush alerted her that Billy was finished. He came out of the trees, zipping his pants and buckling his belt.

As he sat down and lit another cigarette, Scott thought about the M-16 in the chopper. It had a clip in it so he guessed it was loaded. Getting to it was another challenge, however. He figured that Billy had a boss, but he didn't know who that would be. Whoever it was, when he or they arrived, it would be next to impossible to escape. He had to think of something while Billy was the only obstacle.

"Can you put our cuffs in front?" he asked out loud. "I think our wrists are broken anyway," he continued. "Come on, man; you can't hate us that much—you're an American for Christ's sake."

Billy jumped up, stepped on his cigarette, and shouted, "Hey now, writer boy, don't be takin' the Lord's name in vain!"

Scott had to laugh. "Oh, I'm sorry," he said sarcastically, knowing it was better to have him engaged in conversation. "I didn't know you cared. If you care so much about Jesus, you'll undo these handcuffs or, at least, loosen them a little. It's something Jesus would do, I'm sure."

Scott wasn't religious, but he figured he would take a chance and see just how crazy this man was. He had taken him for an uneducated redneck racist so he couldn't put that together with his defense of Jesus, but then none of this made any sense.

He stared at Billy, waiting for a tell, any emotion. Billy fingered his automatic and stroked his chin—he was thinking, a good sign. Scott was thinking of the M-16 only a few yards away in the back of the chopper. He looked at Mai and blinked his eyes once. She took that to mean, yes, you are thinking the same thing I am.

"Well, alright. I guess I can cuff you in front. You go sit over there on that other rock while I change the gook's cuffs," he said, pointing in the opposite direction. "And don't try anything, not even a twitch," he said, patting the .45.

God, this guy is as stupid as I thought.

Billy turned Mai around by her shoulders, "Turn around real slow and get down on your knees."

Scott gave Mai a single blink.

Mai slowly lowered herself to her knees, her face more swollen than before. Her dry, cracked lips were trembling, but she did as he said. When she was on her knees, Billy turned around and made sure Scott was still sitting on the rock. He stepped closer until his legs were almost touching Mai's face then he unzipped his pants, fumbling with his genitals.

Mai's eyes grew as large as eggs. She was terrified and still helpless. Now Billy didn't have his hand on his gun. Scott jumped up and charged as fast and hard as he could; putting his shoulder down, he hit Billy with the full force of his 215 pounds. Billy went sprawling, kicking up dust as he slid three feet. Before he could stand up, Scott was standing over him, and before he could recover, Scott kicked him in the face so hard it splashed his nose open and tore apart his upper lip. Scott kicked again, then again, and then stomped on Billy's temple. He was out or dead, but Scott didn't care. He turned and went to Mai, who was shaking, tears streaming down her face.

"Oh, baby, are you okay?" he asked, kneeling with her.

"Yes, I'm okay. Just shaken."

"We don't have any time. The sun is going down and whoever is behind this is going to be here soon. This guy didn't bring any rations or water, so he wasn't planning on staying here long. I'll get his keys and undo your cuffs. Hang on."

Scott stood and went back over to Billy. He was still breathing, but his face was a mess. His body was crumpled in a fetal position so Scott sat down next to him, turned around, and felt in his pockets. The pain was white-hot, shooting up his entire arm as he contorted his hands to pull out the small key.

Holding it gingerly between his index finger and thumb, he got up and went over to Mai.

"Stand up and turn around."

He fumbled with the key, trying to look over his shoulder to find the right spot on the cuff. After several attempts, he managed to find the keyhole, jam the key in it, and turn. Just as her cuff snapped off, Mai instinctively held one wrist in her hand. Both wrists were bleeding and raw, nearly to the bone.

"Here, take the key," he said.

Mai held the small key in her hand and looked at Scott's cuff and then heard something in the distance. It startled her and she dropped the key.

"Hear that?" she asked.

"Yeah. It sounds like trucks. Hurry up; we've gotta get out of here."

As he spoke, Billy began to groan and his feet moved.

"Hurry, baby."

Mai was shaking so hard she could barely pick up the key as the sound of large transports rumbled closer. She could feel the ground start to shake as Billy slowly brought his hand to his face.

"Come on. Come on!"

"I am," she said as she finally got the key in the cuffs and one of the clamps sprung open. Scott turned, grabbed the key from her, turned it again, and the other side opened as he bolted to Billy, who was beginning to get to his knees. Scott reared back as if he was about to kick a field goal. His deck shoe caught Billy under the jaw, probably shattering his teeth.

As Billy fell to the dirt, Scott pulled the .45 out of his holster, pulling the slider back, forcing a round into the barrel, and then shot Billy point blank. His body jerked once then went limp, blood pouring out of his wound.

Duyen Nguyen

"Come on. Whoever they are, they'll be here in a minute. Grab his duffel bag. There might be some water in it. I'll get his rifle out of the Huey."

Scott gave a thought to taking the chopper. He'd flown enough so that he was pretty sure he could do it, but it was too late. He could see the trees rustling less than a few hundred yards away. It sounded like a convoy. The engine in the chopper was off; it would take too long to get airborne. His next thought was to hide somewhere nearby in the jungle and wait to see if they were Americans, but he didn't want to chance it.

He raced to the chopper, climbed in the bay door, grabbed the M-16, jumped out, grabbed Mai, and the two ran off into the trees. When they were far enough away, Scott climbed a tree and looked back. He could just barely make out the clearing as the four large army trucks lumbered into the encampment. They weren't American. They would find Billy immediately and keep coming.

As Scott scouted from the limb high above, Mai crouched to her knees to rest, her hand on the tree for support. She didn't want Scott to see her fatigue or the occasional dizziness so common with the first trimester of pregnancy.

* * *

The Central Highlands were once dominated by the Fulro. Early in the war, the Americans began to train them in unconventional warfare, hoping they would become allies who could slow Viet Cong activity in that area. Special Forces troops developed base camps in the Highlands and recruited 40,000 Montagnards, as they were also known, for fighting alongside them.

Scott was getting another history lesson from Mai as they climbed higher into the mountains and further away from their pursuers. There was a full moon, but the jungle was dark and fearsome with menacing sounds and movements. Mai thought of snakes and the large carnivores that stalked this area of the country.

Scott had seen that the moon was west of the sun before it set, so he kept bearing to the right, hoping to stay on track for a northerly direction.

"We'll stop and camp here," Scott finally said.

"Camp? We don't have anything to camp with."

"He had a canteen in there; maybe he had some blankets."

Mai began digging through the duffel bag, despite the pain it caused in her bruised and bloodied wrists. There was one can of rations but no sign of an opener. There were two shirts and a pair of jeans as well, so they decided to use those to cover the ground as they settled in thick foliage far off the trail.

Lying on the makeshift bedding and speaking in a whisper, Mai told Scott more about the Montagnards.

"My father spent a lot of time up here. He worked with the Special Forces teams with the Montagnards, translating and training. They're good people who have been converted to Christianity. A group of theirs was slaughtered up here just before you came to Vietnam. They love the Americans."

"That's good, could be a lot worse. We're lucky for now. How does your head feel?" Scott asked, stroking the other side of her face gently, wanting to make it all go away for her.

"It hurts," she paused, "a lot, but I'm more worried about your cut. This guy had nothing in his bag other than these clothes and a canteen, no first-aid stuff. That needs about fifteen stitches," she said, touching the edge of his forehead in the moonlight.

The two managed to sleep a couple of hours before the roar of a large cat woke them. It seemed far off, but Scott knew he had to stay alert. He settled back down when he then heard the rustling of the bushes not far away. He put his hand over Mai's mouth and whispered, "Shh. Something in the bushes. Stay very still."

The sun was just beginning to creep into the valley below and as Scott turned to the sound, he saw four men standing twenty feet away with rifles. Each had a blanket-like cloth over his shoulders and was wearing army fatigue pants.

Hopefully, they were Montagnards.

Mai sat up quickly. The four men were silent, staring at the two odd visitors sleeping on the ground. She stood up and said something to them, but it wasn't Vietnamese. One of the men jabbed his rifle at Scott and replied in the same language. Mai answered with what Scott thought was a comment about him.

"Người Mỹ?" he said in Vietnamese. "Is he American?"

Mai replied yes in Vietnamese and then asked the man if he spoke the language. He nodded his head that he did.

Scott stood up but did not attempt to reach for the M-16. He still had the .45 tucked into the back of his waistband. He glanced at the rifle at the same time the man did and then both their eyes met. The man turned his head and gave Scott an expression that said, Better to leave it where it is.

Scott nodded affirmatively.

The quick conversation continued between the two as Scott stepped closer to Mai but did not touch her. He assumed she was explaining their situation and asking for help.

After the two had talked for a minute, and the man had drawn a simple map in the dirt with a stick, she turned to Scott and said, "It's okay. Their village is nearby, perhaps only a mile. He will take us there and give us water and food. He says there is a Green Beret camp, maybe ten guys about four miles north of their camp. He can take us there later."

"Thank God. Maybe we'll get out of here in one piece."

"He wanted to know how we got here so I told him we were kidnaped. Didn't say it was an American. That would be too confusing. I said you were a journalist; that seemed to satisfy him. I also said my father was Lieutenant Colonel Trinh. He said he knew of him as a great legend, a good man. He also said there are many VCs in the area, mostly loose groups, so we have to be very careful.

"I think we'll be just fine for now. Follow them."

Chapter 30

The four Montagnards led the way up the steep slope. Each of the men with a machete, an M-16 slung over their shoulders and a handgun in their holsters. All provided by U.S. Special Forces. Mai and Scott were close behind, trying to keep their footing.

The sun was halfway up in the sky, but a thick mist still hung over the hills and the valley far below. As they reached a summit, the leader turned to Mai and said something in his native language. "We are near the village," Mai translated. "You will be safe here for the time being, but we must get you to the American camp tomorrow," she continued, adding her own addendum. "He wants to take us to a Green Beret camp tomorrow."

"Good idea," Scott agreed.

"He also said there is a large unit of U.S. Infantry about ten miles to the north, near Kontum. It's the 4th Division.

"Sounds like we're surrounded by friendlies. I told you I would take care of you."

267

Mai looked back over her shoulder, smiled, and patted Scott on the shoulder.

Coming upon the village was like walking onto a football field from the bleacher tunnel. Though they were in the mountains, the area suddenly opened up into a vast flat plain, perhaps half a mile in all directions backed up on all sides by even higher mountains. To Scott, it was like night and day. The foreboding dense jungle and forest abruptly gave way to an entire village of Montagnards, which Scott learned was pronounced "mountah-yards."

The two had spent the three hours climbing and talking about these people, where they came from, and why they weren't like any of the other Vietnamese.

Scott learned they were comprised of more than twenty different tribes, each with their own dialect. Montagnard was French for "Mountain people." They were the original settlers of this area now known as Vietnam long before the Chinese, most likely from Malaysia and Polynesia centuries ago.

"We must look strange to these people," Scott said to Mai. "Here I am in California deck shoes and Levi jeans and you are in a red satin dress, not exactly the kind of garb you would wear to harvest the crops."

He looked out across the field where women in cotton dresses or baggy black pants carried enormous baskets of firewood on their backs. Others were working in a nearby sugarcane field or a small rice paddy. As far as he could see, the village was self-sustaining, irrigated by rain and runoff from the mountains into this flat valley—ideal for these crops.

There were ten or twelve houses built up on stilts, which told Scott that the rain and overflow must get deep in the season. The sides of the houses and huts were made of laced bamboo or other tree branches.

As the group walked into an area next to the huts, he could see two men sitting on their legs, carving the meat off a leg Mai said was water buffalo. Underneath the houses, he could see chicken coops, stored firewood, and baskets of grain. These people seemed to be far better off than he'd imagined. It appeared as though they had everything they could ever need. No wonder they didn't like the Communists. Life had been ideal here. What they cultivated, they used and shared with each other.

The leader of the four men motioned for them to come to an area where there had been a recent fire in a ring of rocks outside one of the huts. Apparently, he was the leader of the entire village and this was his hut, the place where he delegated, a sort of public meeting place.

It seemed that everyone in the tribe had a specific task and was hard at it, not giving much attention to the newcomers, not even the blonde American. They almost seemed blasé about the visitors, trusting implicitly that the leader had everything under control.

Near the fire pit, several women sat together rinsing garments in a tub of water.

The sun was beginning to set as the leader brought Mai and Scott to a hut, which he indicated would be theirs for the night. Inside were two cots made of thick tree branches with mattresses made of fabric stuffed with the same straw they fed the water buffalo. Above each was draped a gauzy mosquito net, though Scott had seen no insects yet. There was a bowl on the floor and a straw mat that separated the two cots. On the floor next to the cots were two vessels filled with water. Stark but functional, Scott thought. He had expected to be sleeping on the ground again this evening.

The leader left and as Scott put the duffle bag and the M-16 against the wall, an elderly woman came in through the cloth-covered doorway.

"Hello, my name is Cam. I am here to clean your wounds," she said in halting English. Scott was surprised any of these people could speak English.

The elderly woman with thick dark, wrinkled skin sat down slowly, a pottery bowl in one hand and several towels in the other, along with a small wooden bowl filled with a brown paste. She then began to converse with Mai in her tribal language, telling her she had learned some English from the Green Berets over the last two years. Mai told Scott her name meant 'orange like the fruit.'

To Scott, the woman was gentle and serene, about seventy-five he guessed though she could've been even older given the hardiness of these people. Cam explained to Mai that it was a traditional herbal antibiotic, that it would help Scott's gash heal faster but not do much for Mai's face, which had to heal on its own. "The swelling will go down in a couple of days," she told her.

Cam then scooped a handful of the brown paste out of the bowl and put her hand on the back of Scott's neck to hold him as she smeared it over his wound and most of his forehead. It immediately began to sting, almost like hot coals, and Scott instinctively pulled back.

"Yoww!" he screamed. "What is that stuff?"

The woman spoke in her language. "Don't be a baby, big boy. It's only roots. It will heal your wound."

Mai laughed and patted Scott on the arm as if he were a child on his first visit to the doctor. After the woman was done, she sat on the cot and spoke with Mai, telling her about the men and some of the battles they had been in with the Special Forces.

"Since we are so close to the Ho Chi Minh trail, the VCs are always lurking. They've killed many of our people, not in our tribe but the others, for working with the Americans. Mostly, they leave us alone. The route is about seven miles to the north. Warrior was brave to bring you here.

"They've come to the village several times, but Warrior is an adept ambassador. He pretends we don't hate them. He keeps the weapons hidden in small graves we've dug and then covered, so they don't see the army rifles. He feeds them and then sends them on their way, but it's a precarious balance, very shaky. I know they would kill us all if they suspected."

"That is his name?" Mai asked.

"Yes, Warrior."

After Mai had translated, Scott began to be troubled. If the VC ever found them here, all of these gentle people would be killed. He'd heard about the atrocities almost too graphic to think about. He didn't say anything, but he knew they would have to leave in the morning and join the Green Berets at their base and then find their way back to Saigon. He handed the water vessel to Mai and she nearly emptied it before handing it back to Scott.

"We will get you more water. Drink all you need. We will also feed you tonight at the fire," Cam told them.

As the two women continued to talk, Scott walked out of the hut and down the steps. Looking down between the slats, he noticed a black dog, probably only a year or two old, curled up underneath the steps. The image took him back to California, so far away and yet, at this moment, as clear as if he were there. He had a black Lab he adored as a boy. The two were inseparable. He'd named him Chubasco after the Pacific storms for his high energy and he had died of old age the year before Scott shipped out for Vietnam. They'd had an incredible journey growing up together and Scott had been depressed for weeks after his death.

He stood staring at the dog, thinking: These people are so real, so far outside all the fighting, the death and destruction, and the complete unhappiness of this country. They have no want or need to hurt anyone. They're self-contained, a family and community-oriented tribe of people who have inhabited this area far longer than the Chinese, French, or anyone else. This is truly their land. Despite what is going on all around them, they are so peaceful.

As he stood gazing across the field, Mai and the old woman came out and said good-bye to each other. Scott had a large gauze bandage wrapped around his head, brown paste dripping over one eyebrow.

"You look like a sultan with that thing around your head." Mai used her index finger to wipe the paste and then licked it. "Hmm, not bad. Tastes like hot sauce."

Scott dipped a finger in and tasted. "Oh God, Mai, that stuff is awful." He grimaced and then looked down. The dog was still asleep. "Look, Mai, it's a puppy," Scott said, pointing between the slats.

"Aw, what a cutie," Mai said, scrambling down the steps as the dog came alive at the attention, springing up and leaping onto Mai's legs. Scott came down and put his outstretched hand in front of the dog that immediately began to lick his hand and arm, wagging his tail furiously.

"Looks like he eats well," Scott said. "He's healthy and happy. Ask them what his name is."

Mai tapped Warrior's arm and asked him the dog's name.

"His name is An," Mai translated to Scott. "In Vietnamese, it means 'peace'"

From that moment on, Peace, as Scott called him, did not leave his side. Scott even leaned over at one point when he was alone and asked the dog, "Is Chubasco in there?"

That night, Mai and Scott joined most of the people from the village around the large fire for a traditional evening meal of buffalo meat, rice, and vegetables. Scott did not know what the vegetables were, some sort of roots, but the buffalo meat was good, not unlike venison, only fattier. He noticed the village children at another fire ring about twenty feet away. Each of them in a traditional outfit of baggy black pants and white sleeveless cotton tops that looked like potato sacks with holes for the head, neck, and arms.

As the night progressed and the fire grew smaller, one of the Montagnards tossed on more firewood. Under each house was a space almost five feet high and there seemed to be enough firewood crammed under each one to last several years.

Scott noticed that the women were as engaged in the conversations as the men. These people seemed to be on an equal footing, each villager doing his or her own work all day and then joining in the evening for conversation around the fire.

Scott followed the expressions of all of them as Mai talked as easily as she did with him. Her father had taught her about these people that he loved and she'd picked up their language on their visits together when she was young. He could observe firsthand what she was telling him about their culture. They hated the Communists. They tolerated and, in some instances, liked the South. And they loved the Americans, probably because of their involvement with all the Special Forces training they'd received.

Scott noticed their skin was much darker than most Vietnamese and they did not have the folds around their eyes. Mai talked with the leader for a long time, who seemed to want Scott to understand more about them. When he was done, Mai turned to him and said, "His name translates to 'Warrior' in English. He is the de facto leader of his tribe and is considered a leader as well in the surrounding areas.

"He said his people, more than forty thousand strong, have been fighting alongside the Americans and are considered an important part of the Special Forces' efforts in the Central Highlands. He seems to be very proud of this, as he should be."

Using Mai, Scott asked Warrior, "How long have you and your people lived in this village?"

"From the beginning of time. Our ancestors came from Malaysia and nearby islands," he answered, smiling.

Mai added, "He likes that you are interested in them."

"How many villagers are here?" Scott asked.

"Thirty-eight now. We had been more than fifty before the war began."

"I'm sorry for your loss," Scott replied, guessing those people might have been casualties. "Have you had many encounters with the VC?"

"Yes. Before the war, we were a quiet village. We have everything here we need. There is no reason to go out into the world of the Communists of the North. We have fresh water, healthy soil, temperate weather, and all the food and firewood we need, but now, we must fight."

Mai interjected again, "They love my father because they make a distinction between the North and the South. They see the South as benign at best, to be tolerated. They feel these mountains are their home, their property, and the VC are trying to take it from them.

"Scott, you could liken these people to your Native Americans. They don't have a common language with us; they share no traditions with perhaps only the exception of one."

"What's that?"

"Courage. That's why they were so close to my father. He fought the French and now the Communists, and he was very brave. Warrior says he knows him well. They're both very courageous and would fight to the death without retreat. That is why they are so fond of the Green Berets and, by extension, all Americans. They see you all as brave warriors."

Warrior interrupted as the children finished their meals and began dancing and chanting around another fire.

"One of the reasons the VC hate us is that many of us are Christians; others are Catholics. We had posed a threat before you Americans came, but now we disrupt their supply lines. They don't know it's us, but they suspect. As long as we feed them and appear stupid, they leave us alone."

"The VC massacred two hundred and fifty of his people in a village about fifteen miles north of here called Dak Son," Mai added.

"No more! No, more!" Warrior yelled when he heard the words Dak Son. "Someday we will have our own independence. Now, we help the Americans and perhaps they will help us. There are many Green Beret bases nearby and when you are ready, we will take you to them."

"Thank you, Warrior," Scott said, a little sad that these people weren't integrated with the South Vietnamese, who was just as courageous as they were. He wished he could express that, but there wasn't time for political discussions.

Scott was becoming more and more enamored of Mai. His affection and love already ran deep, but each day that he watched her, he was filled with more admiration. She wasn't only the mother of his unborn child, she was courageous, unyielding in the face of adversity, adept at so much, even as an ambassador here tonight. He was beginning to see how life would be impossible without her, not just here, but in the States.

He put his arm around her and not knowing if it was correct under the circumstances, but also not caring, he leaned over and kissed her on her good cheek. Suddenly, all the villagers jumped up and began dancing in circles around the fire, chanting and laughing.

Mai looked at Scott, kissed him gently, and said, "They approve. They cherish love. Warrior says it's what makes their world, so they celebrate."

Peace was curled up beside Scott, his long nose and ears resting on Scott's thigh. It was a surreal moment. It was as if he was with family and the whole world was in harmony. The puppy almost made him forget where he was.

After a while, the fire was extinguished and Scott and Mai returned to their hut. The night was still lit by a quarter moon; the only sounds coming from the tree frogs. Peace jumped up on Scott's cot and curled at his feet. The three were asleep in minutes.

With the sun barely creeping up the mountain, the fog outside was dense, hanging over the rice paddies just inches from the shoots and casting a white blanket of humidity over the valley. The women were just beginning to stir, set up fires, and already starting to work at their chores.

Peace yawned at the foot of Scott's bed, barked once, jumped down, and ran outside at the smell of food. The two lovers woke in separate cots—too narrow for two—got up, and embraced.

Suddenly, the quiet country ambiance was shattered by the sounds of shouts and gunfire. Scott instinctively grabbed the .45 and told Mai to stay in the hut as he ran through the doorway, taking the five steps in one leap.

In the distance, emerging from the fence line and the trees were, at least, fifty VCs, firing automatic weapons, shouting, and running toward the village.

Scott knew they had no time; they had to run, to get back into the jungle. If the VCs found them here, all the villagers would be killed. The village men raced out of the houses and huts with their rifles and machetes. It was going to be ugly and bloody.

Scott left the duffel bag, grabbed Mai by the sleeve and began to run, but then thought better of it. The VCs were too close; he and Mai would never make it to the tree line. He pulled her under the house, dragged her back further and then they crawled toward the back of the house behind a large pile of firewood and bags of rice. It was dark and wet. Scott held the .45 at the ready, holding Mai down, her face almost in the dirt.

As he put his finger to his lips to quiet Mai, he peered out under the steps. The village men were charging into the field, screaming some kind of war cry to match the VCs' screams. Some of the women had rifles, others scattered to run into the forest.

As a full battle ensued, it was chaos: some of the village men in hand-to-hand combat with the VCs, others swinging machetes, automatic fire going off from both sides. He could see Warrior shooting from behind a tree, taking out four VCs singlehandedly, but there were too many of them. He could even see the expressions of hate on their faces as they bayonetted several of the villagers. When the men fell, the VCs would slice their throats open so deep they almost beheaded them.

One VC grabbed a village woman and tore off her dress. She broke loose and began to run but the VC shot her in the back, and then unzipped his pants right in the heat of battle, rolled her over, and jumped on her.

The massacre didn't last long and it was all Scott could do to remain silent. With every fiber in his body, he wanted to crawl out and take them all on but Mai felt his anger and held onto him tightly.

It was excruciating to watch and be so helpless. Women and children screaming awful sounds Scott had never heard, a primal sound like feral dogs dying in agony. The VCs killed every one of them: men, women, and children. When the village became quiet, the VCs walked around and took all the rifles, knives, machetes, and ammunition from all the villagers; some they shot again in the head.

Scott wanted to vomit in the dirt. He held his hands over his mouth as Mai clutched him. She didn't even want to breathe. The two waited for what seemed like hours before coming out. When they did, the village was decimated, so many dead. The children with their throats slashed, one man with a knife in his eye were more than Mai could bear. She ran behind a nearby hut and threw up.

Scott stood stunned, beyond comprehension, as if his mind had been run over by a train. He was in another world. The sadness couldn't be understood. None of it was human. These were beasts born on another planet, he thought.

He put his hand against a tree and vomited into the dirt three times as he cried. Wiping his tears, he walked toward the hut where Mai had run. There, by the front of the hut where they'd slept, was Peace. He was lying next to the steps, his eyes still open, his tongue hanging out, and four bullet holes in his heart.

Scott knelt down and picked the dog up, taking him inside and placing him gently on the cot, then sat next to him and cried until he had no more tears.

Mai stood over the two, weeping with her hand on Scott's shoulder. The village smelled like gunpowder; outside the doorway, the bodies of the Montagnard painted the ground with blood. Thirty-eight people had been slaughtered. The only remaining living thing was a hen and her chicks huddled under the steps. It was as if Mai was having an out-of-body experience, standing at the gates of Hell and peering in at insanity.

It was time to leave, Mai told Scott, tugging on his sleeve. "There will be others coming," she said.

They walked down the steps to several bodies. He grabbed an M-16, two clips, and another .45 automatic pistol, which he shoved into his waistband. Mai picked up two M-16 clips as well.

"Here, let's go this way. I know this area a little. We should go northeast. We have to reach the ocean. It's the only way. Otherwise, we'll be captured or die in the jungle without a guide," Mai said, taking charge.

They began to run, leaving the duffel bag behind. They carried two canteens of water, ammunition, one machete, and no food.

The late morning sun was heating up the jungle canopy, creating a dense mugginess. High in the trees above, monkeys chattered at their passing and it seemed the bush came alive with animal communication warnings of their presence. With the sun directly overhead, it is hard to determine their location, but Mai felt sure they were better staying off any worn paths that might indicate VC traffic. They had no idea which direction the murderers had taken, and it didn't really matter. They just needed to keep moving.

Scott led the way, slashing at the hanging limbs and dense undergrowth. The trek was going to be slow. He estimated from his time in Pleiku they were about seventy-five miles or more from Quy Nhon where a South Vietnamese battalion had taken back the beach area city from the VC after Tet. From there, they could get help to go to Cam Ranh Bay down the coast and then hop an army transport to Saigon.

"Watch out!" Scott yelled back to Mai. "Snakepit up ahead," he added, turning to hold her hand and guide her around a nondescript area on the trail.

"What's the matter?" Mai asked, not hearing what he'd said.

Scott pointed back, "That spot covered with branches and leaves is a VC snake pit. They dig a hole about six feet deep and then put sharpened bamboo sticks tipped with poison in them facing up. If you fall in...well let's just say, it's not the way you want to die."

They had only made it a few uneventful miles by the time the sun was beginning to set. Scott thought they should find shelter for the night when suddenly a squad of VC was upon them, coming up the slope to the right of the path. They'd been as silent as a whisper. There were five of them, stabbing at the air in front of the couple, shouting orders.

"Get down," Mai said. "They want us on our knees."

* * *

It was pitch black out when Scott woke up. His head was pounding as he reached up and felt the sticky wetness of blood once again on his forehead. This time, the wound was on the left. He didn't know how deep or how bad. As he tried to focus and get his bearings, he began to recall kneeling on the trail with Mai, five VCs standing around them, poking their bayonets at him and laughing. That was it. Judging from the coagulation of blood on his head and neck, he guessed he'd been out for at least an hour.

His hands and feet were tied in front of him with rope. He was sitting in the dirt in a hut. The only light was coming from a small campfire that he could see through the blanket covering the doorway, along with the sounds of men talking.

Shaking his head, he realized Mai was gone, or maybe they had put her in a different hut. Frantic, he inched himself closer to the opening on his fists and knees. There was no sign of her. Since he spoke very little Vietnamese, he knew if they hadn't taken her to this camp, the chances of finding her were practically impossible. Had she been killed? Thoughts of the VC torturing her made him so angry, he began to pull furiously at his ropes, tearing the flesh from his wrists, but he knew he had to calm down. He would be no good if he lost control.

He sat back, trying to sort out his options: find out if Mai was in the camp, escape or be killed. If he had to make it out alone, how would he ever find her? Dejected, he sat up against the bamboo and took a deep breath, waiting to see what these men would do.

Glancing down at his chest, his press pass was still hanging around his neck. There wasn't much chance, but his credentials as a journalist just might keep him and Mai alive.

He guessed he'd been sitting for about two hours and he'd been given no water. The VCs were still jabbering to each, drowning out the natural sounds of the jungle. There were no tree frogs, no monkeys screeching. The men outside seemed as if they were involved in a heated political argument. Perhaps they were debating what to do with him. As he sat dejected, his head on his knees, a large angry man opened the cloth covering the doorway. In one hand, he had a water canteen and in the other a heavy handgun. He said something in Vietnamese and by his expression, Scott thought he was going to offer him some water.

The man came closer, holding out the canteen with the cap unscrewed. Scott hadn't had any water since they had escaped the village. As the man offered the flask to Scott's mouth, he suddenly pulled it back and took a full swing, crashing the gun butt on Scott's open head wound. Everything started spinning as the man began to laugh uproariously. It was the last sound Scott heard as he slumped over on his side into the dirt.

* * *

The sun crawled over the rocks and ruts and then through the slats in his cage; sunrise and it was already blistering. Scott woke up to the heat and chatter of his captors. His head was pounding as if someone was inside with a sledgehammer trying to break out. The blood that covered his shirt was now dry and crusty.

He tried to swallow but could feel the skin peeling off his lips. He traced his tongue over them only to cause himself more pain. It had been at least two days since he'd been given any water or food, but that was the least of his problems. The ropes were gone and in their place were the solid bamboo slats of a cage no more than five feet square; not big enough to stand in. He was barefoot; his deck shoes, ring, press pass, and chain were gone as he felt to make sure he still had two arms and legs.

Sitting up, he grabbed the three-inch-thick bamboo bars that were laced together with rope and twine. There were no joints, no hinges. Not far away, six VCs stood talking, pointing and laughing at him as they puffed on their cigarettes. He felt like a monkey in a test lab. His entire body ached as it had never ached before, not knowing that when he was unconscious, the men took delight in beating him with a thick rope and bamboo poles.

He looked at his surroundings. Based on the terrain, he felt he was probably still in the Highlands. His captors had pitched a rudimentary camp, the only clearing in the thick jungle and forest. It is hard to tell how high the elevation or where the sun was.

These men were real guerillas. They carried little in the way of supplies, used a single tent to cover the meager things they did carry and appeared to sleep on bedrolls on the ground. Their baggy clothes were filthy; probably outfits they'd worn for weeks.

Scott tried to pick out some of their words. He recognized "transport," "prison," "pig," and journalist." The rest was gibberish to him. Trying to listen intently, he was startled from behind when one of the men rapped his knuckles with a short pole. He snatched his hands back and instinctively rolled up as tight as he could, bringing his knees to his chest with his arms. Then, another man thrust first one pole then a second through the cage past Scott's ears and out the other side; a way for them to carry him somewhere. Two large VCs, the tallest and heaviest Vietnamese he'd ever seen, picked up the poles and walked about one hundred feet to a waiting flatbed truck. They slid his cage on it and then pulled up the tailgate.

One of the men tapped the fender loudly and the truck's exhaust belched out a cloud of black smoke as it rumbled down the dirt road into the forest.

Chapter 31

Midnight had passed. She was finally home after the nightmare and the subsequent wandering in the jungle for days before the Green Beret unit found her and flew her back to Saigon. Her head was still bandaged from the fall down the glassy slope as Scott was taken away. Thank God that patrol found her. She knows she would be dead if they hadn't. At first, they had to be on high alert because she could've been VC, but once she mentioned her father and the Warrior, it was as if she'd used a magic code. They took her back to the base and then on to Tan Son Nhut and the army hospital.

Mai wouldn't allow herself to think of Scott as being dead, nor would she allow her mind to wander and visualize what may have happened to him. Her father's Buddhist wisdom came back to her. In grief, the untrained mind wants to torture itself, to paint pictures, vivid images.

I won't allow it, she thought, but, of course, having the probing, inquisitive, and creative mind she did, the pictures came. So, to banish them, she got tipsy. She did not want the images to keep her awake all night. The only thing keeping her sane was the hope that Scott was alive and the safety of her unborn child. Traditionally, her mother would be tending to her. Medical care was still archaic in Saigon, limited mostly to those few who could use the army hospital or a visit to the local naturopath, some of which were still not much more than shamans who prescribed herbs, special oils, and little else beyond aspirin. Despite all of it, the baby was okay.

Mai couldn't sleep, not even with drinking the last of her father's Bordeaux. The night was calm and cold. She thought of something else her father had told her when her mother was killed: "Replace the bad pictures with good ones. Remember your favorite time and replay that tape every time an evil thought enters."

She sat on the back door steps and rifled through her memories. The best picture appeared without hesitation. She was sitting with her mother at the piano. She must have been five or so. Her mother had taken her right hand and index finger and used them to poke out the first six notes of a Mozart melody. She would never forget the attention and warmth she felt, nor the tune. Her mother was smiling, patient, adoring. Her father sat in this den, smoking his pipe and reading. It was ideal, a memory snatched from the past, a vivid and good picture... but it didn't last long. She wasn't as adept as her father.

Walking inside, she scoured the cupboards for another bottle of wine. There was none. She would have to go it aloneShe longed for stability; for the way things were when they were good. When they were good, everyone was alive and well, all in one place at the same time. A party with Scott, her mother and father—all of them existing on the same plane at the same time. But she knew the scene would not play out; this is the way it would always be—disrupted. Whoever promised it would be otherwise? We are fooled into thinking that the dominant themes of life are dependable, consistent, good, and safe when, in fact, those moments—whether measured in hours or months—are the fleeting ones, like trying to catch a beautiful fragrance in a bottle. Life is nothing but a battle, she thought, a constant one-step forward, two steps back ordeal. We all long for a consistency that doesn't exist.

She turned on the eight-track stereo and slipped Nina Simone back in. The gravelly, yet, sexy voice filled the room, but now the sexiness gave way to darkness; notes that were passionate were now somber and foreboding. She left the tape going anyway; it suited her mood.

Plodding into her father's office in her slippers, she took a deep breath through her nose and smelled not only his pipe but Scott's cigars. His journal laid on the desk, an open invitation from the Devil—read me, it beckoned, be close to Scott; don't be afraid, I will comfort you.

She knew better. Sitting down in the deep-worn, leather chair, she reached over and picked up her father's favorite pipe; drawing it up to her nose, she inhaled the sweet odor of maple and rum and her father. Next to the pipe was the engraved walnut box where he kept his tobacco. She opened it. The fragrance filled the room; it hadn't been opened in perhaps a year, and the smells were intoxicating as she stretched out with her feet on the ottoman, trying to recreate those "good" pictures.

She patted her stomach lightly, knowing in her heart that her baby, just under a month old, was okay. For the tiniest moment, her mind wasn't in turmoil and the soft jazzy sounds softened the pain.

* * *

Where she'd left the drape open, the sun broke through the window and streaked across her face. It startled her and as she got up to close off the day, it took her a moment to remember where she was.

The first order of business was to form a plan.

Having fought a long battle with herself the night before, she was now ready to move on to do something important. There would be no impotence, no bad pictures, no sitting around feeling sorry for herself. She was on a mission. Somehow, she would find the right people, the right direction, and she would figure out a way to free Scott.

Glancing over into the den near her father's desk, she saw the green backpack Scott had brought home. It gave her an idea.

Chapter 32

Bao sat alone in the back of the club in the same booth that he and Scott had shared months ago. It was early and the bar was dark, smelling of the same sour beer and stubbed-out cigarettes. The same bartender performed the same perfunctory labors at the bar he always did at 9:00 a.m. The only thing different was the person Bao was going to meet.

He sat quietly with a glass of soda in front of him, not knowing what to think. His friend, Phong, who owned the Tu Luc Bookstore, had handed him a cryptic note two days before. He'd unfolded the small piece of paper and read, "Meet me at the Siren Nightclub on Nguyen Van Thoai Street, Saturday morning at 9:00 a.m. I have something important to you."

The note wasn't signed. He was leery. Was it a trick? What could anyone have that would be important to him? He took another sip of his soda.

He began to tap his fingers on the table as his old acquaintance, the bartender, smiled at him while mopping the floor around the booth. The only light in the large room came from the open back door and the two overhead lamps. The bar didn't open until noon, but most of the action came later at night when the drinkers and dancers liked it dark.

As he sat, he heard the front door open and saw a stream of light sweep across the dance floor. He looked up immediately to see a beautiful young Vietnamese woman with dark, troubled eyes. Looking left and right, she was adjusting to the light. He suddenly felt as if he knew her though he couldn't remember from where or when. Bao remained silent, watching to see what she would do. In her left hand, she carried a black leather purse. In her right, a dark canvas bag.

He could tell when she saw clearly as she zeroed in on him. As she approached, he realized the bag she was carrying was his backpack. In a split-second, as his thoughts darted around, he realized he'd almost given up on finding it. It had been over a month. There was nothing of value to anyone else. The thing that had worried him was his American passport tucked in the hidden zippered pocket which showed he is a U.S. citizen. Now, it was coming to him. He must've left it here in this booth the last time he'd talked with Scott.

This woman must be the girl Scott had fallen for, the one he'd escaped with that night at *The Queen Bee*. Though he'd never seen her, he knew she was attractive and a student at the School of Literature.

When she was about ten feet from the booth, Mai whispered, "Bao?"

Glancing around the room with his typical caution, he did not answer. He gestured with his index finger to his lips and then waved her over.

Mai sat down and placed the bag between them on the seat.
Without introducing herself, she said, "I think I have something of yours."

Bao looked at the bag and then unzipped the top, seeing his papers, a ball cap, and various other things pretty much as he remembered them.

Mai watched him without saying anything, waiting. When it seemed he was satisfied that she hadn't ransacked his stuff, she said, "I'm Mai. Do you recognize my name?"

"Yes. Now I do. And I know you from somewhere—somewhere before Scott."

Bao realized Scott had taken the bag home that morning of their meeting and he began to piece everything together, everything except where he knew her from.

"Where is Scott? I haven't spoken to him in months," he asked. "I'm assuming he brought this home with him. Did you open it?"

"Yes, but not at first. I wanted to look inside, but Scott wouldn't let me. He's told me all about you, but he always just referred to you as 'the stranger.' Then, when he brought this home, I couldn't stand it though I didn't pry...until we were kidnaped, at least."

"What? By whom? When?" he stammered, genuinely surprised.

"I only know who. It was an American MP named Billy. We don't know why he did it other than maybe Scott's stories were beginning to rub too many people the wrong way."

"What happened?" he asked, moving a little closer to Mai, his interest in who this woman might be to him temporarily shuffled to the back of his mind.

Mai looked around, now with the same sense of secrecy. "We were having dinner one night. We'd ridden into the city on a moped that Scott had been using. When we were finished, we returned to the bike to go home and that was the last thing either of us remembered until we woke up in a helicopter with that MP flying it. Both of us were handcuffed, Scott had a terrible gash on his head..." Her voice trailed off; then she recovered and finished her story.

Bao was sitting on the edge of his seat, trying to make sense of what she was saying, trying to guess why the MP had kidnaped them. None of it was connecting.

"Oh my God. I hope he wasn't picked up by the VC." Bao said as he watched Mai bow her head, apparently not wanting to discuss that possibility.

He sat, waiting for her to respond and when she lifted her head, tears were running down her cheeks. He handed her a cocktail napkin and she wiped her face without any other animation. Except for the trails of tears running down her face, she made no sounds, no movements. As she sat up, straight and stoic, taking a deep breath, Bao suddenly realized who she was. He recognized the expression of a young girl he met at Khai Tri Bookstore when he was only fifteen.

President Diem had just been overthrown in a coup. Looking at her face and eyes, he was transported back to that day when he first spoke to her. She was about his age. It was on his birthday, November 1, 1963. They were in the bookstore on Le Loi Street. He'd just heard the gunfights, the news of the coup on the radio, and the voice of the General telling the people of Saigon that Diem was out and the military was in control. He remembered days before the tension that had filled the air and permeated the streets of the city. He would never forget the scene when the Buddhist monk sat calm and quiet, cross-legged in the street, pouring a can of gasoline over himself and his bright orange robes, and then set himself on fire in protest.

He thought he'd pressed all of those things into his never-to-be-opened-again vault of memories. Seeing Mai was bringing it all back. Suddenly, their meeting took on a whole new meaning. There was so much he wanted to ask her, not only about her and Scott but about the time that had passed since he'd last seen her.

"I need your help," she said, breaking his trance, waiting for a reply.

"Certainly. God, where do we begin?"

"With your backpack, I suppose."

Bao was going to respond but decided to let Mai reveal what, if anything, she'd been able to put together from the files he'd left in the bag.

"I need to find Scott. I need to talk with some of your people," she said, emphasizing the word, your. "I need to get Scott out of wherever he is, which is probably a VC prison camp."

Still playing it safe, Bao said, "Uh, like who? What people?"

"Like this Jacobs guy at the embassy. Like your cousin..."

Bao's heart sank; his breathing became a little labored. He'd hoped he hadn't left any trail of his cousin. The only other person who knew the identity of his source until this minute had been his father.

"Well...," Bao started to say something slowly but Mai cut him off.

"Look, Bao. There's no sense in pretending. I know you've been working with Scott, that you were feeding him a lot of those stories—you and his friend Hank, and Jacobs. I'm not stupid. I read everything in your files. It all fits together."

"The only thing that didn't make any sense was where you were getting the information. Then, when I got here and saw you, I immediately remembered you, though it took me a moment. When I saw your cousin's name and your meeting dates with Scott, I realized that was where you were getting your information. I recognized your cousin from the newspaper—he's President Thieu's interpreter. He's in every meeting. It's perfect."

Bao shifted nervously in his seat. What would he say? Would she threaten him? Under no circumstances could his cousin be revealed. He tried to think. He felt like he could trust her. She was obviously distraught and he wanted to help but without exposing himself, his father, or his cousin. For the moment, he wanted to get a better sense of her and as he rifled through his instincts, it all started coming back to him, the days when he'd first met her.

Mai sat quietly, seeing that Bao was lost in his memories. There was no rush. She needed to convince him to be part of her team; if that meant living in the past for a while, then so be it.

"Do you remember when we met?" Mai asked.

Bao thought for a moment, looking at the ceiling.

He did a quick rundown in his mind: Mai needed help to find Scott. She now knew who his source was. He still didn't know what else he'd left in his bag that she now knew, but it seemed a moot point. It was time to switch gears. It was time to find Scott—not that he wasn't sympathetic, but Bao still had the same motivation for feeding Scott the stories. President Thieu had never trusted Nixon and Kissinger and, as it was turning out, rightly so. Scott was the only way the Americans and the people in Saigon who read the papers and listened to the news could have any semblance of truth.

Scott was the one who unknowingly was keeping the playing field even. None of the other journalists had his temperament or his talent, and the cycle had already been cemented, a very symbiotic relationship all the way around.

With his backpack in hand and their conversation concluded for the time being, the two left the bar, going in different directions. Bao decided not to discuss the meeting or his cousin. His father, Professor Phan, always became irrational when Bao brought up his mother and her side of the family. For now, it was best to be silent and immediately talk to his cousin about Scott.

Another meeting was set at Mai's house. The wheels would start turning soon... very soon.

* * *

Bao went back to his Saigon apartment that night, the tiny two rooms that he shared with a University student on Cong Ly Street. He began to make a list of contacts, including Jacobs, his cousin, Hank and Phong, who owned the Tu Luc Bookstore. And finally, his friend Tai, the driver who was so adept at listening to his passengers, while all the time pretending to be intent on keeping his eyes on the road.

Sitting near the window, Bao sharpened his pencil and gazed down the street toward the area of town in which he'd grown up. After he had gone to the University, he'd almost had a guilty feeling. He'd done everything right to stay out of the fight. Young Vietnamese men, eighteen and older, were conscripted into the army if they didn't pass "Tu Tai", the high school diploma exam. For his age, he'd always been sharp and more intuitive than most. He managed to finish high school in 1966 at the age of seventeen. Many of his high school buddies were sent off to the battles. When they did manage to return on leave, he would always treat them to drinks and food, trying to "pay back" for the privilege he was conferred upon.

At first, they regaled him with their awful stories of the fighting, the inhumanity, and their relationships with the American GIs. Though most of them fought in their own separate units, the ones who did fight alongside the Marines and army soldiers were impressed with their courage and often asked them about their feelings toward Vietnam and the war. Most of the GIs felt it was their duty to America, not necessarily Vietnam, but they thought they understood the reasoning and managed not to complain about fighting someone else's war. Of course, there were also plenty who believed the whole affair was pure insanity, didn't want to be there, thought it was an unjustified cost of American lives, and could only pray for the day they went home and were done with it.

Bao often thought about those guys. Regardless of their politics, he respected and praised them. A lot of them had enlisted and understood what they were in for, believing in Vietnam's right to democracy.

Bao's closest encounter with the fighting only came as a result of his Boy Scout troop. He was a scout master the year he entered the University. When the 1968 Tet Offensive was over, his troop had helped care for the wounded. He remembered the carnage and ugliness he hoped he'd never, ever see again. One incident in particular stuck with him. As he and two of his fellow Scouts were carrying a litter with a wounded MP out of a burned-out building, he looked over at a smoldering Jeep that was parked nearby. Inside at the wheel, there was a body that was burned almost beyond human recognition. The Jeep was nothing more than a steel frame with a black human skeleton sitting in it, his bony fingers still melted to the steering wheel.

It was time to do more than feed stories to Scott and to being a Boy Scout. Bao was going to combine forces with this very strong-willed woman, and they were going to find Scott.

Chapter 33

I'm writing letters that will never be mailed.

That's because I have no paper, pen, or pencil; the words are all saved in my mind. I'm a writer, so this is one of the ways I keep my sanity. They can imprison my body, but they can't board up my brain.

I sit here staring at the bamboo bars, smelling the fouled dirt I've felt every day now under my feet for who knows how long. Keeping the boogeyman at bay by writing inside my head.

Mai, if you can hear my spirit, I miss you terribly. I love you more than life. I'm in agony not knowing if you're okay. If our child is okay. That's the real torture. Did you make it out? Did you find the Green Berets? I wish more than anything, if nothing else, to know. And to somehow have you know that I'm alive and okay.

If I could write a real letter, I wouldn't tell Mai, or anyone for that matter, what is happening here to me, to the others. There are maybe six of us. I'm not

305

sure because we are only allowed a few minutes a day together, and aren't authorized to speak because the reprisals are horrific. Most are GIs, probably army, maybe a Marine, and one Air Force pilot. They seem brave or at least very stoic. I don't feel so brave, but I try.

The cruelty has become just another way to spend part of the day. My mind has become so numb to it; my body barely feels it. It's like some kind of out-of-body experience. It wasn't that way, of course, in the beginning. At first, I didn't think I would survive. They asked me questions about the secrets I knew as a journalist and, of course, I had none. All of mine had been published. So they tied my wrists together behind me, laced another rope through that binding, and threw it over a tree limb. They made the others watch as they hoisted me. First with a series of jerks so painful I passed out. Then they perfected their method by starting slowly and ending with a vicious yank. As the slack is taken out and the rope becomes taut, at first, my wrists ache, then my elbows and, finally, as my feet leave the ground, my shoulders feel like they're being ripped out of their sockets until they are at a 45-degree angle to my body. They can't go any further without snapping off. The two men pulling me up know that, so they stop when I'm suspended about four feet off the ground. It is like pulling the leg away from the carcass of a fried chicken, complete with the tendons, veins, and meat.

There are other unsavory and inhuman things they do to us. I think it's just for their amusement. They pretend to want my so-called secrets, but I believe they know I know nothing about the military.

In my 6 x 6 x 6 box I think over and over again about the day I went to the LA Times and begged them to hire me as a stringer. I had the fire and energy to convince them to take me on. Enough of that and a knack for research and tracking down my own stories got me a paid position with them. I wanted to catch the liars and the cheats—not that I was a choirboy—because I loathed those who stole authority. Vietnam seemed an example of that written on a global scale. I never gave a thought to the risks. I just didn't think it all out. Arriving at Tan Son Nhut wasn't bad. But it didn't take long to turn my rides with the 633rd into seeing a small piece of what war really was. With rounds whizzing by my face as I leaned out of the Huey to help throw the propaganda leaflets, or when I pitched in to help a medic lift a stretcher with yet another young American boy near death, lying there without his legs, blood everywhere...everywhere. What happened at the University that night of the concert, during Tet in Saigon and escaping with Mai. Or being captured and being here. That's what I didn't plan for, didn't see. I now know what war can do.

They're coming. Time to hide my mind from them.

Mai, I miss you with every fiber of my being.

* * *

U.S. Embassy, Saigon

Mai had continued her fight to gain Scott's freedom, alternating her investigations between Bao, Hank, and Jacobs. She knew nothing yet about one key player, the one who would tie all her loose ends together. As she sat in the embassy lobby, waiting yet again for Jacobs, she asked the receptionist to turn up the volume on the television. There was an NBC broadcast live from Hanoi. She walked closer to see the telecast. The commentator speaking off camera tried to sound editorial, dispassionate. But in reality, this was live and anything but objective. All the cameras were trained on the street.

The air-raid siren was so loud, it seemed to push the air away, bullying through the Hanoi sky and reaching everyone who wasn't deaf. The government had warned all civilians with nonessential posts to leave the city. Hanoi had placed sirens around the city to warn of the B-52 raids, which were frequent and devastating. To be sure, the north was far from passive, firing surface-to-air missiles by the hundreds almost nightly. Between the blaring siren's scream, emergency warnings were barked out with details. "Enemy aircraft now approaching southeast Hanoi," and then a verbal countdown followed… "100 km… 80 km… 50 km. Everyone evacuate to the closest bomb shelters. Antiaircraft forces, be ready for action," and so on into the night. They called it the rain of death as swarms of B-52s blanketed the skies and unleashed a Hell on earth. The bombs were massive, weighing 500 pounds each; the sheer magnitude to an observer stupid enough to watch was surreal. I can only describe it as gray raindrops under a blanket of bombers, nothing more than specks growing larger and larger as they raced to their targets, interspersed with red tracer trails from the antiaircraft missiles zigzagging upwards at more than 700 miles an hour. Hanoi called it, the Dien Bien Phu of the Sky, and the fierce and deadly nature of the battle made it rightly comparable. B-52s not accompanied by fighter planes exploded into flames and break into thousands of pieces, plummeting to the ground with regularity, but the damage on the ground was devastating—factories, munitions storage, building and entire city streets evaporated or turned to cinder and ash. When the airstrikes were over, the speakers announced, "Enemy aircraft now leaving Hanoi," as if declaring the North-South train was leaving the station.

Mai could tell the newscaster was struggling to keep his real feelings inside. Certainly, he was being watched carefully. He continued.

"The day after the latest raid, Hanoi told the citizens via the announcement system that they had prevailed once again and that another victory over the B-52s is always the pride and spiritual strength of the good-willed and wise Vietnamese people." The commentator whispered as if his voice wouldn't be heard by the troops standing next to him. It didn't take wisdom to see the devastation and destruction the raids had inflicted: crumbling buildings, concrete strewed everywhere as just so much litter, bodies partially obscured by the fallout, and streets blasted asunder or just simply gone.

Mai watched intently and then in horror as Scott came into focus. He was being paraded through a portion of the city not destroyed, in fact, a place left nearly intact. Along with Scott, two Air Force B-52 pilots, one Marine officer, and one Army Major were being forced to walk through the street waving the North Vietnamese flag. Later, they would give short interviews to the press. Scott's press pass had magically reappeared around his neck just for the occasion. All five men had been given clean clothes, were shaven and bathed, and presented as generally healthy. They were told to smile and wave as if they were in the Macy's

Thanksgiving Day Parade, and to wave the flags provided.

Crowds always lined the streets for these displays. It was a way to kill several birds with one stone for Hanoi: They could rally the spirits of the populace after being pummeled from the sky, reinforcing the propaganda that accompanied the sirens. Remind them the Americans had taken their licks in kind, and degrade the American GIs and America, in general. They could show the world that the raids did little to stifle their resolve and perhaps most importantly, the confessions of the soldiers who were given written scripts to follow. They asked for forgiveness and pledged their loyalty to Hanoi and Communism, in general, all the while smiling and waving the flags.

Scott did not smile. He did not wave his small flag though he did trudge in line behind the four others. He, like the others, had lost a considerable amount of weight. As the men progressed slowly through the streets barefoot, the crowds jeered and threw bottles and anything else they could find as the cameras rolled, recording every inch of the march.

* * *

The tears streaked down Mai's cheeks. She still had not wiped them away when Jacobs finally showed up. He hadn't seen the broadcast.

"Mai, what's the matter?" he asked, seeing that she was obviously in pain.

Mai jerked herself out of her sorrow. "Did you see that? Did you see it?"

"See what?"

"The NBC telecast from Hanoi. I just watched it. They paraded Scott along with some other prisoners down one of the main streets in Hanoi. People threw garbage and bottles at him. But he's alive! Do you realize? He's alive! I just saw him with my own two eyes. We have to do something. We know where he is. We must do something immediately," she was yelling.

"Come over here, Mai. Let's sit down," Jacobs said, pulling his handkerchief out of his coat pocket. "I know how difficult this is for you, but we can all have some relief now that we are confident he's alive," he said, trying to put the most positive spin on the situation.

"But, it isn't that easy. We know he's a POW and we have been in negotiations over all of our prisoners since we began the Peace Talks. It's a daily part of the process."

"Screw the Peace Talks. They're going nowhere and you know it," Mai said, knowing more about them through her talks with Bao than Jacobs did.

"They're going nowhere, and they aren't doing anything to get our guys back," she said, wiping her eyes with the white handkerchief Jacobs had handed her. She couldn't stand him, but right now, Jacobs was an important part of her process and her only real connection inside the diplomatic corps, and about as close to any government official she had talked with though she couldn't share any of what she knew yet. It struck her as odd how little he knew, in fact how little all of those in the government outside Nixon, Kissinger, and Le Duc Tho knew.

"We are trying our very best. Trust me, Mai. We know there are more than five hundred POWs. Scott isn't alone. We are doing everything we can to effect his and their release."

Mai wanted to tell Jacobs he was an idiot. She was beyond frustrated. The more she learned from Bao, the more she knew she had to fight through the lies and find her own path to freeing Scott.

Not answering Jacobs, she took a deep breath, put his handkerchief up to her nose, blew hard, then rolled it up, grabbed his open hand, placed it in his palm, stood, and walked out.

* * *

The following week, she met with Bao in a quiet café they had never used. She related her brief talk with Jacobs. He could feel her anger in the room even before she approached him.

He listened patiently, knowing she'd probably come up against another brick wall at the embassy.

Okay, take a deep breath. What happened?"

As Mai related her story, he waited and nodded, about ready to offer some news of his own.

"Here," he said, handing her his napkin. "I have news. It's good and bad."

"Oh please, I can't stand any worse news."

Mai stopped wiping her face and leaned forward as she glanced around the room.

"What is it?" she whispered.

"The Paris Peace Accords will be signed soon."

"Oh God. When? Tell me more, tell me more!"

Now Bao was looking around carefully. He'd gotten more involved with this woman than he ever dreamed possible, especially after they'd both realized how common their lives had been despite the disparities in their family status.

"Don't know exactly when, but very soon. The good news is the POWs will be released. The bad news is that this is a betrayal by Nixon and Kissinger to the South, or at least, that is what President Thieu and many military leaders believe."

"God. When will we know for sure?"

"Soon. I'll keep you posted. By the way, how is your baby?"

"She is two now and doing fine. Before all this, we named her Kim-Phung. She is now my sunrise and sunset every day. All I can think of is keeping her safe and getting Scott home. He must be going crazy thinking about us."

"Thank you for sharing, I must go now."

Chapter 34

Scott Reynolds had not been accounted for since his appearance on television the previous year, but there was no doubt, he had been among those captured.

Mai could do no more, not a single note, letter, or a visit to the embassy. She'd worked so hard for almost three years to get Scott released. She was exhausted mentally, emotionally, and physically. Everything she hoped for hinged on that one television appearance of Scott and the other four being marched down the center of Hanoi, paraded mostly for the Western media, looking emaciated, lost, without hope, but nevertheless alive. That was almost three months ago to the day.

Now, her only hope was that he would be coming home along with all the others, both Vietnamese and Americans, but she had no idea that the very next day, March 29th, they would all be released.

Mai's only mental attachment to anything outside her house was with Assistant Ambassador Jacobs who would be notifying her if, when, and where Scott would go. She guessed Tan Son Nhut but did not want to get her hopes up before she knew for sure. Maybe today, tomorrow, or maybe never, she thought, wiping a tear from her cheek. A tear she couldn't identify as either elation or depression so deep she feared she would never return from it.

Mai didn't have the energy to even pace within her anxiety. Instead, she withdrew her journal from the shelves, which by now was nearly filled with thoughts, memories, longings, and a hundred notes of anger about the war, her father, her country, and Scott that almost jumped off the page.

Scott was the writer, she was the musician; but the more she read her own thoughts, the more poetic they seemed to her now. There was a lyricism about these emotions dating all the way back to her first days at the University, even before she met Scott. There was a certain music to the musings of love, hope, and hate.

Writing an entry in her journal Mai intended for Kim-Phung, she began to feel even more bonded to Scott. The little girl had Scott's temperament and his hair. Though her features were more Vietnamese, her hair was a light brown, almost blonde when the rays of the sun caught the top of her head.

Chapter 35

Dear America:

Most of us are familiar with the Serenity Prayer: God grant me the serenity to accept those things I cannot change and the courage to change the things I can.

I want to emphasize the second half of that. Though acceptance of other people, places, and things is a key to our serenity, we can change anything we choose about ourselves and, in turn, alter the world around us. That is why God gave us free will. It's our choice; always has been, always will be. We are the compilations of the decisions we've made in life.

The biggest choice we make, in my opinion, is to be a victim or a survivor.

I'm a survivor. When I was held a prisoner for three years, I had a lot of time to think. I was nearly broken. My defiance and resolve were worn out. I was in the very darkest corner of my being; probably only a few heartbeats from the end. My wife and child were so far out of my reach I thought I would shrivel up and die. And death was better than the agony of my own thoughts of what was happening to them. Courage and hope abandoned me, or I abandoned them. Yet, somehow, I chose to gather what strength I had left and to carry on a minute at a time.

We are all living in a time of great potential harm, not just within a war or because of the lies we have been fed, but within ourselves. We don't have to accept these circumstances to find serenity and peace. The very challenge of non-acceptance, noncompliance is what allows us to live a life of anticipation and hope, against any and all odds.

We are like a young, green, plant pushing its way through the solid concrete of a sidewalk to reach the sun. Unbelievable but true every day, everywhere. Unlike the plant struggling

Duyen Nguyen

alone, our roots are even stronger
because they are intertwined, working
together to overcome harsh conditions. We
Americans and Vietnamese may have
different cultures and languages, but
together, our bond can withstand the
fiercest winds and the most inhospitable
conditions known to man.

I was never one to accept the status
quo and never will be, but I almost did
in that cage. When I realized I had a
choice, I found the power of my own
courage I thought had been steadily
crushed over three years. That power
showed me we can change ourselves, our
outlook; and, yes, we can change this war
and our two great countries.

All of us need to stand up, take a
close look, be honest, and say, "My God,
the Emperor has no clothes." We are being
used as pawns in a game so vital and
deadly, it's difficult to wrap our brains
around it all. Our leaders (and I use
that term lightly) have gone far, far
beyond failing us. They are chipping
pieces of God from our souls little by
little with their insidious lies, their
arrogance, and sociopathic intentions.

If we let them take God out of us, surely only the Devil will have us in the end. All of us.

President Johnson lied. The Gulf of Tonkin that started all this was a setup and a lie. The bombings in Cambodia were kept secret. Nixon, Kissinger, and McNamara all lied.

It doesn't matter now, though. What I'm saying does: We can change everything. Don't let anyone, including those people in their cushy offices in Washington or Hanoi, tells us otherwise. We do have a choice. We do not have to accept this. We do not have to continue to be a victim. We can be not only survivors but also be courageous beyond any proportion of which we think we are capable.

Let's make angels in the snow. Let's watch spring move north at 13 miles a day. Let's enjoy rainbows, and the courtship of songbirds, and the sparkle and smile of the one we love. In America, we say that we only want a little peace of mind, a bit of happiness now and then, and the ability to love and be loved, to play and to work hard. That is not too

```
much for any of us to ask. That is what
the people of South Vietnam and America
must not ask for—we must demand it.
    It is our choice.

    Scott   J.   Reynolds,   for   the   Los
Angeles Times
```

Scott and his daughter sat on the couch, Mai on the chair facing them. It was surreal not seeing him for over three years. He was gaunt, white, and frail, but she could still see that spark in his eye. He was at peace.

Mai did not know what to say. Scott was hospitalized for scurvy at the army hospital and debriefed for a week. He was still exhausted. Mai looked into his eyes, searching for the light and wondering if she would ever understand his pain, wondering but not asking what they had done to him. If he wanted to talk about it, he would and she would listen.

For now, he wanted to rest and walk – something he hadn't done since his capture. He'd been tortured relentlessly. When they weren't inflicting physical pain, they were trying to destroy his mind. Either way, he was only out of his small cage for about an hour a day. He wanted more than anything, when his legs and stamina allowed, to just walk. That was his way of emptying his thoughts though he knew he'd never forget. Back only ten days, he was already having horrible nightmares he couldn't shake for hours after he woke up.

Nevertheless, he couldn't find hatred in his feelings. Perhaps he'd become numb entirely, but he didn't feel that emotion. Mai tried to tell him what she and Bao had done to get him freed, but he understood, that wasn't an issue. It was what it was.

He'd had plenty of time to write hundreds of his mental diary entries, and he'd looked at himself, the war, the U.S. government, and fate from as many facets as the Hope Diamond. There were plenty of others, especially combatants that had died in prison or were treated far worse than he was. It was time to move on. The only thing he wanted Mai to know now was that he loved her more than ever before. Being without her and not seeing their baby for more than three years were the things that had been nearly the most unbearable. He didn't want to tell her that he'd once tried to kill himself. That would have been to admit defeat and in his mind would have meant he didn't love her enough.

Mai knew that given time, Scott would be right back at his investigations and writing, but she didn't share that with him. It was strictly his call what he wanted to do. She would be there for him every day and every night and if he was distant, so be it. She would adapt, that was the very least she could do. Her job was to keep this family together now.

EARLY 1975

Scott had recovered enough to start writing again, albeit slowly. Two years had passed since the POW release. Though his column was still being read, nothing ever seemed to change. The world around him in Saigon seemed as normal as ever and politics at home were pushing the news of the war to the back pages. All the attention was now on Nixon. The stories of Watergate, Nixon, Agnew, and all the other dirty tricks dominated the newspapers. That night, after he tucked Kim-Phung into bed, he sat making notes in his journal:

- Charges against the Ohio National Guardsmen stemming from the 1970 tragedy were dropped.
- Allegations of illegal CIA and FBI activities were leveled by his competition, The New York Times, alleging that during the Nixon administration, the agencies had maintained files on 10,000 U.S. citizens and had engaged in illegal domestic operations.
- Vice President Agnew resigned and pleaded no contest to a charge of income tax evasion.

Scott continued to recall the stories and he laughed when he noted that the Nobel Peace Prize had been awarded to Kissinger and Le Duc Tho for their efforts to end the war. The more he thought about it, the more he laughed and continued to make notes.

It was all obscene and beyond comprehension. His country was falling apart, but it was still where he needed to send Mai and Kim-Phung. Scott's focus was to get them out of Saigon, either to Singapore as an interim point or directly if he could do it, to America. He began his plan after Hank told him he'd been assigned to head up security at the embassy. He knew then that he would finally be able to retrieve his letter.

Chapter 36

Colonel Trinh wasn't one to retreat. He'd been awarded Bao Quoc Huan Chuong, the South Vietnamese equivalent of America's Medal of Honor, the highest honor for any officer during the war for extreme acts of bravery. He'd left it for Mai, hanging in a frame on the wall in his den years ago. He never considered himself brave or courageous, even after he singlehandedly killed three VC, who had his unit pinned down by machine gun fire. He went on to rout a full platoon about to overrun his men and his position. Charging into the face of the enemy, engaging in hand-to-hand and bayonet combat they said he'd saved every man in his unit.

Sitting in a foxhole, his index finger on the muddy trigger of his M-16, a momentary lull in the battle, it pained him to know they were running from the fight, from the Communists. It pained him more to hear that some of the many loyal officers he'd come through the ranks with were deserting. How could these men he thought he knew so well be abandoning their troops?

He was troubled by what he saw. He sat in the mud his finger perpetually on the trigger, his boots filled with water, and reached his soggy hand into his upper left pocket and withdrew a piece of cellophane. Painstakingly he unfolded it and placed it on his lap with his free hand. While never losing sight of the ridgeline in front of him for longer than the blink of an eye. The sound of a twig breaking caused him to catch his breath, scrunch down lower in the hole, and listen intently. After a minute, one of his men signaled from a nearby foxhole that it was clear.

* * *

OUTSIDE HANOI

Bach had been given a second-in-command position. His superior was a Lieutenant Colonel, the veteran of many years of fighting. Together, they led a battalion of about 300 men outside Pleiku, looking for one fight after another, advancing from the west to the southeast.

The people in Saigon were truly in denial. They'd heard rumors that there were many hotspots well north of the city, but that didn't seem unusual. There had been no official announcements from Thieu's regime, no serious talk from the American or

Vietnamese journalists, nothing that would indicate any real danger. Still, many people were agitated, even though they believed that a settlement between the two sides was imminent. They'd put their hopes and dreams on the Americans rescuing them, of making a final resolution once and for all, and they believed that would happen.

However, there were also many who were concerned. If anything were to happen, they wanted to be with their loved ones. They wanted to bring their family members back to Saigon from all the outlying provinces and cities, and so there was an exodus of sorts as people rode bikes, walked, took boats, or made their way to Danang, Nha Trang, and Cam Ranh trying desperately to reunite. In turn, people to the north were moving south, walking, riding bikes laden with bags and cases of meager belongings. There was something in the air that didn't feel right, even though they were convinced that the sides would negotiate.

Chapter 37

Scott's sources had all but dried up. His last story for the Times had been in early February, which revolved around President Ford's commuting Nixon's sentence.

There was an odd sense of foreboding in Saigon, a feeling he couldn't identify, a vague collective anxiety to which no one seemed able to pinpoint a cause.

He and Mai stayed home most of the time; Scott's forays into Saigon became fewer and farther between. He couldn't find Bao. His one attempt to get into the basement at the embassy had failed. He thought that after a meeting with Jacobs one afternoon, he could pretend to use the men's room in the back of the lobby, and then use the fire escape staircase to investigate. Upon reaching the intimidating steel door, he met with an even more daunting Marine who did not smile and did not allow him access. He wondered what they actually kept in there.

Duyen Nguyen

This afternoon, as Scott and Mai sat reading in the den, there was a knock at the door. Scott got up and peeked out the curtain. Seeing that it was Sang, he went to open the front door.

"May I come in?" the old woman asked.

"Certainly. Come, come in," Scott said as Mai stood.

"Hello, Sang. How are you? Can I get you some tea?" Mai asked.

"No. I'm fine. I have something of great importance to talk with you about. May I sit down?"

"Of course," Scott and Mai said simultaneously. "What is it?"

The frail woman sat on the couch and dabbed a small white kerchief from her dress pocket to her head. It was hot out and she was perspiring and breathing hard.

"Is something wrong?" Mai asked. "Are you okay?"

"Yes. I'm just hot and winded. But there is something wrong. They won't tell us, and maybe they don't know, but many people are going to the central provinces to bring back their loved ones or to be with them. Many think this is the end."

Scott spoke up. "I don't believe you should worry, Sang. I would know if something was happening. One of my best friends, Hank, is an MP at the embassy. He'd tell us if anything was going on," he said and then to himself wondered if Hank or any of them really would know.

"I don't know. I can feel something in the air. I just know there are plenty of people going north and my nephew Hai...you remember him, don't you, dear?" she asked Mai.

"Yes. What about him?"

"He's a helicopter pilot in the army. He is going to go to Pleiku to bring back his cousin. He knows the general area where your father is, it's not far from the Green Berets he works with. Have you heard from him lately?"

Mai sat for a moment not answering, trying to recall her last contact. It had been over two months. She remembered sending him a letter in February.

Suddenly, the cry of the baby broke the mood of the room. Upstairs, Kim-Phung had awakened from her nap and Mai excused herself.

"I'll be right back, aunt Sang."

Scott and Sang sat staring at each other until Scott broke the silence.

"So, what are you saying, Sang?"

"I'm saying maybe it's time for Mai's father, Colonel Trinh to come home."

"I don't know, Sang. He's a big boy. He's been through this before. I guess he knows what to do. Besides, from what Mai says, he's not likely the type to leave in the middle of a fight. Besides, we don't know what's going on up there for sure."

"Well, son, I would give you a piece of sage advice. Maybe you should contact the embassy and your friend tonight. Find out all you can. For me, I'm just offering a ride. Hai flies one of those U.S. Army Huey helicopters. There's plenty of room."

As Scott thought about what Sang had said, he heard Mai returning with Kim-Phung.

"Ah, my princess," he said, reaching his arms open for Mai to give the girl to him. Kim-Phung was 4 years old and small for her age, but Scott knew she would grow strong like her mother and be just as beautiful. He adored his daughter and when he held her, he was in a distant place. In fact, his whole demeanor changed. He wasn't as feisty or ready for a fight at the hint of a story.

"Tell Mai what you just said, Sang. I'm going to get lunch for Kim-Phung," Scott said as he stood and walked into the kitchen.

* * *

Colonel Trinh hunkered down, unfolded the plastic, and pulled out one of the two pieces of paper he'd been protecting for so long. He unfolded the first one slowly—the delicate, cracked, brown one—and placed it on his lap. He began to read carefully the copy of the letter he'd written to his wife, Constance, a French name that meant consistency and fortitude.

Dear Constance,

We will move in days and lest I cannot write you again, I'm compelled to say a few words in case I don't survive.

I have no misgivings about what I'm engaged in. I lack no confidence, as I hope you know. My courage, as yours, but perhaps not in the full measure of that, is unfaltering. Oh, how we have for so long struggled to make this our country – and what a great debt we owe to our fighting men!

I wish with all my heart to come home to you. It has been such a long, hard struggle. However, I'm willing—perfectly willing—to lay down all my joys in this life for my country and for my men. My love for you is eternal and deathless. Yet my country binds me nearly so irretrievably to this fight and to this field.

All the memories, the blissful moments I have spent with you, come over me like a wave of warm sunshine; peaceful, loving, and full of gratitude for having enjoyed them so much time with you.

If God is willing, I will join you and our beautiful Mai soon. However, remember, death is not the end. Our spirits will rejoin and the past and present will be one. With every atom of my being, I love you.

Your devoted husband,
Hung Trinh

He survived that battle and returned home. The Indochina War was over and the French had been banished. Constance had put his battlefield letter to her in a frame and hung it in his office the day he came home. Two years later she had been killed in crossfire between Nationalists and VC during a period of unrest.

There was a precarious peace for several years after that and he'd been chosen as the Deputy Province Chief of Pleiku. It was 1967 and Mai attended the University, she had lived in the house where she was born, and the new war, with the coming of the Americans, hadn't begun yet. He took the post, returning home only twice a year. When he left, he took the frame off the wall, removed the letter, folded it carefully; put it in a cellophane bag, and kept it in his pocket.

Trinh had always been fascinated with America, its own wars, and its history. In particular, he couldn't read enough about the Civil War, the astounding courage of so many men on both sides, and what so futile an exercise it seemed with so many lives lost, just like this one. He read everything he could about General Lee, General Meade, and Gettysburg, the decisive battle that changed the entire war. He had hoped Pleiku was like a Gettysburg; but, sadly, that wasn't to be, at least not here and not now. The Southern armed forces were pushed toward the sea in a massive retreat.

He had managed to write to Mai on several occasions in the last year, but had received only one reply, albeit a long one. It came months ago. Thank God, he thought, she was alive and now he knew, fiercely in love with an American journalist, of all things.

Trinh glanced at his watch covered in mud. He'd taken his finger off the trigger, losing his concentration on the hordes of VC just over the hill. He wiped his eyes and then the face of his watch. Twenty minutes had passed in silence and the sun was going to set in two hours, which is when they would return. He had no reinforcements and not much of a perimeter. He estimated the number of VC in the hundreds. He had twenty-five men, all with light automatic weapons and only two mortars.

For a moment, he allowed himself to let go, but only in his mind. There was no way in his heart and soul he would give up. He knew his men would fight to the death for him and for their country and he would be with them, the first to charge. He was disgusted with his fellow officers who were fleeing. It made him want to vomit.

Knowing it would remain quiet, he gave hand signals to his nearest Lieutenant to pass along—have every man ready. They will attack at nightfall.

He looked at his letter to his wife a final time, imprinted Mai's memory and face permanently in his mind, folded and replaced it to his pocket. As he slumped in his muddy hole, he wondered if she remembered much of him from these last couple of years. He wanted her to know he went out fighting; down to his last dying breath. He felt for the grenade. If all was lost and his men no longer needed him, he would not be captured. He was prepared to take his own life and as many VC with him as he could.

APRIL 21, 1975
HANG XANH, MAI'S HOUSE

Sang sat, waiting for an answer.

"Hai is leaving early in the morning from Tan Son Nhut. I can stay here with Kim-Phung, of course. I already anticipated that. You two go. You need to see your father. Maybe you can convince him to return," Sang said.

Mai looked at the old woman's face. It was the face of history, patience, understanding, dignity, and fortitude. She wasn't going to give up. She knew best. Her droopy eyes belied a determination that only another generation had, the generation that had lived through two wars.

Mai could hear Scott talking and playing with Kim-Phung in the kitchen. She heard her laugh, the kind of giggle that makes everyone in the room laugh. She began to drift off as Sang sat quietly and patiently, thinking about their future. She wanted more than anything to have her family in one piece—her father, Scott, and Kim-Phung—here, safe.

Though Sang seemed to know something no one else did, Mai, like so many others, even with her political savvy, felt the Americans would reach an agreement with the North that ordinary life would somehow continue.

Suddenly, Mai broke out of her thoughts, jumped up full of energy, and announced loud enough for Scott to hear, "Okay, we're going. We're going tomorrow morning."

Sang smiled knowingly.

"Good for you, girl. It's the right decision. I will go now and prepare with Hai."

Scott, who had been standing on the other side of the wall, came in smiling, holding Kim-Phung's hand.

"Saddle up the horses, girl. We're takin' a ride," he said with a grin.

Kim-Phung looked up at her father and said, "What horses, Daddy?"

"Just an expression darlin'. Just an expression."

* * *

The next morning at dawn, Sang knocked on the door. She stood with a bag packed for the overnight stay. Mai and Scott were ready. He had dressed in his old set of fatigues and given Mai a fatigue jacket to cover her jeans and sweater. He also gave her the .45 with the ivory handle, grabbing the six-shot Beretta and a 12-gauge shotgun. He stuffed his memo pad and a pen in his breast pocket.

He kissed Kim-Phung good-bye and then Mai knelt down to her and said, "My love, you take care of Sang. That is your job for today. Daddy and I will be back tomorrow night. I love you."

Sang stood with the little girl in the doorway as the two got onto the moped and sped off down the dirt road to Tan Son Nhut. Hai would be waiting outside hangar five.

* * *

TAN SON NHUT AIR BASE, SAIGON

The sun was already hot and bright in the early morning. After a brief introduction by Scott and Hai, Scott put on his Ray-Bans and helped Mai into the Huey. In seconds, they lifted off, climbed to 3,000 feet and headed north. Approaching the central airspace, they could see people coming down the national highways, now streaming in hordes. Suddenly, for the first time, Scott and Mai realized that this was it. The picture below was chaotic with people, motorcycles, cars and convoys of military trucks jamming the routes heading south or to the sea.

As Scott surveyed the scene, Mai sighed and thought how close she'd come to saying no to Sang, how prescient she was, how wise. She was right, and she didn't say it out loud; this was it, but the best possible ending could still be horrific. She couldn't lose Kim-Phung, Scott, or her father.

Several hours later, Hai began pointing down and told Scott who was riding shotgun, "There, see, at the edge of that treeline?" Hai kept pointing as Scott scanned the terrain below.

"See those foxholes lined up at near the trees?"

"Yes, yes. Are you sure?" Scott asked.

"No, not 100%, but if you look several hundred yards to the east, that berm would be a great hiding place for the VC. These are the coordinates my Green Beret friends gave me, at least as close as they could."

Hai brought the chopper down to 700 feet, as low as he dared and began to hover.

"This is it. I'm sure of it. It's now or never," Hai said.

Scott pointed down. "Okay. You're right. We don't have the time to second guess. Bring it down to that clearing just behind them, behind the tree line."

* * *

Crouched low, Colonel Trinh heard the familiar whirring of helicopter blades not far off behind the trees. A helicopter had landed there. His first thought was that he was being flanked by another VC unit. His plan was about to unravel. There was no way he could hold off an enemy coming from two directions. There was nothing to do in that instant but stay down. Suddenly, out of the tree line, two figures emerged. He aimed his rifle. Over the sights he could see one of them was a female and as they approached closer, he could hear his daughter's voice, yelling. "Father, Father, it's Mai."

He knew her face so well; he identified it immediately under the green and black camouflage. For a second he couldn't make sense of it. Who was the man with her? They were close now.

"Get down. Get down! What in the world are you doing here? Are you crazy?" Trinh asked in hushed anger and confusion.

"Not important, Father. This is Scott and we came to get you out of here. It's time to leave...now!" she said emphatically.

Trinh looked at Scott then back at Mai. So many thoughts raced through his mind as he touched his daughter's face gently. Hearing a rustling in the brush, he turned abruptly.

"Colonel, you must leave with us now," Scott said as Trinh gestured to his Lieutenant, who had crawled toward them, to stay put; that it was okay. Though he couldn't see them all, Trinh's men were ready, waiting for any signal from their leader.

Trinh held Mai's hand. "I cannot leave. I won't leave. Too many of our men have already deserted. That is dishonorable. I will not fail my men," Trinh said.

"Father, you have too much to live for. We need you. Your men need you. Your country needs you. You have a granddaughter," she blurted out and with that, Trinh's eyes widened with surprise.

"Oh my God," he said. "Oh, my beautiful girl. But I must stay. You must go back and begin a new life. You must return now. It is late. Gather your mother's things, her keepsakes, and go with your daughter and this young man to the American embassy and get out of here. That's an order!"

The tears began to pour down her face so fast she couldn't wipe them away as she began to heave and try to catch her breath. Scott put his arm around her, his other hand holding the Beretta, and said quietly, "Mai, it's time to go. We can't do anything more here. Your father is right. This is where he belongs. He's a man; a leader, and a hero. Heroes don't abandon their men. We have to leave him," he said as he pushed Mai ahead of him. She stumbled toward the tree line shielding the helo. Scott turned to Trinh, who was still hunched down in the foxhole, and saluted. Trinh returned the salute, reached into his pocket, pulled out three photos, handed one of them to Scott, and then gestured for him to go.

He grabbed Mai by the elbow and the two ran as fast as they could, Mai still crying. Within two or three minutes, they'd reached the clearing where the Huey waited. Near the chopper, he could hear the RPMs increase and see the blades picking up speed. Behind them, he heard rapid shots from where Trinh was dug in. The firing seemed like it would never end. Scott shoved Mai in and fixed her harness running around to

342

the other side. Hai pulled back on the stick and slowly raised the Huey. His skills were still shaky, but he knew once he got up about 300 feet he'd be in the clear. Hai quickly figured out what must have happened as Mai continued to weep in the backseat. No one said a word. The next stop was to pick up his cousin. They flew east toward the sea and then back to Saigon.

During the long flight, Scott had time to reflect. At first, he'd simply thought, that's it. The end of a hundred years of Mai's family. Her father had been the patriarch of a once large family, but two wars had taken their toll. All the males–the uncles, brothers, and sons–had been killed. He and his daughter were the last of the Trinhs. There were no surviving males to continue the name, but there was something far more important; there was Kim-Phung, half-Trinh, half-Reynolds. Part-Vietnamese-French, and part-American. How ironic, he thought. The Americans who fought the Vietnamese were actually incorporating them into the American bloodstream, into their DNA. So many Vietnamese killed, far more than Americans and yet, the two countries would forever be inextricably tied together.

Chapter 38

The physical world was closing in—rapidly. Trinh was in the lead position, his men as ready as they would ever be; some in foxholes, others behind berms of dirt or thinly hidden behind bushes and trees, each left with perhaps only sixty rounds of ammunition from the nightlong battle. Only two of them had fallen, and Trinh guessed they'd managed to kill at least fifty VCs who were temporarily in retreat. The numbers reminded him of Greek history. The Spartan 300 who withstood an onslaught of Persian forces, 100,000 strong. Not only did they resist the attack, but they also drove them back ultimately, along with the Athenians, preserving their freedom.

Like Sparta and Athens, South Vietnam had been free. Now, the Communists were threatening that freedom. Like the Greeks, they would fight to the death. The odds were of no consequence to them.

None of Trinh's men had eaten in two days and few had any water left. His unit—along with many of the others–was in full retreat to the sea. Trinh had lived with the shame he felt for other commanders who abandoned their men and their posts. It was a shock to his core, that which he had embraced so thoroughly about his fellow Vietnamese.

He would never abandon his men. He would ensure they were safe in whatever way he could manage. If they chose to retreat, so be it. If they wanted to surrender, that was their reality, which was out of his control. He hoped they would return to the Highlands, to the mountains and disappear or regroup with the Montagnards if that was to be. At least, he would give them a choice, a chance.

Lying in his foxhole, Trinh knew the VC would wait until it was nearly dark again, probably as the sun was setting over their shoulders so that it would be at its brightest and in Trinh's eyes as they came in hordes over the slight ridge 200 yards in front of him.

Though he was hyper-vigilant, he was also at peace remembering that nothing ceases to exist. Only the appearance of a thing ceases as it changes from one form into another. His mind was quieted with the image of fire, the native wood as hard as concrete, quickly turning into flame and then evolving into smoke. The smoke then drifting off, breaking up, and returning to the air where it began. And then eventually, with the rain, back to the soil, perhaps to nourish the growth of a new tree.

He was unafraid. He hoped his daughter would know his state of mind, his real intent, his promise to return to her so that death when it came, wouldn't be a noteworthy change. Trinh dug his fingers into the soggy mud around him. He loved the feel of the soil, his soil, the smell of it as he let it crumble and fall between his fingers. He looked up, wondering if this night sky would allow the stars to return, and then he took a twig and scribbled some words in the sand. He guessed it was near 6:00. Sundown would be in less than an hour and they would come. Packed tightly together, they would roll as one unit, a solid wall of humanity, maybe several hundred of them, grinning as they always did the way a mad self-satisfied hyena appears over his dying prey. They would take great pride in the slaughter, no matter how many of them went down.

The last of the birds chirped, signaling the death of the sun. It was directly in Trinh's eyes when he heard the war whoops. The savages were coming. Trinh signaled to his Lieutenant to draw back, for him to command his men to retreat. His Lieutenant signaled back in the negative. Again, Trinh gestured with force and with an expression his officer could clearly see from forty yards away. Once more Trinh nodded for him to move and then the Lieutenant understood. There was nothing he could do and he knew it. He had served under Trinh now for three years. He could hear the VC coming, perhaps a quarter of a mile away, as he crawled out of his hole and kept a crouch as he heaved the .30 caliber machine gun over to Trinh and scrambled back to his men, waving his hand frantically in retreat.

Trinh stretched his arm out and retrieved the machine gun. He had one hand grenade attached to his jacket, a .30 caliber, and his M-16 with two clips. It would only be enough to slow them down for a few minutes, maybe keep them pinned until they realized he was alone. When he knew his men were gone, he squirmed around to face the coming onslaught, pulled back the slide on his rifle, and put the hand grenade on the ground next to him. Taking a deep breath and grabbing one last fistful of dirt, he squinted into the disappearing sun and heard twigs breaking behind him. Quickly, he turned and aimed but held his fire—it was his Lieutenant. "Không thể bỏ rơi ông thầy được. Can't leave you alone, boss," he said.

"Thì theo tao về miền vĩnh cửu," Trinh replied. "Come join me for eternity."

The two men lay and waited and then it began. They looked like locusts, Trinh thought. Hundreds of VCs poured over the ridge yelling, screaming like banshees, an awful, sinister sound meant to instill fear. Shoulder to shoulder they came with the last rays of sun peaking over the horizon. The Lieutenant grinned, an odd, satisfied smile as the first bullet went through his helmet, clean—in and out. Trinh began firing the M-

16 with one hand as he pulled the pin from the grenade with the other, heaving it into the center of the line. Five or six attackers easily went down, but that did not slow the flow. They poured across the field like a black tsunami. He emptied his clip and then picked up the .30 caliber and did not take his finger off the trigger until the barrel was glowing.

Now, they were very close, only seventy-five yards he guessed as he turned to make sure there were no other stragglers from his unit. He knew they would stay together and keep running until they were safe or fell down trying. It was okay. The world was good again. The M-16 was empty, but the .30 caliber probably had twenty or so rounds left. Smoke was pouring out of the hot barrel as Trinh continued strafing the onslaught; their bullets so close to him he could smell them go by his head. A grenade went off just to his right, but he was dug in; the only thing showing was the barrel of his gun and part of his helmet and his eyebrows.

Suddenly, in the midst of it all—his Lieutenant lying dead next to him, blood pooling up in the mud around him—he felt a glow come over him, a feeling of pure solitude and peace. He'd given his men more than enough time to be at least a couple of miles away. He stopped firing as they approached. It was as if he'd gone blind except for one vision. Mai's face was right there, right there in front of him. She was waving to him, "Come, Father. Come home. I need you."

The first VC to arrive was a Lieutenant Colonel, the Commander. Trinh dropped his weapons and stood up as if to say, come and get me. In his left hand, Trinh held his grenade, the pin already pulled. The Commander dropped his weapon as well and pulled a knife. The two men stood motionless; as fifty yards away, the company led by Bach was advancing.

Trinh spoke first. "It is not necessary to kill even one more young man at this point. Too many have died already." Then he slowly reached out to the Commander, who lowered his knife. Trinh grabbed the Commander's fatigue jacket with his right hand and pushed him to the ground. At the same time, he turned away and let his finger off the grenade. Before the Commander could scramble to his feet, he yelled to Bach to hold his ground. "Do not advance," he yelled as Bach signaled to his men to stop. Trinh turned away from the Commander, folded his arms with the grenade close to his stomach, and fell face forward on the ground. The explosion was muffled. For a second, the Commander was shocked as Trinh's body was raised nearly half a foot off the ground. Then he realized the courage of his enemy's choice.

Within seconds, Major Bach stood exhilarated and out of breath. He'd run full bore for more than 300 meters. It was exactly how he'd imagined his return, a conquering hero. He signaled to the company to spread out and find the rest of Trinh's men, but they were long gone and he was very disappointed, signaling his Lieutenant to count all the bodies he could find in the foxholes and surrounding woods. He might have to cheat the numbers a little when he reported back, but no one would know. He helped the Commander up and they stood together surveying the area. It was over and they knew it, even if the South Vietnamese didn't. There was no doubt. He and his comrades would finally be victorious after twenty years of war.

Bach's orders were to move on to Saigon to join the other units. The VC pillaged the weapons from the dead along with anything in their pockets. As he ordered the company to assemble and move out, Bach saw the Colonel's breast pocket was unbuttoned. Though his uniform was soaked with blood and most of his abdomen gone Bach reached into the pocket and pulled out two folded sheets of paper and several small black and white photos. The photos fluttered to the ground as he tried to unfold the document with one hand while still holding his rifle in his other.

'Dear Constance,' it began. He couldn't help but read what he realized was a love letter and a good-bye. He knelt down to pick up the pictures, one of which he immediately recognized as a recent picture of Mai. Another was of a woman he figured was Constance, this man's wife. The third had to be a picture of Mai as a little girl. He couldn't take his eyes off that one. In that five-year-old, he could see every talent, each passion, and all the drive that had attracted him to her. He could see the grown woman as a seed. He had killed her father. He became aware of a glimmer of guilt trying to force its way into his heart, he shook it off, turned, ordered his men to the south, and then stuffed the letter and photos in his jacket pocket.

Glancing down, he noticed several words scribbled in the dirt. He turned his head to read: "Gỗ tan thành khói."

He did not know what to make of it. Wood to smoke. Odd, he thought.

Chapter 39

APRIL 30, 1975
U. S. EMBASSY, SAIGON

The days leading up to the end contained countless stories of courage, bravery, despicable acts. Just about everything human beings are capable of. As Scott and Mai struggled desperately to return to Saigon, thousands upon thousands of refugees joined them. Technically, the war was over, but many of the GIs, especially the officers, knew something was out there. The boogeyman was lurking in the dark corners.

Hank had been the head of security for the embassy now for just a month. One of his subordinates just three weeks before had taken an orphanage north of town that was run by a Swedish priest under his wing. He'd convinced his buddies to help rebuild the stone buildings and bring food to the Vietnamese children. Another soldier under Hank, Sergeant McGilroy, had just returned five days prior from a briefing that Assistant Ambassador Jacobs held on the roof of the embassy building.

"I was so pumped," McGilroy told Hank. "He said we had nothing to worry about. There wasn't a VC within sixty miles of Saigon."

Hank had kept a map on the wall of his small embassy office where he colored in each advance by communist forces. As towns or provinces fell to the north, he'd fill it in with a colored pencil. He, too, was told nothing was going to happen; a negotiated settlement was imminent, one that would allow the embassy and some Americans to remain. Many GIs had married Vietnamese women, they'd helped support their wives' families, and they'd made homes not only on the land but in the hearts and culture of these people. They didn't want to leave. The map didn't lie. Eventually, it became clear. They were coming and it was time to leave.

GIs monitored the news from home. In those last weeks, they looked and looked for the column from Scott J. Reynolds, but the paper had been substituting his byline with another for so long, the GIs assumed he'd been killed or fired. But they still hoped he'd appear with answers.

THE SHELLING OF SAIGON BEGINS

After so many politicians and media had said, "It's the beginning of the end going back to 1965," it finally was.

The shelling quickly became a regular occurrence every morning at 4:00 a.m., they could set their watches to it; and, by then, Hank had looked at his map that was nearly filled with color, and quietly remarked, "There's just too much color in there. It's over."

The American embassy began evacuations and personnel were taken in troop carriers to Tan Son Nhut airport under an MP guard attachment. They, at first, occurred quietly as the rest of the city and the Vietnamese people incredibly went about their ordinary lives. The naïve and opportunistic politicians still believed in a negotiation with the North. They and many of the people still thought "it could all be worked out." Still others felt that if Saigon fell, the Americans would nevertheless return, or, at least, provide help. Others felt there could be no way America would permanently leave South Vietnam. The Vietnamese people believed there would still be a new political solution that would involve the U.S. There would be a new order. Surely, it would come. But it became apparent to the final contingent of South Vietnamese believers of this that, "The Americans are abandoning us" — and they were.

Scott finally gave up on his crusade. He had done what he could do right up to the final days. His priority, his existence for being on this earth on this day was to get his wife and child to safety and beyond that, to America. Getting to the embassy, the Saigon river port, or Tan Son Nhut airport were the three options—and those doors were rapidly closing.

* * *

In the days leading up to the end, chaos, unrest, and panic broke out as hysterical South Vietnamese officials and civilians scrambled to leave. Martial law was declared. The American Operation Frequent Wind, the final phase of the American evacuation, had been delayed until the last possible moment because U.S. Ambassador Graham Martin still believed that Saigon could be held and that a political settlement could be reached.

Air transportation was scarce. Nearly every available chopper and plane were being used to ferry the injured and dead soldiers to Saigon. Farther north in Danang, rows upon rows of coffins sat covered with South Vietnamese flags awaiting transport into Saigon. People were pouring in from Pleiku and Kontum, Hue, Quang Tri, and other cities. And even in this scramble, people were dancing in cafés and nightclubs. Restaurants and theaters were still open. Meanwhile, there was a plan to send the Vietnamese Special Forces in an attempt to retake Ban Me Thuot.

Insanity.

The roads leading to the city were littered with bodies, but still passable as a seemingly endless caravan of vehicles crawled south. If a person had been in a plane up high enough to see the 17th parallel all the way to Saigon, it looked like a giant human body stripped of its skin and bones, the only thing remaining—blood vessels and heart. All of the veins and arteries that were roads or trails were streaming in the same direction—to the heart of Saigon.

More than 100,000 NVA soldiers had advanced on Saigon, which now was filled to bursting with refugees.

Nine thousand miles away, President Ford was giving a speech at Tulane University, saying, "Vietnam is a war that is finished as far as America is concerned."

Buses were picking up people and essentially going nowhere because of the flow of humanity, but most were headed to the Saigon port or the Tan Son Nhut airport.

Blocks away at the U.S. embassy, Assistant Ambassador Jacobs was setting up a reel-to-reel audiotape so that when he and the embassy staff left, it would play a continuous loop, recording over the broadcast horns across the city that would keep saying, "All is well. All is well. All is well."

Insanity.

The message would continue to broadcast loud enough for most of Saigon to hear long after the embassy staff had left. Below and inside the embassy building, Marines locked all the doors and put chairs against them to brace for the inevitable onslaught.

Hank as head of the embassy MPs was the only person left who had access to the basement. Last week, his friend Scott had given him a brother's phone number in California so he could pick up the Bonneville when he got home and then Scott asked for one final favor—if Hank could find the letter in Archer's effects and take it to Mai's house. Hank had honored his friend's request. During the chaos, nobody would care if he took any document from the basement. Following Scott's detailed instruction, he arrived at Mai's house the day before and found a back door unlocked. He entered and put Scott's letter in the top drawer of the big desk in the den. He would do much more to help his friend, but he had not heard from Scott since.

At exactly 3:30 in the morning, President Ford sent a message to Jacobs telling him to halt any and all evacuations of any Vietnamese. Only Americans were allowed to leave—embassy officials and staff, CIA, GIs were first. Once the building had been secured, Marines piled sandbags six feet high around all the doors to prevent the Vietnamese from going up to the roof.

And then they left.

Chapter 40

Scott and Mai had arrived at the Saigon river the night before. They managed to fight their way through the hysteria that had already been building since the shelling began, stealing two bicycles near Cho Ben Thanh, and then figuring out how to make their way to Mai's house nearly forty blocks away on the outskirts of the other side of the city.

Mai prayed as they pedaled furiously, dodging screaming people, lifeless bodies clogging the streets, and the whistle of incoming artillery shells. She prayed that Kim-Phung was alive, that Sang was still protecting her. She was running on pure adrenalin and nothing would stop her as Scott trailed behind by several yards, unable to keep up with her.

Miraculously, the dirt roads leading to her neighborhood were empty. Everyone had long since fled. Mai jumped off the bike before she even stopped pedaling and let it run into a tree. Scott followed in her footsteps to the front door, which was locked. Mai

358

banged on the door until her hands began to swell. Scott ran around to the back.

There was no answer at either door as Mai screamed at the top of her lungs for Sang and Kim-Phung. "Let me in, Sang, it's me. Kim-Phung, it's okay. It's your mother, let me in." Still no answer. Mai ran around the back where Scott was now opening the unlocked door. Scott pushed it open and both slid in yelling, "Sang, Kim-Phung!!"

Mai scrambled through each room and then heard a tiny, frail voice; Kim-Phung was standing at the top of the stairs alone, crying, a small stuffed bear under her arm. Mai took the entire staircase in four leaps, grabbing her daughter and nearly squeezing the life out of her.

Scott came up and embraced the two and then saw Sang hobbling out of the back bedroom, her familiar, creased, face almost white.

"Are you alright?" Scott asked, running to her.

"Yes. Yes, I'm okay. You must leave. Take your family and go and get out of here," she said, gesturing toward the front door.

Mai turned and said, "No. You're coming with us. You cannot stay. You will be killed."

"No. I'm serious; you take Kim-Phung and get out of here. I'm old. I've seen my time. They will do with me as they please. I'm too old to accost or to kill. They will leave me alone. Now go!" she yelled.

Scott grabbed Kim-Phung from Mai and with his other hand grabbed Mai, and ran down the stairs. Before they left, Scott ran to the den and pulled out the only other remaining ammo clips for the Beretta. The ammo was in the top drawer. Sliding the drawer open, he saw four .9 mm clips. There was a file, some pipe cleaners and sitting under the file, the letter; no envelope, just folded with Mai's name on the outside, just as it was in his back pocket the day he had lost it. Hank had honored his final request and accomplished his mission. Scott thought.

He grabbed the clips and the letter, then a backpack that was sitting near the desk. Pulling one side of it open, he pushed in the clips and the letter and fashioned a harness, then returned to the living room, grabbed Kim-Phung, put her in the makeshift sling, grabbed Mai's arm, and they ran out to the bicycles. With the two straps securely around his shoulders, Kim-Phung resting on his chest, they took off on the same road they'd come in on.

Kim-Phung sandwiched between them, looking startled and confused but not crying, Scott said, "I love you," throwing his arm around Mai and squeezing her, perhaps for the last time.

They had seen Saigon during Tet. They'd been a part of the battle. They'd stepped over bodies, seen all the blood, the fires, and the horrors–but that was the aftermath. They hadn't actually lived through it so neither of them could've been prepared for what they were about to see.

If a person has never been involved in a riot, a revolution, any mass exit of enormous numbers of human beings running for their lives from whatever chaos is driving them then they cannot be prepared for the fear. They cannot know what it's like to have no lifesaver, no safety valve, no answers.

As Scott, Mai, and Kim-Phung peddled toward the airport, they came to the center of town, into the heart of the melee. It was as if everyone had gone crazy together, at precisely the same moment. There was no one or place to turn, but Scott knew the second he saw the airport that they were going to have trouble.

Now Kim-Phung began to cry loudly. People were running past them from every direction, gunshots were cracking off in an incessant rattle, grenades were exploding, and body parts were flying.

With all the gunfire and explosives, the air began to fill with a dense fog of smoke. But Scott had ridden this route so many times on his moped, he could almost feel his way there as he held on to the handlebar with one hand and wrapped his arm around his daughter with the other. He didn't feel it, but Mai holding onto him with her left arm used her right hand to slip the medallion into his back pocket.

He also didn't know, but off the coast, the U.S. Navy stationed three aircraft carriers to handle incoming Americans and South Vietnamese, not knowing of Ford's order to leave them behind. However, there were so many people on board the vessels, the sailors and boarders began pushing the helicopters off the decks into the sea to accommodate more people. All of South Vietnam was trying to get on those three ships.

As Scott, leading the way, came up to the familiar entrance to the airport, he saw the hordes of people who were racing toward the two helicopters— one on the roof, the other on the ground were their last hope.

Scott looked up and then back to Mai and saw Assistant Ambassador Jacobs and about ten Marines in the Huey that was lifting off from the roof. The one on the ground contained more Marines and appeared to be bursting at the seams, its rotors beginning to rev up to the correct RPMs for liftoff.

Scott stepped off the bike and let it fall as he unstrapped his backpack and handed his daughter to Mai. Her eyes were crazed as she held onto Kim-Phung, who was screaming. Mai sensed Scott wasn't coming and she couldn't stand it. The world was coming apart at its center.

Scott pulled out the .45 in his right hand and held three more clips in his left as he could see at least twenty civilians running toward them, being chased by some VCs who were firing on them.

"Go! Go! Get on that chopper. Do not let them stop you. I will be right behind you," Scott yelled as the helicopter's blades began to whirl louder and faster and the landing skids began to jiggle back and forth.

"No! You're coming, too. You must come now. Please!" Mai pleaded, tears streaming down her cheeks.

"Daddy, Daddy!" Kim-Phung screamed, stretching her arms toward him.

"Go now!" Scott yelled again as he glanced back at the onslaught and then embraced his wife one more time.

Before he let go of Mai, he reached into his backpack and pulled out the letter, stuffing it in her jacket pocket. "Go, Mai. Please go," he said, pushing her from behind.

Automatic weapon fire continued from what seemed like every conceivable direction. Masses of people were running just a hundred yards behind them; he knew all of them had the same idea: Get on that chopper! He had to get Mai and Kim on board.

"I'll meet you at Ruby's," Scott shouted, but the noise was so loud he wasn't sure if she heard him.

When Mai was close enough to nearly touch the Huey, Scott turned and shot two VC coming from his left then turned one last time to see Mai climb up with the help of a Marine. He didn't want to look, to hear her scream for him to come. He knew he couldn't. It was too late. He would have to stand and fight. Somehow, he'd known long ago that it might end like this and in an odd way that was okay. He turned quickly, shot another advancing VC and then glanced to his right. Two VCs stood alone, staring at him.

One short man had a sniper rifle aimed at him. He recognized the other, taller VC immediately. All three froze.

Bach exchanged weapons with his Lieutenant; making sure the powerful gun was loaded, he brought it up to his shoulder. Time stood still as he turned and aimed at Mai, a Marine with his arm around her in the Huey. He closed his left eye and focused with his right. Mai was climbing up into the chopper, which was beginning to lift off slowly under twice the weight it should've been carrying.

As he raised the rifle slightly to put her in the middle of the crosshairs, he could see the intersection of the crosshairs dead center in Mai's back, the face of a small child with her tearful chin on Mai's shoulder, one arm in the air screaming for her father. Suddenly, Bach remembered the picture of Mai that her father had kept.

He held the rifle tightly and pulled very slowly on the trigger but couldn't bring himself to shoot her. He lowered the gun and realized Scott was nearly on them. Scott had dropped the .45 and was bent on strangling Bach with his bare hands.

Everything was happening too fast, mere seconds. His Lieutenant had a bead on Scott with his pistol. The crowd was surging and stumbling toward them as those who were shot fell and three more behind them tripped over their bodies. Mai was inches from the edge of the Huey as four Marines held their hands out screaming, "Come on! Come on! Hurry!"

Then in a split-second, Bach realized Scott was going to kill him with his bare hands. He was prepared to fight to the death. He dropped the rifle on the ground and steeled himself, turning to his Lieutenant, who was about to pull the trigger of his .45.

He could see the man's finger coming back as if time were standing still. "No!" Bach screamed. "No!" And as he plunged at the Lieutenant and reached for the man's wrist, the gun went off twice.

Like a slow-motion scene in a movie, Scott's legs turned to mush and his body dropped to the ground like an empty bag of sand. At the same time, he felt levitated and detached from his body. A white velvet curtain wavered gently, giving him a feeling of total serenity. He saw Mai's sweet face, smiling at him and sailing farther, farther away.

Another half second and Bach could've deflected the pistol. As he stood over Scott, the blood pooling up around him, he turned to see the Huey finally lift off, struggling to share the cramped space. The chopper was lumbering with the load, passengers' legs hanging over the edge of the bay door opening as it stubbornly lifted into the air.

Mai watched below as the entire scene unfolded. She screamed when she saw Bach drop the rifle to the ground. She pulled Kim-Phung's face to her chest and stifled another scream as she watched Scott go limp and hit the ground. In an instant, the chopper was on the other side of the building and she could see the port off in the distance. The man who was holding on to her and Kim-Phung, looked familiar to her.

He watched Mai's expression of horror and realized the skirmish below involved her, perhaps her husband, a friend, or a family member. He pulled his bandana from around his neck and held it in front of Mai who couldn't hear what he was saying but could read his lips, "Không được nói tiếng Việt. No Vietnamese allowed," he said, quickly wrapping her face in it and placing his ball cap on her head.

Then he leaned closer to her ear and said, "It's Hank. You're going to be okay."

* * *

U.S.S. MIDWAY, OFF THE COAST OF SOUTH VIETNAM

Over an hour later, when Mai and Kim-Phung landed on the U.S.S. Midway, people were screaming for medics. The chaos was only slightly tempered from the fighting in the harbor or at the airport.

Mai found a corner on the deck next to a utility cabinet. Kim-Phung sat on her lap in shellshock, unable to cry any longer. Mai took a deep breath and pulled the letter out of her pocket. As she unfolded it, she felt as if her heart would explode. She could barely breathe as she read:

```
Dear Mai,
Even though we haven't been together
long, I feel as if I've known you a
lifetime. Perhaps the fighting has
only increased our awareness of how
fleeting life can be. I want you to
know that I adore you. I want you to
marry me, and I want us to go to
America when this is over.
```

Mai quickly realized Scott had written the letter seven years ago. Before she could read further, two small photos fell from the envelope. She frantically scrambled with her free hand to grab them before the wind that was gusting across the carrier deck claimed them.

One was of a small girl about four years old. At first, she thought it was a picture of Kim-Phung, but that wasn't possible. Suddenly, she realized it was her, a picture her father had taken years ago with a Kodak Brownie camera; the resemblance took her breath away. Then, she looked at the little boy, probably about five in the other picture. Though he was a towhead blond, she couldn't help but also notice the similarities to Kim; the nose and mouth were nearly the same. The young boy was sitting in front of a sign that read, Ruby's Diner.

She continued to read, her tears now running, dripping onto the flight deck:

Mai, for whatever reason, if I do not make it out of this, there is something very important I have to tell you. If the war ends and we have not won, you must somehow leave and go to California to my brother.

Her chest heaved as she tried desperately to finish the letter.

Julian's address is 8001 Claytor Mill Ave., Los Angeles. I've written to him about you so he knows. There is so much I couldn't tell him through the mail. He will know what to tell you and how to help you.

I know if you are reading this, I was killed because there is no other way on this earth that I would not be with you. I also know that if

that happens, I will have written
the truth, the things that America
and the Vietnamese people had to
know. Whatever we talked about that
didn't see the light of day you need
to share with the world, especially
the story about the plot in which
South Vietnam was betrayed and
delivered to the Communists. The
following pages are copies of the
classified memos evidencing what I
told you.

I love you more than life.
Scott

Mai turned the page over and found an almost blank
sheet of paper with a terse note:

REMOVED FOR NATIONAL SECURITY
Henry Jacobs

She burst out crying. Scott was gone. A
civilization she cherished had crumbled into ruins.
Everything else was meaningless.

Epilogue

The guest speaker Joe Bateman looked out on an audience that included families of former POWs and many of those that died in captivity and in the conflict.

"The United States made a promise in connection with the Paris Peace Accords. We promised to continue to support South Vietnam with weapons and other aid to the same extent the Soviets supported the North." He paused to scan the crowd.

"We didn't.

"We promised we would return to help.

"We didn't.

"We all know what happened instead: Watergate—the scandal whose very roots were in America's policies. The President's ability and desire to keep the promises he had made evaporated. Congress took away his right to use air power and slashed aid to Saigon. The North Vietnamese, delighted by this turn of events, launched new offensives. In April 1975,

Saigon fell after its under-supplied troops fought bravely for over a year against an enemy still fat with Soviet and Chinese largess.

"For the first time in its history, the United States let an ally it had sworn to defend run out of bullets. However, our men didn't make that decision, our government did.

"Kissinger admitted he'd misjudged the willingness of the American people to defend the agreement when he said, 'What we misjudged more than anything was our ability to effect peace with honor.'

"However, my friends, that admission statement is another the lie of Kissinger's. In April 1975, while some remaining units of South Vietnam's army continued to fight bravely, Kissinger said. 'Why don't these people die fast? The worst thing that could happen would be for them to linger.'

"So this is what it comes to. Over fifty thousand Americans and millions of Vietnamese dead, countless wounded, a hundred and fifty billion dollars in military aid, the U.S. ripped apart by years of violence on the campuses and in the streets—now this from Washington—'Sorry, Vietnam, but I have another engagement. Let's have lunch someday. Don't call me. I'll call you.'

"April 30th, 1975 is the day South Vietnam was sold to evil by betrayal and abandonment. Lest you have never been told the real ugly stories of that fateful day..."

Two Asian women sat quietly in the third row, one middle-aged, the other in her late twenties. The older woman had her hands placed gently over, the younger woman's hands.

"Thank God for the Freedom of Information Act. It's too bad this young journalist, Scott J. Reynolds, never made it back. Though he wasn't a GI, he was a warrior. He told the truth. As he did in so many of his Los Angeles Times posts during those years."

As the man finished speaking, in the back and away from the crowd standing near a tree tears running down his cheeks a middle-aged man listened and nodded in agreement. He wasn't dressed for the occasion. His sandy hair under his ball cap, perhaps a bit long for an older man and a mix of more silver than blonde, was blowing in the breeze. His full beard grew patchily high on his cheeks and was almost completely gray. He had on worn jeans, a t-shirt and a pair of Ray-Bans.

As the crowd began to disperse, he wiped the tears from his face, pushed himself along with a cane, and began to move away as quickly as he could. The two women were moving faster and came alongside them. When he realized it was them, he started to move at an angle away. Now was not the time.

The young woman was nearest to him. She brought a hand up to brush long, lustrous, black hair from her face. Her blue eyes, clearly Caucasian, complemented rather than contrasted the lighter olive tone, with just a hint of natural burnt umber, in her cheeks. He couldn't help it and stopped to look at her.

The face of the older woman was a darker tint but the high planes of their cheeks were the same. She removed her glasses to reposition them and he saw that only the crinkling of lines around her eyes showed all the years that had passed. Suddenly he smelled the scent of magnolia and he remembered the texture of her skin as he touched it. He bowed his head and shuffled further out of their way.

# # #

AUTHOR'S NOTE:

Perhaps the most ironic part of this love story and the relationship of the Vietnamese people to the Americans was the treatment of America to its own men, all the GIs. These returning veterans weren't only shunned by America but were also spit on, pelted with rocks and other debris, vilified in the press, and basically blamed and forgotten for the entire mess.

It wasn't for at least another ten years that the American veterans from Vietnam were accepted and the country began to realize the astounding sacrifice these men and their families had made for them and the Vietnamese people—and the country truly began to heal.

Today, regardless of the politics of the conflict, we honor our soldiers because we know that it isn't the people or those who serve who start the wars.

ABOUT THE AUTHOR

When South Vietnam was delivered to the evil North in April 1975, after many failed attempts Duyen Nguyen finally escaped and came to the U.S. in November 1984. Mr. Nguyen was one of the almost 800,000 refugees known as, boat people half of which settled in the United States. He now practices law in San Jose,

California. Mr. Nguyen is currently working on the sequel to *Behind the Smoke Curtain*, a novel about Vietnam after the fall of Saigon in April 1975, titled *When the Heart Cries but Never Breaks*. He is also the author of the novel *CHIEF | The Story of a Pit Bull*.

A summary of both those stories accompanies on the following pages.

ABOUT *WHEN THE HEART CRIES BUT NEVER BREAKS* [THE SEQUEL TO *BEHIND THE SMOKE CURTAIN*]

"When the evacuation is ordered, the signal will be read on Armed Forces Radio. That signal is: 'The temperature in Saigon is 105 degrees and rising.' This will be followed by the playing of, I'm Dreaming of a White Christmas."

That announcement triggered Operation Frequent Wind, the almost unbelievable evacuation plan executed by US forces on 29-30 April when more than 7,000 people were evacuated by helicopter from various points in Saigon. The total number of Vietnamese evacuated by Frequent Wind or self-evacuated and ending up in the custody of the United States for processing as refugees to enter the United States totaled 138,869.

But hundreds of thousands were left behind that then faced 're-education' by the victors. The re-education camps, modeled on Soviet Gulags (and in some cases operated similarly as a Nazi concentration camp) soon became full. Wives and children of the prisoners were rushed out of their homes to the rural areas under the New Economic Zone programs that were announced as a thinly veiled justification for the confiscation of all assets held by families of the defeated.

The smoke had cleared over Vietnam but the country still ran with blood.

This is the continuing saga of American journalist Scott Reynolds, wounded and left behind as Saigon fell. Imprisoned in a camp—tortured and held secretly in solitary confinement—he and another prisoner, Tuan, a young former South Vietnamese Army officer, escape during a camp uprising. A female North Vietnamese communist cadre at the camp who has fallen in love with Tuan reluctantly helps them. Traveling at night and hiding during the day not long after their escape they find Lan, a teenage girl who is escaping her own Hell. She had killed the Zone Commander that had tried to rape her. Together they evade patrols and informers and try to make their way to the coast and find a boat to escape Vietnam. This is their story.

ABOUT *CHIEF* | *THE STORY OF A PIT BULL*

The story of a very brave dog that saved the life of a young wounded veteran and how she saved his. Both are scarred and damaged... but together -- woman and dog -- find love, trust and peace. The very things they dreamed and wished for but thought they'd never have. Hannah is a combat wounded veteran; her face is disfigured and she lost her left leg. Chief is a dog that escaped from a dogfighting ring that she adopted (against others advice because of his breed) as part of Wounded Warrior Project to help veterans. While traveling in Colorado, at a rest area, Hannah is attacked by a serial killer and rapist. Chief defends her. But the police take Chief from her (permissible under Denver/Colorado law) and plan to put him down. Hannah fights to save his life. Within this entertaining, sometimes heart-wrenching, tale, is a goal to raise empathy, compassion and awareness about animal cruelty... and how dogs that have experienced it can be saved and rehabilitated. And in turn, how they can be a benefit to a human... sometimes even saving them with their love.